Seduction of a Proper Gentleman

"When I look into those lovely green eyes of yours I get the most remarkable sense of—"

"Inevitability?" Dear Lord, did he feel it too?

"Yes! No! I don't know. Possibility perhaps. But know this." Oliver tipped her chin up with his finger and glared into her eyes. "If we had been introduced at a party or your eyes had met mine across a crowded dance floor or you had ridden past me in the park, I would be actively pursuing you. And I have not found a woman I would actively pursue in some time."

"Oh." She swallowed hard. "Now do you intend to kiss me?"

His gaze slipped from her eyes to her lips and back. "Regrettably, no." He dropped his hand, grabbed hers, and headed briskly back toward the manor, fairly pulling her along behind him. "I do, however, want to. Rather a lot. Which does not strike me as wise."

"Because you don't trust me?" Even so, it was delightful to know he wanted to kiss her. "Or because I'm dangerous?"

"Both."

By Victoria Alexander

Chapter 2

It wasn't a bad way to spend the day. Not productive perhaps but then Oliver had always believed that one should, on occasion, have a day in which nothing of note should be accomplished. A day that was simply to be savored, like an exceptionally fine cigar or a wine of rare vintage or a lovely woman.

Oliver leaned on the balustrade on the back terrace of Norcroft Manor and gazed over the gardens and the fields and countryside beyond. While he didn't consider himself a country sort of person, he did love being at Norcroft Manor. There was a peace here one never knew in the city. Of course, nothing of significant interest ever happened in the country, which was precisely why it was so peaceful. This was fine up to a point, but a week or two from now he would be bemoaning that fact. Even so, this was his favorite time of year, right after the harvest. It wasn't late enough in the year for the hint of autumn to come and yet the change of seasons was in the air nonetheless. Or perhaps it was simply in his mind. Anticipation, that's what it was. The feeling that something was about to happen.

It was a silly idea and probably due more to the idleness of the day than anything else. Still, he had earned a bit of rest. In the three days since his arrival he'd met at length with his estate manager, paid visits to all of his tenants, scrutinized the harvest, and agreed to his mother's plans for the annual Harvest Ball. Oliver chuckled. Not that he really had any say in it. The dowager Countess of Norcroft was convinced her true calling in life now was as a hostess, though she had once been skilled with a bow. Oliver conceded she might well be right. Besides, he rather enjoyed a good party himself and the Harvest Ball, always held out-of-doors, under the stars, was a longstanding tradition on the estate. Mother was also awaiting the arrival of her three nieces by marriage who would join in the festivities. The girls had lived with them until the end of the season when they had left the city to spend the summer months with their sister, the Marchioness of Helmsley, at her husband's family estate, Effington Hall.

never knows what might happen that would be fodder for gossip and I do so like witnessing such incidents first hand."

"I haven't been to Lord Darlington's party for years." A wistful note sounded in his mother's voice. Utter nonsense, of course. His mother had an extremely active social calendar. She had nothing whatsoever to feel wistful about.

"Perhaps that's where we've met," Lady Fitzgivens said. "Although admittedly my memory has dulled along with the rest of me through the years. Still." A naughty twinkle shone in her eye. "I daresay we have a few good years left."

Mother laughed. "One can only hope."

"I shall take my leave then." Lady Fitzgivens turned to go then turned back, concern on her face. "Do let me know how the young lady fares. It did not appear that she fell that hard. I'm rather surprised she has not come to her senses yet."

"While Dr. Miller's is a country practice, he is a more than competent physician," Mother said firmly. "She is in very good hands."

Lady Fitzgiven's gaze searched his mother's. "Excellent. I should hate for my . . . my good deed to be for naught." She turned again and started for the door.

"What about baggage," Oliver blurted. "If she arrived on the train she must have had bags of some sort."

Lady Fitzgivens shrugged. "I didn't notice any

unclaimed bags but surely if she had bags they will turn up eventually. Good day, my lord." She nodded at his mother. "Lady Norcroft." With that she swept from the room.

Oliver met his mother's gaze firmly. "Do you think this is wise?"

"I'm not sure wisdom has anything to do with it, Oliver," Mother said lightly.

He folded his arms over his chest. "You do realize Mother, this young woman could be anyone."

"Precisely, why it was our duty to take her in."

"But she could be a thief or a criminal or a—"

"Don't be absurd, Oliver." Mother scoffed. "One can tell just by looking at her that she is obviously a lady as well as a young woman of substance. And did you note the bracelet around her wrist with the little gold charm? I should like to get a closer look at that. It was exquisite."

"Stolen, no doubt," he muttered.

His mother continued as if he hadn't said a word. "Her clothes are of an excellent quality, the latest style and in perfect taste. Her gloves were exceptional. You can always tell a true lady by the quality of her gloves."

"Yes, yes, I know. Lady Fitzgivens said—"

"And she was right. Did you by any chance look at our guest's boots?"

Oliver huffed. "No, but—"

"They are lovely and suited for travel but not overly practical. They are the kind of boots purchased by someone who doesn't give a second thought to the

"Certainly not of a romantic nature."

"I do not discuss my romantic adventures with my mother," he said in a lofty manner.

"Four of your friends have wed since the start of the year and yet gossip hasn't linked your name with anyone." She shook her head. "Caring about nothing but family business and your responsibilities as earl is not the way to find a wife, my boy."

"Accepting a stranger of unknown origin into our house simply because she's the bearer of an empty envelope is not the path toward adventure either." A note of triumph sounded in his voice.

"Oliver Leighton, I doubt that you would recognize an adventure of any sort if it came right up and bit you on the a—"

"Mother!"

"I was going to say arm." His mother stared at him for a moment then laughed. "Adventure, like beauty, is very much in the eye of the beholder. Regardless of how we view this situation, I suspect we shall know everything soon enough."

Hollinger cleared his throat from the door. "My lady, Dr. Miller has arrived."

"Very good, Hollinger." She headed toward the door. "One way or another, Oliver, this unknown lady has provided a bit of excitement. And you are always complaining about the tedium of country life."

"I like the tedium of country life," he called after her. "It's peaceful!"

"You hate peaceful," she threw back over her shoulder then stepped out of the room.

"Not at the moment," he muttered and suspected very soon he might well long for peaceful and tedium.

Still, his mother was right. Unless his suspicions were correct—and even he realized he was more cautious than was perhaps warranted—they would know the identity of their mystery guest as soon as she awoke. And unless she was seriously injured, not likely given the short distance of her fall, that might be at any minute. He had to admit to a bit of curiosity himself. After all, her gloves and boots aside, she was quite lovely.

And he couldn't help but continue to wonder about the color of her eyes.

nearly everyone who will be in attendance, if not by sight, then by reputation."

"Even so, I would think—"

"Beyond all else . . ." Lady Fitzgivens dug through a large reticule dangling from her arm and pulled out a crumpled envelope with a flourish. "She had a letter addressed to Lady Norcroft." She handed the envelope to Oliver with a triumphant gleam in her eye.

It was indeed addressed to his mother. He raised a brow. "It's open and it's empty."

"Is it?" Lady Fitzgivens plucked the envelope from his hand, shook it and peered inside. "So it is. The letter must have blown away in the confusion." She returned the envelope. "How very awkward. I gather then that you don't know her?"

Oliver shook his head. "I've never seen her before."

Lady Fitzgivens shrugged. "Well, perhaps Lady Norcroft . . ."

"I've never seen her before either," his mother said, sailing into the room. She gave a cordial nod to the Clarkes, crossed the room to the sofa, and studied the unconscious woman. "Still, she could well be a distant relative or the daughter of an old friend or any number of things. I really have no idea but she is our responsibility now."

"Why?" Oliver said without thinking.

His mother and Lady Fitzgivens exchanged glances as if basic hospitality wasn't something one could expect a man to understand. Which was most unfair. Oliver considered himself quite hospitable.

"Hollinger, have her carried to one of the rooms in the west wing, the green one I should think." Mother nodded at the butler who immediately signaled to a footman every bit as up to the task as Tom. The young man cast a regretful look as the footman gathered up the lady and carried her off. "Joseph, I'm sure Cook can provide you and Tom with some refreshment in the kitchen for your troubles. You've been most helpful."

"Weren't nothing, my lady." In spite of his words, Joseph looked pleased at the compliment. Hollinger ushered father and son to the door and directed another footman to take them to the kitchen.

Mother turned to Lady Fitzgivens. "I am his lordship's mother, Lady Norcroft. I don't believe we've met, although you do look vaguely familiar."

"I often do." The lady laughed. "I am Lady Fitzgivens." The other woman smiled pleasantly and it struck Oliver that the two older ladies might have a great deal in common. Aside from a similarity of age, they both seemed to think he was somehow lacking in the social niceties.

"Might I offer you some refreshment as well?"

"No, no, I must be on my way. I've delayed far too long already." Lady Fitzgivens leaned toward his mother. "I should hate to miss so much as a moment of the festivities at Lord Darlington's. One

"Beg pardon, my lord." The butler's voice sounded a few steps behind him. In all the years Oliver had known Hollinger, he had never been able to figure out how a man as solidly built as the butler managed to approach without making a sound.

Oliver turned. "Yes?"

"There is . . . that is to say there are . . ." Hollinger's usually unflappable demeanor seemed just a touch ruffled.

Oliver bit back a smile. "Go on."

"My lord." Hollinger drew a deep breath as if to brace himself. "There are . . . *persons* in the front parlor."

"Persons?" Oliver raised a brow. "Of a disreputable nature?"

"I didn't say that, my lord." At once Hollinger's aplomb returned.

"No, I simply gathered as much from your expression."

"My apologies, sir," Hollinger said in his usual cool manner. "It will not happen again."

"I'm certain it won't." Once more Oliver resisted the urge to smile. Hollinger prided himself on being the perfect butler and such perfection did not lend itself to allowing his opinions to show on his face. "Who are these persons?"

"Mr. Clarke, from the village, and his son accompanied by an older woman, obviously of quality, and a young woman. They seem to feel she belongs here."

Oliver drew his brows together. "Who belongs here?"

"The young woman."

Apparently, having permitted his usual stolid façade to slip, Hollinger now felt the way to redemption was to reveal as little information as possible. "Why would they think she belongs here?"

"I'm not certain, sir. It's rather convoluted and most curious."

"Is it?" Oliver stared in confusion. "What does the young woman say?"

"Nothing, my lord." Hollinger paused. "She does not appear to be conscious. You might wish to—"

"Yes, of course." Oliver started toward the house then stopped. "How did she get here?"

"Young Mr. Clarke carried her, sir."

"I see." Tom Clark was a strapping lad hovering on the brink of manhood. While he was well able to carry damn near anything, he had a look in his eye that indicated he wouldn't be at all reluctant to haul unconscious young women around the countryside. "You might wish to mention the fact of a visitor's unconscious state before any other details should the occasion ever again arise."

"Indeed, sir."

"It is somewhat intriguing though," Oliver said more to himself than the butler and again started for the door. "An unknown woman, unable to speak for herself, brought to our door."

"Yes, sir." Hollinger made it across the terrace a scant step in front of Oliver and quickly opened the door. "And a very attractive young woman at that," he said pointedly.

"I know that you, and every other servant in the house, are firmly aligned with my mother in the shared goal of seeing me wed but you needn't drag in half-dead women off the street," Oliver said under his breath. His mother had long wished him to marry but ever since the first man had fallen in the blasted tontine, she had become relentless in badgering him about his failure to wed. He had noticed as well that Hollinger and Cook and other household servants, who were as much a part of the family as they were employees, had not so subtly joined in her crusade.

"My lord, I would never consider such a thing." Hollinger's shocked voice sounded behind him. "And, might I point out, that her arrival is through no fault of anyone here at the manor."

Oliver snorted in a manner indicating his skepticism. He was well aware that Hollinger and the rest of the staff had only his best interests at heart. Still, it was an annoyance to realize that the personal details of his life were of as much concern below stairs as they were above. It was irritating as well for the man who had won the tontine to be made to feel by those around him as if he had somehow failed.

Oliver reached the parlor and paused. Joseph Clarke and his boy, Tom, stood off to one side

looking at once awed and uncomfortable. Certainly, villagers attended the Harvest Ball but they rarely visited the manor at other times.

The young lady had been laid on a sofa. Hollinger was right. She was indeed lovely, with dark red hair, the color of good mahogany, and fine features. Oliver wondered what her eyes would look like. He rather hoped they would be green. He'd always had a fondness for green-eyed redheads. But what man didn't?

"Lord Norcroft, I presume." A well-dressed, handsome woman, about his mother's age, stepped forward.

"Yes." Oliver nodded a bow. "And you are?"

"I am Lady Fitzgivens but it scarcely matters." She waved aside the question. "At the moment I am simply a concerned passer-by. A good Samaritan as it were. I had just departed the train from London and was about to enter the carriage I had arranged to meet me here to take me the final way to Lord Darlington's estate. It was extremely shortsighted of Lord Darlington not to have his estate located closer to the railway, although I suppose the railway is to blame, as Lord Darlington's property has probably not moved for generations." Her brows drew together in a considering manner. "No, it definitely has not moved. I could have taken a carriage the entire way I suppose, but excessively long carriage rides are so tiresome and I find a train is much more interesting. Don't you?"

"Yes, I suppose but—"

She smiled pleasantly. "Do you know Lord Darlington?"

"I have made his acquaintance," Oliver said slowly.

"Lovely man. As I was saying, moments after my arrival I saw this unfortunate young woman trip and fall off the train platform." She cast a concerned look at the young lady on the sofa. "Fortunately, it wasn't very high. Unfortunately, the poor dear appears to have hit her head. Still, by the looks of her, she has a healthy disposition and should come to her senses in no time. What time is it?"

"Half past three, my lady," Hollinger said.

"That late? Well, I imagine she will be fully recovered and back to her normal state within a day or two." She nodded thoughtfully. "Or three. Perhaps even a week. Possibly longer." She paused. "Or less. There's really no way to know how long something like this might last. It's all remarkably imprecise."

Oliver stared. "You can't possibly be a physician."

"Don't be absurd." She leveled him a hard look. "I am simply an astute and wise observer of life." Her gaze shifted to his unconscious guest. "Although one would think she would have at least awoken by now," she added under her breath then met Oliver's gaze firmly. "You might wish to provide her some assistance, young man."

"Yes, of course. I had certainly intended—Hollinger," Oliver glanced at the butler, "send for a physician at once."

"My wife went to fetch Dr. Miller, my lord," Joseph said quickly. "But we thought it best to bring her here without delay."

"Quite right." Oliver paused. "Why?"

"It seemed a good idea," Lady Fitzgivens said quickly. "We didn't want to leave her lying on the ground. Why, it wouldn't be at all the right thing to do."

"Of course not, but why here?" Oliver asked.

"Oh, to Norcroft Manor you mean? It seemed obvious. Her hat and gown are of the finest quality and in the latest fashion, indicating she is well bred and certainly of means." She leaned toward Oliver and lowered her voice in a confidential manner. "The gloves, you know. One can always tell a lady of quality by her gloves." She straightened. "We thought she belonged here. A houseguest perhaps. Goodness, where else might she be going?"

"The same place you are. To Lord Darlington's perhaps," Oliver suggested.

"Excellent point, my lord. How very clever of you to think of it," she said with a smile that seemed oddly forced. "Nonetheless." Lady Fitzgivens waved away his comment. "She's entirely too young for Lord Darlington's gathering. At least this particular gathering, although I daresay like most men of his age, his lordship appreciates the companionship of a lovely younger lady. However, I know

I would rather the nefarious perpetrator be a handsome, dashing rogue rather than a lovely young woman."

"Mother!"

"I do love it when you're shocked, Oliver, and it doesn't bother me in the least. It's been a very long time since I've had an adventure of any sort—"

"Well, I should think—"

"What?" She narrowed her gaze and Oliver felt as if he were again a small boy and had done something naughty. "I should forgo adventure given my age?"

"No," he lied. "I wasn't going to say that at all."

"Then you were thinking it. I know that look. It's that *I know better than you and therefore I am responsible for you* look. Your father had a very similar look although he probably would have understood." She paused and her gaze seemed to focus on something entirely out of sight. "He and I had several grand adventures in our youth."

"Perhaps now is not the time—"

"I have no intention of filling you with tales of what is long past." She sniffed. "Besides, you don't deserve to know. However, you should know this." She pinned her son with a firm look. "By virtue of an envelope that might or might not be legitimate, this unknown visitor, for good or ill, is now my adventure. I daresay you could use a few of your own," she added under her breath.

Indignation washed through him. "I have adventures."

fact that they won't last. And quite expensive as well, I would say. I can't imagine a thief or a criminal wearing such shoes." Mother shook her head. "If thieves and criminals are wearing shoes like hers, then we are all wasting our time abiding by the laws of society."

"Mother!"

"Oh, don't look so outraged, dear. The lure of fine footwear is not about to entice me into becoming a highwayman." She rolled her gaze toward the ceiling.

"That's absurd, Mother. I never thought . . ." He clenched his jaw. He wasn't the one had who suggested highway robbery for shoes so why was he the one who now felt like something of an idiot? He drew a deep breath. "I'm simply saying—"

"She had a letter for me, darling. Don't forget that."

"She had an envelope for you." Oliver's voice rose. "An empty envelope at that."

"Yes, that was a shame."

"She could have addressed it herself."

"The paper was of excellent quality. The handwriting refined and possibly familiar although I can't be sure. So many people I know have a similar hand. It's most annoying. If she wrote it herself, she did a very good job. Which only begs the question of to what end?"

"Nefarious purposes no doubt," he said darkly.

"What an exciting idea. I wouldn't at all mind being the object of a nefarious purpose although

renewed." Perhaps wicked was more accurate than wistful. "Regardless, it's always memorable and a great deal of fun."

Kathleen studied her aunt, the truth at once becoming clear to her. "You didn't agree to accompany me to England because it might be an adventure. You wanted to come because of this party."

"Which I have no doubt will indeed be a most extraordinary adventure." Hannah cast her niece an unrepentant grin.

"Very well."

"Very well what?"

"We'll go." Kathleen waved at the file. "You're absolutely right. I do need to put all this out of my head for a few days."

"I scarcely think a few days is sufficient—"

"A few days," Kathleen said firmly.

"Very well." Hannah thought for a moment. "We could stop in Norcroft. It is on the way."

"I don't know—"

"Nonetheless, it might be beneficial to see the place where you will spend the rest of your days. I would think . . ." Hannah paused for a long moment.

"You would think what?"

"I have an idea," Hannah said slowly.

"What kind of idea?"

"An idea . . ." Hannah's forehead furrowed in consideration. "An idea that will allow you to get

not wish to follow him tonight and I have no intention—"

"Kathleen," Hannah said with a sigh. "You haven't been the least bit amusing ever since you agreed to marry Norcroft. You're entirely too serious and grim and—"

"It's a grim and serious matter." Kathleen glared. "You may be willing to sacrifice me, my life and my future but as much as I have come to accept this as being inevitable, I remain both reluctant and uneasy."

"Precisely why you need a . . . a holiday. Yes, that's it." Hannah beamed. "In the country I should think."

"Near Norcroft's estate?"

"I believe it may be on the way but that's not our destination."

Kathleen narrowed her eyes. "Then what is our destination?"

"We, or I should say I but you are most welcome of course, have been invited to join a dear old friend of mine at his estate. Every year at this time he gathers together the most amusing guests for a house party, although that seems a somewhat insufficient term for it as it goes on for a month or more. Guests stay for a few days or a few weeks. They leave, others arrive. We have all known each other for decades now but I haven't been able to attend for years." A wistful look drifted across the older woman's face. "One never knows who one might meet or what old friendships might be

This is a work of fiction. Names, characters, places, and incidents are products of the author's imagination or are used fictitiously and are not to be construed as real. Any resemblance to actual events, locales, organizations, or persons, living or dead, is entirely coincidental.

AVON BOOKS
An Imprint of HarperCollins*Publishers*
10 East 53rd Street
New York, New York 10022-5299

Copyright © 2008 by Cheryl Griffin
ISBN-13: 978-0-7394-9949-8

VICTORIA ALEXANDER

Seduction of a Proper Gentleman

AVON

An Imprint of HarperCollins*Publishers*

"Never fear, Kathleen, and leave it entirely to me." Hannah smiled the sort of smile that would strike fear into the heart of anyone who knew her well. "You shall be the Countess of Norcroft in no time." Her smile widened. "The curse will be broken and we shall all live quite happily for the rest of our days. No matter what it takes."

to know his lordship without his knowing your true purpose."

Kathleen drew her brows together. "I don't like the sound of that."

"I didn't think you would. Precisely why I have no intention of telling you until it's absolutely necessary. This match has been five hundred years in the making but obviously needs a bit of assistance. Do remember, dear, *extremis malis, extrema remedia*."

"What?"

"The family motto, Kathleen? Surely you haven't forgotten?"

Kathleen held up her wrist and shook her bracelet. "That would be nearly impossible."

"Extreme remedies for extreme ills," Hannah intoned as if her niece hadn't said a word.

"As excellent a motto as it is, in this instance, I don't like the sound of that either."

"We can leave first thing in the morning. No." Hannah shook her head. "It shall take a few days to make arrangements."

"What arrangements?"

Hannah ignored her. "It's an excellent plan, really quite brilliant. I can't believe I didn't think of it sooner."

"Hannah." A warning sounded in Kathleen's voice even though she knew it would do her no good. Once Hannah latched on to an idea, it was impossible to dissuade her.

This book is dedicated with affection to
Adrienne Di Pietro,
for her wicked wit and wisdom
and because she's who I want to be
when I grow up.

"If I may be so bold." He bowed and held out his hand. "I hope, dear woman, these will bring you better . . . luck if you will, than they have me."

She hesitated, then held out a gloved hand. He dropped the shillings into her palm, noting that the gloves were of exceptionally fine quality. A cast-off, no doubt.

"Good day." He nodded, turned on his heel and continued toward his carriage.

When only he and Sinclair had remained in the tontine, Sinclair had suggested, given the speed with which the others had succumbed to marriage, that perhaps they, or the shillings or the cognac, had been cursed. Oliver had thought it utter nonsense then and no less ridiculous now. Regardless, the shillings had now been put to a good and charitable use. The cognac would not be opened until the time was right, which had nothing to do with any concern about luck, good or bad. Perhaps he would save it for his own wedding.

No, Oliver Leighton, the Earl of Norcroft, did not believe in silly things like curses or superstition or magic.

Unfortunately, Oliver smiled in a wry manner, he very much believed in love. And that might be as difficult to find as magic.

father had loved his grandmother and so on and so forth. Why, marrying for love was every bit a part of his heritage as his blue eyes and brown hair. And every bit as impractical.

Regardless, he was who he was.

He signaled to a waiter, requested the cognac be stored for a later time, then rose to his feet. Oliver made his way through the lounge and the foyer beyond, absently jingling the shillings in his hand, accepting the well-meaning congratulations of acquaintances, the jovial comments regarding his skill at avoiding the marital trap that had caught his friends and the observations about his good luck. He nodded at the doorman and stepped out into the deepening twilight. Odd, he hadn't thought it was quite this late. He had lingered longer at the club than he had planned. Not that he had any other plans at the moment.

He started toward his carriage, ignored a twinge of guilt at how long his driver had had to wait and brushed past a woman shrouded in an ancient cloak. A beggar no doubt. At once, Oliver was struck by the enormity of what he had that so many others did not. He had no legitimate reason to feel sorry for himself.

He turned. "I beg your pardon, madam."

She didn't say a word. Her face was hidden by her cloak and that, coupled with the approach of nightfall plus the long hours of savoring the club's best whisky, produced the strangest feeling. As if she weren't quite real. Or he wasn't.

to do its work has always struck me as being somewhat less than lifelike. Oh certainly it is exact, but it fails to capture . . ." Kathleen thought for a moment. "The humanity of a subject, if you will. The subject of a photograph might as well be an apple for all the life expressed in the resulting image." She shook her head. "It is not at all like a living, breathing person."

"And you found the living, breathing person . . ." Hannah paused in an annoyingly pointed manner. "Acceptable?"

"Yes, Aunt Hannah, I did." More than acceptable but she wasn't at all sure she wished to confess that yet. While his eyes had never met hers, even in the deepening twilight she had seen they were a rich blue and she had wondered in that instant what they would look like when he laughed. Or when he was angered. Or in the throes of passion, although that was not something it would be wise to dwell on at the moment and certainly not something she would tell her aunt. While the photograph allowed her to recognize his features anywhere, the lack of color coupled with the firm, unyielding expression that was mandatory for a photograph did not do justice to the Earl of Norcroft in the flesh.

His hair was not as dark as she had thought given the photograph, more a rich brown than a black. He was taller than she had expected as well, his shoulders broader, his stride determined. Oh yes, he would do.

"Oh." Hannah's expression fell, then brightened. "Are we following him then?"

"No, of course not. We're returning to the hotel. My intention was not to accost him, you know."

"Not to accost him yet, you mean."

"I don't mean that at all. I simply wanted to get a good look at the man." Kathleen shrugged as if that was truly all that she had intended. Of course, they both knew better. Indeed, when he had stopped before her, Kathleen had been perilously close to throwing caution to the winds and introducing herself. Even in that brief moment, there had been the hint of something inevitable about the man. Utter nonsense really and attributable to nothing more significant than her grandmother's never-ending pronouncements and her own newfound belief in destiny and the absurd. Regardless, such a first meeting might be awkward and would be highly improper although she had never been overly concerned with propriety unless it suited her.

But he was a British lord with a long and distinguished title and it would not do to get off on the wrong foot with him. Still, Kathleen doubted there was a right foot. She sighed and settled back in her seat. Nothing about this venture was going to be even remotely less than awkward.

"But I thought you had a photograph?"

"An image captured in that excruciatingly long time one has to remain motionless for the camera

"Humph." Hannah mumbled something else Kathleen couldn't make out and thought that was for the best. She assumed it was, as always, a comment on the sensible nature of Kathleen's long-dead parents and how their daughter was just like them. Kathleen had no desire to become involved in yet another debate about magic.

Her grandmother and her aunt had dabbled in magic for as long as Kathleen could remember without any significant results as far as she could tell. Oh certainly both women claimed success with whatever potion they had concocted or spell they had cast, but the results were, in Kathleen's eyes, debatable and more often than not easily explained by rational means. She had long suspected her female relatives liked the idea of magic and thought they were practitioners of the mystic arts when, in fact, they weren't. Their belief was just one of the reasons why Kathleen considered herself the only practical, and therefore responsible, female member of the family.

Magic, spells, charms, and curses were all utter nonsense. Although, admittedly, in recent years, Kathleen had come to accept that possibly her family might have a point, at least when it came to ongoing events that had no other explanation.

"I should think, as you have finally come to your senses regarding the cu—"

"Don't say it," Kathleen said quickly. It was one thing to accept something you had never believed in and quite another it say it aloud as if

"I assume, given your reluctance to do so before now, you were simply waiting to see the gentleman in person before proceeding with a plan. You do need a plan, my dear."

"Yes, you've mentioned that," Kathleen said under her breath.

Aunt Hannah was a firm believer in plans. She said most of the ills of the world could be laid at the foot of poor planning and claimed her first marriage to a wealthy Scottish lord was the direct result of a well-laid plan. That she had loved him with a passion that had lingered far beyond his death at a tragically young age had not been part of her plan. In the nearly quarter of a century since his demise, she had had any number of lovers but not another love. When pressed, she would say that was part of a grander plan which was not, on a divine level, especially well thought out.

"I shall think of something," Kathleen murmured.

"I would be happy to mix up a potion," Hannah said casually. "Concoct a charm or something of that nature. It would make all this easier."

"No," Kathleen said firmly.

Hannah shrugged. "It was just a thought."

"I think this situation is best left to more ordinary methods."

"I don't see why." Hannah sniffed. "The situation is not the least bit ordinary."

"Nonetheless, I prefer to handle this in my own way."

While it had taken Kathleen a number of years to move from utter disbelief to reluctant acceptance, she now believed with a passion that rivaled her grandmother's, even if said belief was in opposition to the type of sane, sensible person she had always thought herself to be.

"For good or ill," Kathleen murmured, absently rubbing the place on her finger where her wedding ring had once been. It seemed if one was about to save one's family through marriage, one should leave the past behind.

"Did you say something?"

"No, nothing at all." She rested her elbow on the desk and propped her head in her hand. "I should have thought of a plan before we left home but there didn't seem to be any time."

"Of course not." Hannah snorted. "The very moment you agreed to pursue Norcroft, my mother was ready to send you off to London. You're lucky she allowed you time to pack a bag."

"She was probably afraid I'd change my mind."

"And with good reason." Hannah studied her niece. "You don't really believe in all this, do you?"

"I certainly didn't at first. Now . . ."

"Now?"

"Now . . ." Kathleen shrugged. "I'm not entirely sure what I believe but whether it's the result of years of listening to grandmother or the events surrounding us all, I am afraid not to believe. And not to want to do something about it. And I sup-

less. Grandmother had staunchly attributed that to the curse, especially since, as Malcomb was exceptionally fond of the ladies, there were no bastard grandchildren running about. Nor had Kathleen's year-long marriage resulted in children, which left Kathleen as the last descendent of the original ill-fated groom and the only one remaining who could end the curse. Grandmother claimed the lack of offspring to carry on the family heritage plus the untimely demises of Kathleen's parents and husband, as well as Hannah's husband, were all due to the curse, and it could no longer be ignored.

Still, when Grandmother had first spoken of the curse, nearly a year after Kenneth's death, Kathleen had demanded to know why she hadn't been told sooner. After all, her poor husband should have been made aware of the risk he was taking by marrying her. If this was indeed real, why hadn't Kathleen been warned?

Hope, grandmother had said firmly, and love. Hope that the curse was, in fact, more legend than truth. She had admitted she had long thought it nothing more than a story herself until circumstances convinced her otherwise. She had hoped as well that, regardless of Kathleen's position as the last of her line, the love she'd shared with her husband would prove more powerful than the faded magic of a centuries-old animosity.

Now, Grandmother was as firm a believer in the curse as she was in anything else of a mystic nature.

Scottish, one English, were to be joined in marriage to end the bloodshed. For whatever reason, the marriage did not occur and an old woman who had lost most of her family to the violence had cursed both families. They had—according to the story that Kathleen viewed as more legend than fact—five hundred years for the families to join in marriage or both lines would end and terrible, dreadful things would happen. When pressed, Grandmother was never explicit about just what kind of terrible, dreadful things—steadfastly maintaining that the specifics were lost in the mists of time— only that they would be very, very bad. Even the five-hundred-year deadline was not certain, only that it would be reached sometime in the autumn in the year of our Lord 1854, before the autumnal equinox.

And wasn't life proving her point? Weren't things getting progressively worse for nearly all of Kathleen's relations as they grew closer to the end of the five hundred years?

Grandmother pointed to the fact that of her three children, Kathleen's mother Glynnis, Hannah and her twin brother Malcomb, only Glynnis had had any children whatsoever and had died long before she should have. Hannah's marriage had been childless and tragically short as well. And, in spite of the fact that Malcomb was a hale and hearty sort and had been wed for thirteen years to a woman who had appeared healthy and sound as well, un- til her death nearly a decade ago, he too was child-

"He did see you," Hannah said under her breath.

"And thought I was a beggar." Kathleen shook her head. "Not an auspicious beginning."

"Nonsense, there are any number of quite happy couples who have had an even worse introduction than yours." Hannah paused. "Although admittedly I can't think of one at the moment."

"You're not helping, Aunt Hannah." Kathleen rubbed the spot between her eyebrows that had throbbed on and off ever since she had agreed to marry Lord Norcroft. She was fairly certain the recurring headache was the direct result of at long last surrendering to and indeed embracing the idea that there might be some validity to the curse, which she had always thought of as absurd. Still, it had become harder and harder in recent years to deny at least the possibility of its existence. There seemed no other explanation for the unpleasant turns life had taken.

Kathleen couldn't recall even hearing of the curse until after her husband, Kenneth, had died in a freak accident nearly nine years ago. Her grandmother had not been opposed to the marriage. After all, Kenneth was of good family and sound fortune and an excellent match. Besides, Kathleen had loved him, which her grandmother had later said was precisely why she had held her tongue. It wasn't until after Kenneth's death that Grandmother had at last told her the rather vague story of how, long ago, two feuding border families, one

"Perhaps." Hannah shrugged. "But it is an answer, an explanation of sorts." She smiled wryly. "And sometimes even an absurd answer is better than no answer at all." Her smile widened to a wicked grin. "And I, for one, am willing to sacrifice you on the altar of matrimony to break this curse or change our family's luck or accept fate or whatever one wishes to call it. Now then, Kate."

Kathleen raised a brow. Kate had been a childhood name that she had quite grown out of and no longer especially liked. Kenneth was the only one who had ever dared call her Kate and he did so mostly because he knew it drove her mad. Still, it had become a term of endearment and a private joke between them.

"My apologies. Sometimes I forget that you have grown beyond Kate. As I was saying." Her tone turned brisk. "What do you propose we do next?"

"I'm not sure there's anything we can do at the moment." Kathleen gathered the papers scattered over the desk. "Apparently our quarry is leaving for his estate in the country tomorrow."

"Excellent."

Kathleen frowned. "It's not the least bit excellent although I suppose it gives us some time to decide what our next step should be."

"Our next step should be to go to the country ourselves."

"Follow him?" Kathleen shook her head. "I did

pose there are worse things to do with your life than marry a handsome, wealthy British lord." She met her aunt's gaze. "What of you? You have always believed in magic and superstition and the like. Do you believe we are cursed?"

"Cursed has such an unpleasant sound but I much prefer it to fate or destiny. At least a curse implies there might be something to be done about it. That it is not inevitable. As for belief . . ." Hannah drew a deep breath. "I believe that I once found the love of my life and lost him entirely too soon. I believe my sister and her husband should not have died so very young. I believe the loss of your husband was unfairly premature. I believe that there is no rational reason for the lack of offspring in our family. Nor do I believe there is any rational reason why any man you have shown even a smattering of interest in through the past nine years has met with, for lack of a better phrase, ill luck."

"I do feel badly about that," Kathleen said under her breath. The fates of each and every one of her occasional suitors had, more than anything else, helped to convince her of the reality of the curse.

Hannah leaned toward Kathleen. "I believe as well in a just and righteous creator who would not inflict a single family with all this of his own accord. Therefore, to me, the only logical answer is this long-ago curse."

Kathleen stared. "There's nothing logical about it."

Kathleen answered without opening her eyes. "I can see it now. Presenting myself at his door—"

"Presenting yourself to his mother," Hannah corrected. "Armed, I might add, with a letter of introduction from my mother, a countess of no little stature."

"In Scotland perhaps," Kathleen murmured.

She heard Hannah settle on the sofa. "I wouldn't let her hear you say that. I daresay my mother considers herself a force to be reckoned with throughout the empire which might well be more in her own mind than anyone else's." She chuckled. "And I wouldn't let her hear me say that either."

Regardless of their comments, the Countess of Dumleavy did indeed have the presence and power that went hand in hand with great wealth and equally great heritage. The only complaint Kathleen had with the woman who had raised her was her staunch belief in nonsense like magic and superstition and, God help them all, curses.

"As I was saying, I present myself at his door and announce that I have come to London with the express purpose of marrying him in order to break a curse that has been on the heads of both our families for five hundred years and is now about to destroy us all." Kathleen raised her head and opened her eyes. "Yes, that should do it. I can't imagine Norcroft won't immediately agree to marriage to break a curse he might not be aware of or, if he does know of it, more than likely does not believe in it, to a woman he's never even seen before."

last year alone she had shepherded three nieces through their first season and had hosted two weddings, both for yet another niece, the circumstances of this the investigator was unable to explain. She had also organized what appeared to be a quickly arranged, but successful, masquerade for charity just last month.

Norcroft had been an adequate but not exceptional student. His lordship was obviously no scholar. Rather a pity as Kathleen had always been fond of debate of an intellectual nature, especially as it pertained to the culture of the ancient Romans. Indeed, study of Roman civilization had long been a quiet passion of hers and she considered herself quite well versed on most aspects of ancient Roman life in the British isles. Apparently, intellectual pursuits were not something they had in common. Not that it mattered.

She sighed and pushed the file away then rested her head on the back of her chair and closed her eyes. Seeing him in person today had been surprisingly unsettling.

"Well?" Hannah's brisk tone sounded from across the room. "Have you come up with something?"

"I can't think of a thing. How does one go about convincing a total stranger to marry you?"

"I haven't the vaguest idea. I have never had to entice a man into marriage nor have I ever wished to." She paused. "Perhaps then it is time for," Hannah could barely choke out the words, "a forthright, direct approach."

"The nerve of the man." Hannah chuckled. "I can't imagine how he might have thought that."

"I can't imagine how he would have thought otherwise," Kathleen muttered. How could she have been so stupid as to so much as consider approaching him outside his club? Especially wearing that blasted cloak. As plans went, this was not well thought out. Not that it was a true plan but she would certainly have to do better. No, this encounter was an impulse on her part and not a particularly clever one at that.

Hannah's tone was casual. "Do you think he will recognize you? When next you meet?"

Kathleen shook her head. "Between the hood and the shadows, he didn't see my face."

"Well that's something to be grateful for." Hannah shook her head. "Surprise is always an excellent element of any successful plan."

"I did however see his face." She glanced at the older woman. "He was significantly more attractive than I had expected."

"More than merely acceptable?"

Kathleen surrendered. "Yes, Aunt Hannah, definitely more than merely acceptable."

"Then this wasn't a complete waste of time." Hannah leaned toward her in a confidential fashion. "We've no time to waste you know."

"I'm well aware of that. And I did manage to learn quite a bit about the man."

"And what, pray tell, did you learn other than he is possessed of the arrogance that is the birth-

its veracity was not in doubt. In that and that alone she acknowledged a certain amount of superstition on her part. Indeed, while she had not admitted it to her family (such an admission being an acknowledgement that they were right and she was wrong) she had come to believe with the fervency of a drunkard renouncing spirits or a heathen come to God. "And you're right. I can use any and all help available and it was impolite of me to refuse you."

"Then you'll allow me to—"

"No, but should it be necessary, I will reserve your offer for a later time." Acceptance of forces beyond reason and control was one thing, belief in her aunt's as yet unproven ability to influence the world through magical means quite another. "For now, however, I am open to any advice you might have for a plan."

"I'll accept that." Hannah beamed at the younger woman. "Although I know what a stickler you are for annoying things like honesty and a forthright manner and a direct approach. Few of my plans have ever included honesty. Indeed, it seems contrary to the very nature of plans."

Kathleen laughed in spite of herself. "This is perfect for you then, as I suspect a forthright, honest approach will not work at all with an arrogant British lord."

"They're all arrogant, dear." Hannah patted her niece's knee. "Is he arrogant then?"

"He thought I was a beggar."

two days, but already she had been through the dossier that had been delivered upon her arrival a dozen times or more. The investigator her grandmother had hired through her Glasgow solicitor had been exceptionally thorough. All the details of the life of the Earl of Norcroft were precisely arrayed on these pages and painted an interesting picture.

The information compiled ranged from the ordinary: the location and date of his birth—he was a mere two years older than she—to financial circumstances—aside from a questionable investment in railroads in America, his fortune was considerable and stable—to what might be considered gossip but was nonetheless most illuminating. It seemed the Earl of Norcroft and three of his friends had had an odd wager, the winner of which was to be the last man left unwed. Apparently, against all odds and contrary to conventional wisdom in society, his lordship had won. The smart money had been on him being the first to fall as, according to the report, he alone among the group was not considered to be particularly averse to marriage. Although Kathleen wasn't sure exactly what the victory said about the man, she found it most interesting.

The earl's given name was Oliver, his family name Leighton. His father had died when he was but a boy, leaving him the twelfth Earl of Norcroft. His mother was active in any number of charities and considered an accomplished hostess. In the

right of nearly every titled gentleman and that he is a fine figure of a man?"

Kathleen glanced at the other woman. "I didn't say he was a fine figure of a man."

"I have eyes too, you know, and, in my opinion, he is a fine figure of a man," Hannah said in a lofty manner. "And I have always been an excellent judge of flesh be it horse or man."

"I quite agree and I suspect he is a good man as well."

"I thought he was arrogant."

"I daresay a man can be both." Kathleen thought for a moment. "In spite of the arrogance of his attitude, even in this brief encounter, he has shown himself to be kind to strangers and generous to those less fortunate."

"My, this was a fruitful evening then." Hannah paused. "Does this alleviate your doubts, Kathleen?"

"Not entirely but it is a relief to learn the gentleman has a good heart and a generous nature." Kathleen turned her gaze back to the window and smiled wryly to herself.

In spite of the circumstances, it was indeed a good thing to know about the man you intended to marry.

Kathleen sat at the desk in the well-appointed parlor in the suite of rooms she and Hannah occupied in the Claridge Hotel and paged through the document before her. They had been in London a mere

for generations and therefore had a certain inherent power—perhaps it might be possible, if one were paying scant attention, to mistake a lady of quality for a beggar. And perhaps, if one incorrectly assumed a woman in an overly large, faded, well-used cloak was not a lady of quality, then the apparent lack of any kind of feminine accompaniment in the form of a forbidding chaperone might confirm that mistaken impression. Very well then. Kathleen started toward her carriage a scant few yards from where the Earl of Norcroft's vehicle had been parked no more than a minute ago. Perhaps the man wasn't an idiot, which was rather nice to know, all things considered.

She instructed the driver of her carriage to return to the hotel, then climbed in and settled in the seat across from her aunt and alleged chaperone Lady Hannah Fitzgivens. If truth were told, it was often difficult to tell just who was chaperoning whom. Not that, as widows, either really needed a chaperone. Necessity aside, Hannah had insisted on accompanying Kathleen because, as she had said before they had left Scotland, it might be an interesting adventure.

"Well?" Hannah raised a brow. "Did you see him?"

"I did," Kathleen said slowly.

"And?" An eager note sounded in Hannah's voice.

"I didn't say a word."

Chapter 1

He thought she was a beggar? Kathleen Mac David, granddaughter of the Countess of Dumleavy, stared at the coins in her hand. Indignation swept through her. *A beggar?* The arrogance of the man. No, the stupidity!

"I beg your par—" She looked up, the words died in her throat. The earl was already climbing into his carriage.

She watched it pull away and her annoyance faded. To be fair, and Kathleen was nothing if not fair, in the deepening shadows of the approaching night, and wrapped in the hooded cloak her grandmother had insisted she wear for luck—it had been passed down from grandmother to granddaughter

But if Warton had been the favorite of those who preferred to bet on a sure winner, Cavendish had been close on his heels. Viscount Cavendish, Nigel, had spent much of his adult life in the fervent avoidance of responsibility of any kind and the equally fervent pursuit of women and a good time. Cavendish had lived his life on the edge of scandal and disaster. It was inevitable that one day he would be found in a compromising situation with a young woman of good family—precisely why Cavendish had usually avoided young women of good family. But regardless of the circumstances, it was obvious Cavendish too had lost his heart. And obvious as well that his new wife had played an enormous part in bringing about a change in the viscount. Cavendish had grown in the last few months and any fears Oliver might have had that his friend would come to a bad end had vanished. Cavendish was a changed man and a happy one. He and Lady Cavendish were currently traveling, Cavendish had explained with a laugh, to wherever the stars were brightest.

Daniel Sinclair, the American among them, had been the third to fall. He had entered their circle of friends when his father had arranged a marriage with Oliver's cousin. Although that arrangement had proved unsuccessful, a second matchmaking effort had succeeded, even if the manner in which it had come about was not what anyone had expected. Sinclair and his new bride were now in America, where Sinclair was poised to create a railroad empire. As the other men had invested heavily in the endeavor, they wished him well.

Now, Oliver was quite alone. Admittedly that might be somewhat overdramatic. Certainly Oliver had other friends. Among them, Jonathon Effington, Marquess of Helmsley, although he was married now as well. Indeed, even though Helmsley was not part of the tontine, it had been his marriage that had prompted it in the first place.

This was nonsense. Oliver glared at the innocent cognac. His friends weren't dead, merely married. He hadn't been abandoned, they had simply moved on with their lives. The fact that his was essentially unchanged was no one's fault but his own. It was past time he made a concerted effort to find a bride. It shouldn't be especially difficult. By anyone's estimate he was an excellent catch. He was of good family and equally good fortune, better than average in appearance, indeed, some would call him rather handsome, even dashing. And no one had ever complained about his manner. Why, he could be quite charming. No, there was certainly nothing wrong with him. Now that he had apparently decided what he really wanted, he should have no problem finding just the right woman. No problem at all.

Although there was that bothersome character flaw of his that had kept him from marriage thus far. The twelfth Earl of Norcroft was an unabashed romantic. He didn't just want to marry, he wanted love. His father had loved his mother. His grand-

Prologue

August 1854

It was a sad state of affairs when a man's only companion was a bottle of cognac. And an unopened bottle at that.

Oliver Leighton, the Earl of Norcroft, sat at his usual table in his favorite club and stared at the bottle, absently jingling the four coins in his hand. Who would have thought it would come to this? Certainly not Oliver. He never imagined he'd be the last man standing. When he and three of his closest friends had formed a tontine a mere six months ago, Oliver never dreamed he'd be the ultimate winner. Nor, if truth were told, did he especially wish to be.

The tontine was a wager of sorts. At stake was a shilling contributed from each of the men and the fine old bottle of cognac that now sat before Oliver in an odd sort of silent reproach. Not that there was anything to reproach him about. No, Oliver had emerged victorious through no fault of his own.

It had been Warton, Gideon Pearsall, Viscount Warton, who had originally proposed the tontine. The winner of the stakes, admittedly meager but symbolic nonetheless, was the last man to marry, although freedom was the true prize. If any one of them at that time had been told all but one would be wed within half a year, the teller of such a tale would have been denounced as a lunatic. Of course now he would be seen as prophetic.

The tontine was not a secret among members of the club and other gentlemen of their acquaintance. In private wagers around the city, the smart money had been on Warton. That he had been the first to fall was no more a shock to observers than it was to Warton himself. But fallen he had. And, as he was currently in the midst of planning an expedition to South America with the lovely Lady Warton to indulge her passion for the study of orchids, one might say he had fallen particularly hard. Even if the viscount was more resigned than enthusiastic, he had never suggested the journey not be attempted at all, which was a testament to the charms of the new Lady Warton as well as to the depth of her husband's affection.

Chapter 3

$\mathcal{S}$he opened her eyes and stared at the coffered ceiling high above her head. A very nice coffered ceiling. Not one she had ever seen before but lovely and elegant, bespeaking of an age well past. Where was she?

She sat up and a dull pain washed through her head. She groaned and felt the back of her skull. There was no apparent bump. Still, her head did ache and she didn't know why. She sank back gratefully onto the soft pillow and glanced around. She was lying on a chaise lounge in what was apparently a sitting room. A bedroom could be seen through an open doorway. Both rooms were decorated in cool shades of green and gave the most serene and soothing impression of a forest glade. She had no idea where she was but it was certainly lovely.

"You're awake," a pleasant feminine voice sounded from the direction of the door.

She struggled to sit up.

"Oh no, my dear, you mustn't try to move too quickly." A motherly sort of woman bustled over to her accompanied by two maids who immediately positioned pillows behind her for support. "There, that's better. How do you feel?"

She rubbed the back of her head. "My head . . ."

"Dr. Miller said it will probably ache for a day or so but you will be fine." The lady settled in a chair beside the chaise. "He recommends complete rest for at least a day."

"Who is Dr. Miller?" she said slowly.

"Our local physician. He left a few minutes ago. He's very good and quite well regarded. I have long considered us lucky that he prefers life in the country to what would certainly be a more lucrative practice in London although that's scarcely here nor there at the moment. He will return in a day or two to see how you're coming along." The lady shook her head. "I must say you had us all worried. Why even that nice Lady Fitzgivens—"

"Lady Fitzgivens?"

"She brought you here. You're quite lucky, my dear, that someone as thoughtful as Lady Fitzgivens saw you fall off the train platform."

"Yes, lucky." Odd, she didn't feel the least bit

lucky. If she felt anything at all it was apprehensive. And that was odd as well. Shouldn't she feel something, well, *more*? "I fear I am somewhat confused. I fell off a train platform?"

"Admittedly that part is a bit muddled but apparently Lady Fitzgivens, who had just arrived from London, saw you trip and fall off the platform. You had an envelope addressed to me. Unfortunately, whatever it contained was missing, but she had you brought here."

"And where is here?"

"Forgive me, my dear, of course you have no idea. You're at Norcroft Manor. I am Lady Norcroft." Lady Norcroft smiled in the gentle manner that one might use with very small children or those with feeble minds. "But a more pertinent question is, who are you?"

"Who am I?" she said slowly.

"Yes, my dear, what is your name?"

"My name?" It was a simple enough question. Why didn't she have an answer? Simple or otherwise. The apprehension that had nibbled at her a moment ago now settled in the pit of her stomach.

Lady Norcroft laid a hand on her arm. "Perhaps it would be better if you start with what you remember."

"What I remember," she repeated. No wonder Lady Norcroft looked at her as if she had lost her mind. Apparently she had. She drew a deep breath. "I don't seem to remember much of anything beyond opening my eyes a few moments ago."

"Oh dear." Lady Norcroft studied her carefully. "Are you sure?"

She wrinkled her brow and searched her mind, trying to come up with something, anything before waking up in this lovely green room. She nodded. "Very sure."

"I was afraid of that," Lady Norcroft said with a sigh.

Dismay widened her eyes. "Afraid of what?"

"Loss of memory," Lady Norcroft said in a mournful manner but there was a spark of excitement in her eyes. "There's a word for it." Lady Norcroft's brows pulled together. "What is it? Something Greek sounding, I think."

"Amnesia?" she said without thinking.

"Yes, that's it. Very good. At least you remembered something."

"I didn't remember anything. It just popped into my head."

"Well, my poor dear child, you have amnesia." Lady Norcroft's tone was firm although one might have suspected she was a bit pleased. "One hears of such things but I never imagined to encounter it in person."

"Never?" Panic raised her voice. "You don't think it's something that happens all the time then?"

"Oh, I doubt it."

"Surely it can't be that unusual." This couldn't be happening to her. "No doubt people fall off train platforms every day, bump their heads, and forget who they are." What was she to do? "They're probably right as rain in no time." She stood, the ache in her head dashed away by the fear squeezing her heart. "Perhaps that's why you don't hear about this sort of thing."

"My dear, I don't think—"

"Perhaps it's so common—" An overwhelming desire to flee gripped her. Instead, she paced the width of the room. After all, she had nowhere to go. "People getting knocked on the head, losing their memory one moment and it's back the next—that no one thinks it important to mention it."

"Now, now there's no need to get upset."

"No need?" She pulled up short and whirled to face Lady Norcroft. "I beg your pardon, but I think there's every need! It's most disconcerting not to remember who you are!"

"You remembered amnesia. I would say that's progress." The older woman smiled in a confident manner. "It's a very unusual word."

"But I don't know my own name!" The reality of her situation threatened to overwhelm her and she wanted nothing more than to throw herself into the sympathetic lady's motherly grasp and weep uncontrollably. Abruptly she realized she was not the type of person to throw herself into anyone's arms and weep, uncontrollably or otherwise. Which was at least more than she knew a minute ago. Still, it was scarcely helpful. "I don't know where I'm from. Who my family is." She gasped. "I don't know if I have a family! Or a husband. What if I have a husband?"

"He isn't much of a husband, I'd say, to have misplaced you like this."

"But I don't know." She wrapped her arms around herself and sniffed. "And I don't know what to do now."

"Of course you don't dear," Lady Norcroft said smoothly. "You have amnesia. However you also have me." She nodded at the maids. "Ellen, Mary, tea will help I think." The maids scurried off.

"I really don't think—"

"Nor should you. I suspect thinking will only confuse you more."

"I daresay I can't be any more confused." She sank back down on the chaise. "Lady Norcroft—"

"Very good." Delight sounded in Lady Norcroft's voice. "You remembered my name."

She stared at the other woman. "You introduced yourself no more than a minute ago."

"Yes, but I should think the very fact that you did not forget is of some significance. That coupled with your recollection of the word amnesia and I would say you are certainly on the road to recovery." Lady Norcroft beamed. "However, that's probably more than enough for now. While I know little about problems of this nature, I suspect it would be best if you conserved your strength. We shall speak to Dr. Miller about this when he returns tomorrow. Don't worry about a thing."

"Lady Norcroft—"

"You know, my very dear friend, Marguerite,

Lady Cutchings, once had a prince stay at her country home. This is so much better."

"This?"

"Or rather I should say you. An obviously well-born lady, who has completely lost her memory, arrives with my name on her lips—"

"I don't think it was—"

"Figuratively, my dear. Lips, envelopes." Lady Norcroft gestured in a blithe manner. "One and the same. And a lovely woman at that. Oh, it's quite the type of adventure the Duchess of Roxborough would write in one of her novels." Her eyes widened. "I have an idea that might help." She rose to her feet and held out her hand. "Come with me."

"Where are we going?" She took the older lady's hand and trailed after her into the bedroom.

Lady Norcroft stopped before a large cheval mirror. "There now, what do you see?"

She stared at the face reflected in the mirror. It struck her that one rarely had the opportunity to examine one's own features with an objective eye and perhaps there was a good reason for that. The face that stared back at her was nice enough, even rather pretty, which came as something of a relief. She didn't think she was particularly vain, although she had no idea. Still, it seemed a good thing to like one's face even if one's nose was annoyingly pert, one eyes a bit large for one's face, and one's chin rather pointed. All in all, it was a heart-shaped sort of face and not a bad face to live with. Her eyes were a nice shade of green and went well with the dark red color of her hair. Hair, she noted, that had a suggestion of curl and a definite air of unruliness about it. She suspected it did not behave willingly. Her gaze traveled down the full length of her image.

"Well?" Lady Norcroft said eagerly.

"A bit on the thin side, don't you think?"

"Not at all." Lady Norcroft cast a critical eye on the image in the mirror. "Perhaps a little but you do have a nice bosom and that's important."

"Yes, I suppose," she said and studied her image. She was of average height and wore a well-tailored traveling dress of obvious quality so her slender frame wasn't due to poverty. That too was a relief although it did beg the question of whether she might be shallow as well as vain. Still, she might not remember her name but she couldn't imagine anyone not being pleased to discover they weren't poor.

"You could be a little younger for the proper heroine of a novel although you are scarcely in your dotage." Lady Norcroft perused the woman in the mirror. "You're nearly thirty I would think."

She cringed. "That old?"

Lady Norcroft laughed. "My dear, that isn't the least bit old. However, if you wish, we shall hope for *nearly* rather than *thirty*." She paused. "Well?"

"Well, yes nearly is better."

"No, I meant—well, who do you see?" Lady Norcroft waved at the mirror. "Do you look familiar? Do you recognize yourself?"

She met the gaze of the older lady in the mirror and wrinkled her nose. "Unfortunately, no."

"I was hoping but, of course, you wouldn't." Lady Norcroft's eyes twinkled. "This is the most interesting thing that has happened in a long time." She paused and her brow furrowed slightly. "Although, upon reflection, it has been a most interesting year. I shall have to tell you all about it."

"I'm not sure that's wise, Mother." A gentleman stood in the doorway behind them. He was tall with nicely broad shoulders and dark brown hair. His jaw was square, his features even, his nose straight and aristocratic. He was handsome but not overly so. Dashing was the word that came to mind. His eyes were a deep, rich blue and when his gaze met hers in the mirror, an awful sweet feeling of inevitability swept through her and took her breath away.

"Why ever not?" Lady Norcroft asked.

"You don't know anything about her." He directed his words to his mother but his gaze remained locked with hers. "And from what Ellen told me, she doesn't know anything about herself either."

"He's right." She couldn't seem to pull her gaze from his and, oddly enough, didn't wish to. "I could be anyone."

"Anyone at all," he murmured.

She shrugged. "Or no one in particular."

He smiled a rather devilish sort of smile and her heart fluttered. "That I find hard to believe."

She drew a deep breath. "Do I know you?"

"I don't think so."

"Then perhaps you know me?" she said hopefully.

"I'm afraid not."

"Still," she shook her head, "you seem remarkably familiar."

"Where are my manners?" Lady Norcroft turned away from the mirror. She followed suit, reluctantly tearing her gaze from the gentleman in the doorway. "Allow me to introduce my son, Oliver, the Earl of Norcroft."

The earl nodded and without thinking she held out her hand. He raised it to his lips and heat flushed up her face. Again, his gaze meshed with hers. She swallowed hard. "Are you certain we have never met?"

"There is nothing wrong with my memory." A slight but distinctly wicked gleam sparked in his eye. "And I would most certainly remember you."

At once, it struck her that regardless of her initial response to him, or perhaps because of it, this could be a very dangerous man. Possibly to her future, definitely to her heart. Dear Lord, she did hope she wasn't married. She pulled her hand from his.

"Oh my, this is awkward," Lady Norcroft said.

"Which part, Mother?" he said smoothly.

"I can introduce you to her but I can't introduce

her to you." She turned to her guest. "My dear child, I simply cannot keep calling you my dear child, it will make my head ache even worse than yours. We must give you a name."

"I am quite sure I have a name." She might not know her own name but she was fairly confident she didn't wish for a new one. Did that mean she was proud as well as shallow and vain? Thus far what little she had learned about herself was not especially good.

"Of course you do but unfortunately no one knows it. And we do need to call you something." Lady Norcroft smiled in a persuasive manner. "I know I wouldn't be at all happy if someone wanted to change my name. But it is only temporary and nothing more than a convenience really for the rest of us so I do hope you don't mind."

She forced a smile to her face. "That makes a great deal of sense." She squared her shoulders without thinking then wondered if perhaps she wasn't somewhat courageous as well. Which might make up a little for pride and vanity. "What would you suggest?"

"Nothing immediately comes to mind. I only ever had to name one child and I named him Oliver. The gentleman who wrote my favorite play was named Oliver. I saw it for the first time when I was a girl and I have loved it ever since." Lady Norcroft cast an affectionate smile at her only child. "It was an excellent choice, don't you think?"

"It seems to suit him." Indeed, Oliver struck her as a perfect name for his lordship.

"Now we need a name that suits you." Lady Norcroft studied her carefully. "What do you think, Oliver?"

"It scarcely matters as it's only temporary. I have no idea." He shrugged. "Mary?"

Lady Norcroft rolled her gaze at the ceiling. "Goodness, Oliver, you have no imagination. She is certainly not a Mary. Mary is entirely too ordinary. You can tell just by looking at her, she's not an ordinary sort of person."

"Thank you," Not-a-Mary said under her breath then cringed to herself. There was that pride again.

"Very well then." He thought for a moment. "Penelope?"

"Better. It's certainly a possibility." His mother glanced at Possibly Penelope. "What do you think?"

Possibly Penelope shook her head. "I don't feel like a Penelope. It strikes me as a somewhat flighty sort of name and I suspect I am not a flighty sort of person."

"Nonsense." Lady Norcroft waved away the objection. "I am an Edwina which is not the least bit flighty and yet my son will tell you I am very often flighty. Still, I had no say in my name while, at the moment, you do." Her expression brightened. "What an exciting opportunity for you."

"It doesn't seem very exciting." Possibly Penelope sighed.

"This is absurd." Oliver huffed. "We are not naming a child. She doesn't have to live with it for the rest of her life. Any name will do. What about Elizabeth? Or Sarah? Or Anne?"

"You're right, I suppose," his mother said. "After all a rose by any other name . . ."

"Shakespeare." The earl nodded sagely.

"Very good, Oliver. It's nice to know your education was not a complete waste of time."

"He never was much of a scholar," What-about-Elizabeth said without thinking.

His eyes narrowed. "How did you know that?"

"Perhaps a name from Shakespeare," Lady Norcroft said more to herself than to the others.

What-About-Elizabeth widened her eyes. "I have no idea. It just popped into my head."

"It scarcely matters, Oliver. I daresay anyone with the least bit of sense would see that you were never much of a scholar. You simply don't have a scholarly look about you."

He studied What-About-Elizabeth suspiciously. It was most annoying.

What-About-Elizabeth cast him a look every bit as suspicious. "Are you certain we have never met?"

"I have it!" Lady Norcroft said. "My favorite play is *She Stoops to Conquer*, written by Mr. Oliver Goldsmith." She glanced at What-About-Elizabeth. "He also wrote *The Vicar of Wakefield*, which is not nearly as amusing. Dreadful things happen to the poor vicar and his family although all does end well."

"And your point, Mother?"

"I thought perhaps a literary reference might trigger her memory," she said with a chastising look. "However, my point was that in *She Stoops to Conquer* the heroine is mistaken for someone she's not, which seems to me very much like not knowing who you are at all."

"The heroine, mother, is *pretending* to be someone she's not." Oliver's gaze met What-About-Elizabeth's. "She spends much of the play deceiving the hero."

What-About-Elizabeth gasped. "It sounds as if you are accusing me of deceiving you."

He shrugged as if the answer was obvious.

"No, no, he didn't say that," Lady Norcroft said quickly. "Although it did sound somewhat like an accusation."

What-About-Elizabeth crossed her arms over her chest. "That would make you the hero of the piece and thus far I am not at all sure you have displayed especially heroic qualities."

He glared. "I can be most heroic."

She shrugged, mimicking his earlier gesture.

"Kate Hardcastle," Lady Norcroft said abruptly. "The name of the heroine in the play. I think it suits you."

Oliver's jaw clenched. "I took you into my house."

"Kate that is, not Hardcastle," Lady Norcroft continued. "I don't think you look like a Hardcastle at all."

What-About-Elizabeth cast the earl a sardonic smile. "Your hospitality is most kind."

"Once you had been brought here, we certainly couldn't turn you away," Oliver said.

Lady Norcroft pressed her lips together in a disapproving manner. "Not that he didn't want to."

Oliver closed his eyes for a moment as if to pray for patience. "I never said that."

Kate-That-Is drew a calming breath. In truth, she couldn't blame the earl for his suspicions. She'd probably be suspicious herself if a stranger who didn't know his own name had been deposited on her front step, wherever that might be. "I would think erring on the side of caution is rarely a mistake."

"You do?" he said.

"How very sensible of you." Lady Norcroft beamed.

"I must be a sensible sort of person." She sighed. So she was sensible as well as vain, proud, and perhaps courageous. She dismissed shallow. Shallow was a quality one could probably overcome with effort. "Lord Norcroft was simply exercising prudence." Kate-That-Is cast Oliver an apologetic look. "It seems quite understandable to me."

"As it would to any lady of breeding." Lady Norcroft threw a smug look at her son. "I told you as much, Oliver."

Oliver scoffed. "You told me she had fine shoes."

Fine shoes? Kate-That-Is resisted the urge to look.

"And she does." Lady Norcroft nodded firmly. "How does Kate sound to you?"

"Kate." The name didn't sound right but it didn't sound exactly wrong either. *Kate.* "Kate will do I think."

"Excellent." Lady Norcroft looked at her son. "Perhaps if you made an effort to find her baggage, a clue to who she is would be found as well."

"My bags are missing?" Kate said in a weak voice.

"I have already sent a footman to the train station to see if they were simply overlooked in the confusion. Lady Fitzgivens did not strike me as the type of woman one would call overly efficient." Oliver studied Kate for a moment. "You don't remember anything at all?"

"No." She shook her head. "I'm afraid not."

His eyes narrowed slightly. "Then how do you know you had bags?"

What a suspicious creature he was. "Surely I must have had bags. I was found at the train platform. I am wearing traveling attire, therefore I must have bags."

"Where were you going?" he asked quickly, as if to catch her in a lie.

"I don't know," she snapped. "But I should be on my way." She stepped toward the door. Immediately an inexplicable weakness gripped her, the room swam, and she sank down on the chaise. Odd, she had felt perfectly fine a moment ago.

"My dear, you are not going anywhere." Lady

Norcroft glared at her son. "See what you've done now, Oliver. You've upset poor Kate." She turned to Kate and patted her arm. "We can't possibly let you leave. You're obviously not up to it. Besides, you have nothing but the clothes on your back, no money, and no idea where you were going or where you come from."

"Scotland," Oliver said. "She's from Scotland. I can hear it in her voice."

"Yes, but her accent is not pronounced." Lady Norcroft's forehead creased in a considering manner. "It's my guess she was educated here, in a proper boarding school for young ladies."

"You can tell that from no more than my speech?" Kate tried not to stare. Lady Norcroft was apparently far more perceptive than she might at first appear.

"Indeed I can." The older woman's eyes sparkled. "I have all sorts of accomplishments one would not suspect upon initial acquaintance." She settled back in her chair. "I am a woman of surprise."

Oliver laughed. "That you are, Mother." His gaze slid to Kate. "And far and away too trusting."

"Although I suspect she is far too intelligent as well to be easily fooled," Kate said coolly.

He shrugged. "She has a kind and generous heart. Such people are often taken advantage of."

"And just as often rewarded for their goodness." Kate forced a smile. "If not in this life, then in the next."

"I consider it my responsibility to make certain

when it comes to my mother, *this life* is as trouble free as possible."

"I can't imagine anyone wishing to cause any trouble whatsoever for your mother. You sir," Kate narrowed her eyes, "are a different matter entirely."

Lady Norcroft choked.

"A different matter?" His lordship glared. "I'll have you know I am considered quite a decent sort."

"Hah." She rose to her feet, any previous weakness washed away by indignation. "If you had had your way I would still be lying in the dust at the train platform."

"I would never leave any unconscious woman lying in the dust at a train platform or anywhere else. However," he clenched his teeth and a muscle on the side of his jaw twitched, "I would not have invited her into my home."

Kate squared her shoulders. "I should therefore be happy to leave your home at once." She turned toward his mother. "Lady Norcroft, while I am most appreciative of your kindness and generosity, I fear my presence here has become quite intolerable to your son."

"I never said your presence was intolerable," he said quickly. "I simply hesitate to invite strangers into my home. Strangers who—"

"Who could be anyone. Yes, yes, you said it before." She drew a deep breath. "Lady Norcroft, if you will be so kind as to arrange transportation for me back to the train station, I am certain I will be able to locate my bags—"

Lady Norcroft shook her head. "But you won't recognize them."

"I am willing to take the risk that the very sight of my belongings will at once restore my memory and then I shall be on my way."

"Good heavens, no," Lady Norcroft said firmly. "I can't allow that."

"Nor can I." Oliver blew an annoyed breath. "Regardless of the circumstances, you have been brought to our home and therefore are our responsibility."

Kate glared at him. "Is it your responsibility then to shelter every . . . every stray creature that wanders to your door?"

"In this small corner of the world, yes," he snapped.

"Oliver takes his position as earl very seriously," Lady Norcroft said in an aside to Kate. "He's quite good in that respect."

"Still, I would prefer not to stay where I am not wanted."

"It's not a question of want." Oliver's jaw tightened. "You said it yourself. It's a question of prudence. You could be anyone."

"I do hope so," she said sharply. "As I seem to be without funds at the moment—" she unclasped the bracelet at her wrist and handed it to Lady Norcroft, "—I suspect my bracelet is worth a great deal. If you would be so good as to keep it as collateral and loan me the return fare to London, I shall send for it—"

"Ah-hah!" Oliver aimed an accusatory finger. "How do you know you've come from London?"

"I don't know that I've come from London." She huffed. "I simply surmised that given that your mother said Lady Fitzgivens had just arrived from London. I would imagine that I must have arrived as well. It certainly makes sense. It seems to me a village the size of Norcroft has few trains—"

"Ah-hah! And how do you know how big Norcroft is?"

"I don't know." She gritted her teeth. "Again, it's an assumption on my part as you said this small corner of the world. Am I wrong then? Is Norcroft a great metropolis?"

"Oh, not at all," Lady Norcroft murmured in an absent manner, intent on studying Kate's bracelet. "It's quite small really. Pleasant enough though and charming in its own way."

"Still—" Oliver began.

"Still?" Kate smirked. "No ah-hah?"

His eyes narrowed. "Not at the moment."

"I thought surely he had another ah-hah in him," Lady Norcroft said under her breath.

He ignored her. "But London sounds familiar to you."

"As do Paris and Rome," she said sharply. "I daresay I've lost my memory not my mind."

"I would think someone with amnesia would

have no memory of anything," he said in a lofty manner.

"I do apologize for not conforming to your knowledge of such things. You must find it most irritating to discover you don't know all there is to know about all there is."

"Indeed I do," he said staunchly.

Lady Norcroft laughed. "Always."

He paused and the corners of his mouth quirked upwards as if he recognized the absurdity of the conversation and was resisting the urge to smile. "I rather like believing that I know everything there is to know about everything there is although what I do in truth know is that it's a false belief."

"He can be most modest when circumstances call for it." Lady Norcroft cast an affectionate smile at her son. "He has even been known to admit, on rare occasions, that he might possibly be wrong."

"On rare occasions only," he said in a somber tone that belied the humor in his eyes.

Kate stared. What kind of man was this Earl of Norcroft? Overbearing and arrogant one minute, willing to see the humor and make light of his own behavior the next. It was almost endearing. The man was an enigma and, Lord help her, most intriguing.

"Please accept my apologies." He stepped to Kate and again took her hand and raised it to his lips. His gaze meshed with hers. "You are most welcome to stay as our guest until such time as you regain your memory." His lips brushed across the back of her hand. "And perhaps beyond."

Her breath caught. "I doubt that will be necessary."

"Ah, but you don't know." His eyes twinkled in the same manner his mother's had. But while hers had mirrored amusement, his revealed something altogether different. A promise perhaps, the suggestion of something wonderful to come or wonderfully wicked. Even a hint of magic. "And until you do, you must consider this your home."

"That's most gracious of you, my lord." She tried to pull her hand from his, but he held it firmly.

"Until then, I shall cherish the hope that this was indeed your intended destination." His gaze remained locked with hers.

"How delightfully charming of you, Oliver," his mother murmured. "Sometimes, a mother is so proud . . ."

"And furthermore, I shall do all I can to help you discover the truth as to who you really are." He stared into her eyes. "And believe me, *Kate*, I will discover the truth."

Chapter 4

She stared back at him. "That's sounds like a threat, my lord."

"Not at all," he said smoothly. "It's a promise."

Kate yanked her hand from his and he had the oddest sense of loss. "And do you always keep your promises?"

"Always. But especially when it comes to the truth."

"About me?" Her eyes flashed and it struck him that this was a stubborn and no doubt clever woman.

"Are there are other truths to be determined then?"

"I would think there are any number of truths, as it were, in the universe," Kate said lightly.

"Well versed in philosophy." Lady Norcroft nodded. "I knew she was properly educated." She rose to her feet. "Oliver, I suggest you see if there has been any word as to her bags and I will see to our guest."

"Very well." He glanced at Kate. "Until later then?"

She smiled politely.

He turned and strode from the room.

"Do you like him?" his mother's voice trailed after him.

"I haven't decided yet," he heard Kate say.

"Not an auspicious beginning but not bad, not bad at all," his mother responded. "I couldn't be more pleased . . ."

Pleased? What on earth did she have to be pleased about? Oliver strode down the hall. Just because an attractive woman is practically dropped at his feet doesn't mean he'll take up with her. His mother couldn't possibly think this stranger was marriageable material. Why, they know nothing about her.

Except that she was lovely with fire in her green eyes and obviously fire in her heart as well. He suspected she would be a challenge for any man. The thought popped into his head without warning. *And a joy.* He dismissed it.

"Hollinger." Oliver stopped the butler in the

corridor. "Has there been any word as to our guest's luggage?"

"Not yet, my lord."

He started off then paused. "Does anything about this situation strike you as suspicious?"

"Suspicious, my lord?"

"Do you think she is who she says she is," Oliver said impatiently.

"It's my understanding that she hasn't said who she is, my lord."

"You know what I meant." He glared. "This nonsense about losing her memory. Do you believe it?"

"It's not my place to believe or not believe, my lord."

Oliver clenched his teeth. "I'm asking what you think, Hollinger. Surely you have an opinion."

"I do indeed, sir."

"Excellent. I should very much like to hear it."

"If you insist. I have a skeptical nature, my lord, therefore unusual occurrences often seem to me to be suspicious." Hollinger paused for a moment. "However, I have heard of such things as loss of memory after a blow to the head therefore it also seems to me entirely plausible. *There are more things in heaven and earth, Horatio, than are dreamt of in your philosophy.* Shakespeare, sir," the butler added in an apologetic manner.

"I know Shakespeare!" Oliver started off then turned back. "Hollinger, do I strike you as a scholarly sort of man?"

The butler hesitated.

"Again, I am asking for your opinion."

"As you wish, my lord. Not especially scholarly, no sir."

"Find those bags, Hollinger," Oliver said in a sharper manner than he would have wished and started off. "I am going for a ride. No, a walk. A very long walk."

"Yes, my lord."

So much for the peaceful nature of country life. Oliver stalked down the stairs and through the central corridor to the terrace, passing any number of servants who cast him a curious glance. No doubt news of their mysterious guest's arrival was already the talk of the household. He stepped out onto the terrace, crossed to the far right and down the steps that led to the garden. The house was not especially old as country houses went, a mere two hundred years or so. Palladian in style, it was designed by a previous earl who fancied himself a bit of an architect. Oliver snorted. If he recalled his family history, that particular ancestor was certainly no scholar. Scholarly men did not run in the Leighton family.

He strode along the broad gravel walk between the tall hedges that formed an alley of sorts through the full length of the gardens, intersected at right angles in two places by similar walks. Occasional breaks in the hedges allowed entry into formal planting beds that had been designed nearly as long ago as the house itself. While remaining true to the original plan in spirit, exactly what blooms were grown varied from year to year with the whims of the current countess. His mother was particularly fond of spring flowers, and there was little that could compare with the Norcroft gardens in the spring.

To the side of the main house, and out of sight of the terrace, was a greenhouse dedicated to producing spring blossoms to fill vases in the house all year long as well as the propagation and care of the outside plantings and supplemental care of the plants grown in the conservatory on the south side of the manor. The gardens were Italian and French in style, symmetrical and precise. Classic. He skirted around a large fountain, positioned in the center of the first intersection, and ignored the stares of a half dozen life-size marble statues of nubile nymphs in Grecian garb. Both fountain and statues were installed by his grandmother for no reason other than—as the story went—she liked them.

The formal beds gave way to clipped lawn perfect for games of croquet and his mother's now only occasional foray into archery. Her old target remained stationed at the far side of the wide lawn. Eventually he reached the perpendicular two rows of shaped yews that sandwiched the broken remains of an ancient Roman wall and marked the end of the tended gardens. While the trees hid the offending wall from the house on one side and the countryside on the other, he had long been grateful that whatever earl or countess or landscaper who had originally designed the garden had seen fit to retain this remnant of antiquity. As a child, he had thought it a secret spot built and preserved by magic and had wondered as well if only children could see it. As the current earl, he suspected its retention had more to do with economy rather than anything of a mystic nature. It was less expensive to hide the wall than remove it. Regardless, he was grateful for its presence. It bespoke of a continuity of civilization, an unbroken line of humanity that he liked being part of. As he had done since boyhood, he braced his hand on the stone and vaulted over the low wall. Now, as always, the thought crossed his mind as to the lives of those long-dead Romans and the purpose of this short section of crumbling wall as no one, to his knowledge, had ever determined where it started or where it ended. It simply was.

A half an hour later he reached the top of the gently sloping hill that overlooked the slight valley where the manor sat, the narrow river or broad stream, depending on one's point of view and mood, that ran along the edge of the estate and even, he had always thought, the world beyond. This place was as much a legacy as his land and his title. His father had first shown him this spot when Oliver was very young. It was where he'd said he liked to contemplate his life. Oliver hadn't been up here in years but this was where he too came to sort out the complexities of his own life, and had done so

since the first moment he could escape the watchful eyes of governesses as a boy. From here the
world seemed to take on a proper perspective. He
settled on the ground at the base of an ancient oak
that, as a child, he had thought as old as the Roman wall itself. Now, he knew that was nonsense.
Trees, even oaks, did not live for fourteen hundred
years. Still, the tree was old and venerable and
comforting.

He remembered coming up here when his father
had died. He'd been barely eight years of age at the
time. His father had been not much older than Oliver was now, a healthy, handsome man in the
prime of his life. He had slipped on wine spilled at
the top of the grand marble stairway during a
party in honor of something no one could now recall and had fallen backwards down the stairs. At
first, he had insisted he was fine. But the next day
he had taken to his bed with an aching head. By
nightfall, he was dead.

He'd been a good man and a better father and
had taught his son as much by example as by
words about honor and strength. The day he died,
Oliver had sat by his bed for a few minutes, not
really understanding that this chat with his father
would be their last. Not until years later had Oliver realized his father must have known the end
was near. He had talked to Oliver in those final
lucid moments of the responsibility that went
hand in hand with his title. Responsibility to the
people who depended upon him, his servants and

tenants, responsibility to his country and to his family. And he had told Oliver to take care of his mother.

Oliver had wept under this tree then. Alone, so as not to upset his mother. After all, he was now the earl. But here, he had felt his father's presence and, whether it was a trick of the mind or simply need, felt as well his strength and his wisdom. And he was never alone.

Oliver had come up here before he had gone off to school for the first time and again whenever he had returned home. Here, he had considered the future when he had completed his studies and prepared to fully take over the family finances and estate and all the myriad details that were part and parcel of being the Earl of Norcroft. This was where he had once pondered the vagaries of a woman's heart when the girl he had thought he had loved had loved someone else. And here he had realized that it probably hadn't been love at all, as the pain he had felt had been more to his pride than his heart.

Overlooking his home, his world, through the years, Oliver had considered matters both great and small, those of importance and those of no significance whatsoever. He wasn't entirely sure where the question of Kate fell and wasn't at all sure Kate was the real question.

He stared at the manor in the distance. It was most irritating to discover no one thought he could be a scholar. Certainly he had never aspired to scholarly pursuits, so the fact that no one perceived him as a scholar shouldn't bother him in the least. Perhaps his annoyance came from the very real impression that everyone considered him too lazy or frivolous or stupid to be a scholar. That somehow it was his intelligence they were commenting on. Damnation. He could have been a scholar. He quite liked . . . he searched his mind . . . history. Yes, that was it, history. Why, hadn't he once planned to write a family history? Certainly that was years ago but he had gone so far as to compile old family documents and diaries. No, on second thought, his mother had gathered everything for him. She'd been most encouraging, as he recalled. The papers were probably now in trunks in the attic. He simply hadn't managed to get around to them yet. His life was extraordinarily busy.

Oliver managed the estate and the family's finances. He had any number of quite lucrative investments that he kept a watchful eye on. As the Earl of Norcroft there were constant social obligations as well, especially when he was in residence in London. Besides, his mother and it seemed damn near everyone else he knew wanted him to wed. He certainly wasn't going to find an acceptable bride if he stayed at home and thought about . . . history!

As for adventures, he had had any number of adventures, although perhaps carousing with his friends might not be what his mother had meant. And even that sort of adventure had diminished through the years. He plucked a piece of grass and rolled it absently between his fingers. Admittedly, those adventures had often involved the rescue of his friends and one could argue they had been more their adventures and not his. But his friends depended upon him for assistance and advice. They would do the same for him if need be.

What kind of adventures did his mother think he should have? Should he explore the wilds of Africa or search for buried treasure or slay dragons? How absurd. He was not about to go off to hunt for orchids in the jungle or study the stars in the Southern Hemisphere or build railroads in America as his friends had. He had responsibilities, obligations, people who depended upon him. As for romantic adventures, he'd had more than a few. That none of them had led to anything of a more permanent nature had been, in most instances, for the best. He'd only ever thought himself in love once and even that had not involved the kind of reckless abandon that he had expected then, and still did, surely went hand in hand with true love.

The fact that his mother thought he had no spirit of adventure was only slightly less bothersome than the idea that she did. His brows drew together and he tossed aside the crumpled blade of grass and picked a new one. What kind of adventures did a woman well past her fiftieth year want? Which only begged the question of what kind she had already had? He knew little of his mother's past or his father's either, for that matter, beyond those family details one usually knows in a vague sort of way about one's parents. Now, he wondered if he knew his mother at all. Certainly, they shared the manor and the house in London but aside from finding themselves at the same social events on occasion, their respective circles of acquaintances did not often overlap. The fact that she had brought up the question of romantic adventures was disturbing enough. The idea that she might well be interested in such a thing for herself was more than he wanted to think about. Damnation, she was his mother! And it was up to him to protect her, from herself if necessary. She was kind and generous and far too good of heart which left her vulnerable to those who might easily take advantage of her. Granted, to his knowledge, she had never fallen prey to those with unscrupulous intentions. It was up to Oliver to make certain she never did.

However, if she wished to consider this unnamed guest of theirs as some kind of adventure, it was probably harmless enough as long as he kept his wits about him, resisted the lure of dark red hair and enticing green eyes. Besides, his mother was right about one thing. If Kate was deceiving them, what possible purpose could she have? While his mother did have access to some funds, the vast majority of the family's wealth was under his control. If Kate's loss of memory was a ruse, what besides money could she want? It was an intriguing question. His mother was convinced Kate was a lady of quality. There were certainly ways to determine such a thing. Absently he shredded the blade of grass and stared at the manor. Yes, indeed, there were ways to determine if a woman was a lady that had nothing to do with what she might or might not remember.

And why didn't Kate know if she liked him or not? That too was most annoying. People usually liked him, he was an eminently likeable sort. Most, particularly women, considered him both charming and dashing. And while not the handsomest man in the world, he was certainly not unattractive. He had friends, he was a desired guest at any social gathering, and he was considered quite a catch among mothers of marriageable daughters.

Still, he blew a long breath, it could well be his suspicious nature when it came to mysterious women bearing empty envelopes and claiming not to know their own names had made him somewhat less likeable than usual. Although there had been moments when he had been quite charming in spite of his reservations. Or perhaps he hadn't been charming so much as charmed.

When his gaze had met hers, when he had kissed her hand—twice—there had been something . . . something indefinable. A promise perhaps, although that was an absurd idea and attributable to nothing more than his own romantic tendencies. In spite of his suspicions, and the circumstances were difficult to believe, he found himself casually hoping she was who she said she was. Or rather who she didn't say she was. Perhaps Kate wasn't merely his mother's adventure but his own? It was a silly thought of course. Still, there was something about the woman.

He flicked away the grass in his hand and got to his feet. As always, the mere act of pondering his problems had eased them. And, as always, he felt as if he had talked not only to himself but to someone older and wiser. The feeling was nothing more than a remnant of childhood but reassuring regardless. His innate sense of calm and confidence had returned. The world, his world, had righted itself and life was again in its proper order. He brushed off his trousers and started down the hill. He was in control and he had a plan. Vague and unformed and little more than an idea in the back of his mind, but a plan nonetheless.

He might not be able to determine who Kate was, but he could certainly determine what she was and why she was here. And in the process, determine as well, why he cared.

Chapter 5

*K*ate had bent low to better study the wall. It certainly appeared Roman. She had no idea how she knew this information with the same certainly that most people knew their own names. A knowledge of Roman ruins was one thing she'd learned about herself, although she'd had little time to discover much else.

Lady Norcroft had decreed Kate go directly to bed yesterday afternoon. After all, the older woman had said, losing one's memory was bound to exhaust anyone. Sure enough, Kate had fallen into a surprisingly deep, dreamless sleep and hadn't opened her eyes for a full twenty-four hours. She couldn't recall ever sleeping that soundly before, but then she couldn't recall much of anything. Still, even if there was some satisfaction to be gained by the realization that she had such obscure knowledge, it did seem a rather useless thing to know.

She straightened and met the startled gaze of Lord Norcroft a scant second before his knees smacked into her midsection, and knocked her backwards several feet and flat on her back. A hard thunk beside her indicated he had met the same fate.

She stared up at the sky, decided she wasn't injured, and drew a deep breath. "Do grown men always leap a wall in that manner or is that too something I have forgotten?"

"No?" he said, barely able to catch his breath and it sounded more a question than an answer.

"This is the second time in as many days that I have been knocked to the ground."

"Fell." He gasped. "The first time you fell."

"Did I?" She sighed. "I can't recall." She should probably sit up, although there was something about staring up at the clouds serenely drifting across a blue sky rather than at his equally blue, but not at all serene eyes that made it much easier to talk freely. "Are you all right?"

"I will be. I've just had the wind knocked out of me." For a long moment he was silent. "Have your bags been located?" he said at last.

"Not that I know of."

"But this is not what you were wearing yesterday."

"This dress belongs to one of your cousins. Genevieve, I believe your mother said." She watched a rotund white horse pull an oddly shaped carriage across the sky. "She was so good as to loan it to me."

"I don't it recall it looking that lovely on my cousin."

She laughed. "A charming thing to say, my lord, but I suspect you, like most men, rarely notice what a woman wears from day to day. I daresay you might well have seen this gown every day for a month and yet, the next day, would be hard pressed to describe it."

"Excellent point." He chuckled. "Shouldn't you be resting?"

"I believe I have rested entirely too much already."

"And I believe I owe you an apology."

"For knocking me to the ground or for insincere flattery?"

"The flattery was most sincere, I'll not apologize for that. But yes, for knocking you over and for yesterday as well." He paused. "I was perhaps not as gracious as I should have been."

"Your apology is accepted." She studied a cloud that resembled a frolicking lamb.

"And accepted far more graciously than I have been. Thank you."

"It's understandable really, your behavior that

is. Or at least I seem to understand it." She thought for a moment. "You have all that responsibility."

"It can be a bit overwhelming at times," he said wryly. "Which leads me to take myself and everything else far more seriously than I should on occasion." Apparently his lordship also found it easier to speak candidly while staring at the sky instead of looking at her.

"Still, when one is responsible for a mother or a family—"

"One has to do what is necessary to protect them even from themselves if need be—"

"Especially if they are less than sensible and you are the only one with your feet firmly on the ground."

"Are we speaking of you or me?" he said slowly.

"I wish I knew." The lamb drifted quickly across the sky, pushed by the wind or unseen forces. She shivered and sat up. "It's most exhausting you know, not to know, probably why I slept so long. I keep trying to recall something, anything, about who I am. It's there, just out of reach and yet I can't grab hold of it."

He rolled over onto his side, propped his head in his hand and studied her. "I can well imagine."

"No, my lord, I don't believe you can." She brushed the leaves out of her hair. "All sorts of thoughts keep popping into my head about all sorts of things. None of which seem to be pertinent to the question at hand."

"Who you are."

"Exactly. It does me no good to learn that I am familiar with Roman walls—did you know there are miles of walls in Briton? Hadrian's is the best known of course, but there are countless, shorter structures."

"I had no idea."

"It's interesting enough but useless at the moment." She grimaced. "At the very least, it's disconcerting to know something and not know how or why you have such knowledge. All in all there have been times today when I have wanted to do nothing more than weep uncontrollably."

He sat up, his eyes wary. "You're not going to cry, are you?"

"Not at the moment." Relief washed across his face and she smiled. "I do reserve the right to do so later should the need arise."

"Quite so," he said under his breath.

"However, I suspect I am not the type of woman who does weep, uncontrollably or otherwise."

"You remember that then?"

"It's not a memory." She searched for the right word. "More of a feeling I would say."

"So you still don't remember anything significant?"

"Nothing pertinent. Oh I've discovered a few things about myself but again they are more feelings than facts." She shook her head. "No. I seem to know about this." She waved at the wall. "But that hardly seems helpful."

"Perhaps you're the scholar."

"Me?" She laughed. "But I'm a woman." Still, it was an interesting thought and she liked the idea of it.

"What are you doing here?"

"I was looking at your wall."

"No, I meant should you be out of the house, wandering about by yourself?"

She bristled. "Am I a prisoner then?"

"Only in my—" he started then apparently thought better of it. "No, of course not."

At once the impropriety of her position, coupled with the suggestive nature of what he didn't say, struck her and she had the strangest feeling that she didn't especially care about propriety. And yet, it did have its uses. Sitting on the ground beside the too charming, too attractive, too forward earl was entirely too intimate for comfort. Even so, she regretted the need to move. "Would you be so kind as to help me up?"

"Certainly." He scrambled to his feet and held his hand out to her.

She took his hand and he pulled her to her feet. His gazed locked with hers and for a long, breathless moment they stared into one another's eyes. She could lose herself in those eyes and wondered at the absurd feeling that such a loss would be quite wonderful. And wondered as well why she wanted nothing more than for his lips to meet hers.

"Do you intend to kiss me?" she said without thinking.

"Of course not," he said quickly but she read the lie in his blue eyes.

"You certainly look like you intend to kiss me." Oddly enough, the idea of his kissing her didn't bother her in the least. Indeed, she would more than likely kiss him back. Good Lord, was she a tart?

"If I had intended to kiss you I daresay I would have done so by now."

"If you do not intend to kiss me you should probably release my hand."

"Indeed I should." And yet he didn't. "Still, holding your hand is a far cry from kissing you. We have only just met and, given we don't know your name, that meeting was decidedly one sided."

"Then am I to assume you don't kiss women you've just met?"

"Rarely." He chuckled. "It depends upon the woman."

She pulled her hand from his. "You are quite a flirtatious sort aren't you?"

His eyes widened in surprise. "Am I?"

"Yes, I would say so. Why, even yesterday, in the midst of your suspicions, there were definite instances of flirtation."

He stared at her for a moment then laughed. "Yes, I suppose there were."

She crossed her arms over her chest and tilted her head. "Why?"

"Why?" He raised a brow. "Well, you're a lovely woman. Do I need a better reason than that?"

"Yes, Lord Norcroft, I believe you do."

"Oliver."

"What?"

"As I am calling you Kate, you should call me Oliver."

"That doesn't seem entirely proper to me," she said even though she already thought of him as Oliver.

"No, but nor does it seem fair that I am addressing you as Kate and you are calling me Lord Norcroft. After all." He leaned closer to her. "You did nearly kiss me."

"I most certainly did not!" Indignation colored her voice. She turned away from him and seated herself primly on the wall. "However, I must thank you for proving my point. You are a most flirtatious man and no doubt extremely dangerous."

"Dangerous?" He grinned in a wicked manner and her heart caught. Dear Lord, she *was* a tart. "I quite like that."

"That, my lord—Oliver—is precisely what makes you so dangerous."

He laughed. "You're somewhat flirtatious yourself as well as most amusing."

"Not dangerous?" She picked at an invisible thread on her skirt.

"Oh, I suspect you might be very dangerous."

She glanced at him. "Because you don't know who I am or why I am here or what I might want from you?"

"No, because I don't know what I might want from you."

"Oh my." She stifled a satisfied grin. "You are dangerous."

"If I can't be scholarly, dangerous will have to do." He offered his arm. "Allow me the honor of escorting you back to the house.

She stood and took his arm. "May I ask you a question?"

"Please do."

"What is your impression of me?"

"My impression?"

"Yes, you know." Impatience sounded in her voice. "What kind of person do you think I am?"

"Do you wish me to be completely honest?"

Honesty did seem best. Besides, if she had anything to lie about she couldn't remember it. "I'm afraid I do."

"The first time I saw you, you were unconscious." He shook his head in a serious manner but there was a teasing note in his voice. "Therefore there wasn't much of an impression to be made. I did think you were lovely and I wondered about the color of your eyes."

She stopped. "The color of my eyes? Why?"

"I am exceptionally fond of green eyes and red hair. I must say I was not disappointed."

"Do you think you could stop flirting and answer my questions in a serious manner?" She released his arm and stepped back. "In spite of your tendency toward rudeness—"

"I did apologize—"

"And your overly protective manner—"

"I have a great number of responsibilities."

"You strike me as a man of reasonable perception and intelligence—"

"I'm no scholar," he muttered.

"Nor is one currently necessary although it is obvious that you are not stupid." She resisted the urge to stamp her foot. "We have spent a little time together now. Granted not long but surely you have some opinion. I am lost, Oliver, and I need you to tell me what you think."

He studied her for a long moment then chose his words with care. "I think you may indeed have lost your memory."

"But you're not certain?"

"Not completely."

"I see." She nodded slowly. "Well, then that's that." She started quickly back toward the house.

He hurried after her. "What's what?"

"It's extremely awkward, my lord." She needed to get back to the manor as soon as possible. It was the only haven she had. "I have no way to convince you of the truth."

"What do you expect of me, Kate?" Irritation sounded in his voice. "An unconscious woman is dropped on my doorstep and when she awakens, she claims to have no knowledge of who she is.

Her bags and any identification they might contain, are conveniently lost—"

"Conveniently?" She whirled to face him. "Conveniently?"

"Yes," he said in a haughty manner.

"This is not my dress!" She shook her skirt at him. "It's nice enough I suppose but it's a bit too large and it's not mine. Do you know what it feels like to have to wear someone else's dress?"

He bit back a grin. "I haven't actually worn someone else's dress—"

"Don't even try to be charming! It won't work." She again started off then turned back on her heel. "To what end, Oliver? Have you considered that? Why would I—why would anyone—perpetrate such a hoax on you? No, I can well understand why someone might want to complicate your world but why would anyone want to do such a thing to your mother? She's a very nice lady."

"I haven't figured that out yet," he admitted.

"Well, I have no intention of lingering here until you do so." She turned and started across the lawn. "And I have no intention of staying where my . . . my character is in question."

"Mais vous avez nulle part pour aller," he called after her in poorly accented French.

"Sans se soucier je ne resterai pas où je ne suis pas voulu. Particulièrement pas avec un homme qui me pense suis un menteur!" she said without thinking, then pulled up short. "That was French! I speak French!"

"Most ladies do." Reluctance sounded in his voice. She ignored him.

"You said *But you have nowhere to go*. And not well I might add. And I said *Regardless, I shall not stay where I am not wanted. Especially not with a man who thinks I am a liar.*"

"I never said you were a liar," he said under his breath.

"Hah! It was implied." In spite of her annoyance, satisfaction surged through her. She spoke French! What an accomplished thing to find out about oneself. "Do you think I'm French?"

"No." He took her arm and steered her toward the manor. "I don't know what I think but I am prepared to believe you are not deceiving me about what you do or do not remember."

"Why?" She stood her ground and yanked her arm free.

"I don't think you're that good an actress." He again took her arm and started across the lawn.

"That wasn't the least bit charming."

He ignored her. "And I find myself preferring to think you are who my mother thinks you are."

"And who does your mother think I am?"

"She thinks you are the daughter or relation of an old friend or acquaintance. Someone she knows at any rate. She thinks whatever was in the envelope explained exactly that."

"Why?"

"I don't know. It's the way she sees the world."

"No, why do you prefer to think that?"

"Because my mother is a trusting soul and I do not want to see her illusions shattered."

"She is no more a trusting soul now than a few minutes ago. So the question remains, why?"

"Because you have green eyes," he snapped.

"Come now, I don't think—"

"Because, Kate or whatever your name is." He stopped, pulled her around to face him. "When I look into those lovely green eyes of yours I get the most remarkable sense of—"

"Inevitability?" Dear Lord, did he feel it too?

"Yes! No! I don't know. Possibility perhaps. But know this." He tipped her chin up with his finger and glared into her eyes. "If we had been introduced at a party or your eyes had met mine across a crowded dance floor or you had ridden past me in the park I would be actively pursuing you at this very moment. And I have not found a woman I would actively pursue in some time."

"Oh." She swallowed hard. "Now do you intend to kiss me?"

His gaze slipped from her eyes to her lips and back. "Regrettably, no." He dropped his hand, grabbed hers and headed briskly back toward the manor, fairly pulling her along behind him. "I do, however, want to. Rather a lot. Which does not strike me as wise."

"Because you don't trust me?" Even so, it was delightful to know he wanted to kiss her. "Or because I'm dangerous?"

"Both. I don't trust you and in that, for once, I do hope I am wrong."

"You're being charming again although I would appreciate it if you would walk a little slower. I can scarcely keep up with you."

"I can't help it. It's my nature." He flashed her a grin. "The charm that is." But he eased his pace.

"What are we to do now?"

"Now, you should return to your room and rest until dinner." He glanced at her. "You have suffered two falls and we cannot proceed if you are not well."

"I slept a very long time and now I feel fine. Quite up to snuff I would say although a little hungry." And indeed, at this very moment, she felt more than fine. She was oddly happy although she couldn't say exactly why. There really was nothing to feel happy about except that he had wanted to kiss her. Still, in the scheme of things it wasn't particularly important. And yet, it did feel important.

"I shall have something to eat sent to your room." He shook his head. "Falls are nasty things. You cannot be too careful."

"How very kind of you to—" Her brow furrowed. "Proceed with what?"

"It seems to me the best way to help you regain your memory is to do it one small step at a time. Today, you remembered Roman ruins and French. Tomorrow, we shall see what else you know."

"And you're going to help me do this?"

"I'm going to be with you every minute." His tone was determined, resolute, even slightly grim.

Still, the thought of spending time with him was not at all unappealing. "Every minute?"

"As nearly as possible."

"Oliver." She stopped and he turned back to her. "I am most grateful. I am lost and I should dearly love to be found."

His expression softened. "Before I'm through, I—we—are going to know everything there is to know about you."

She arched a brow. "Is that another threat?"

"Not at all. It's the same threat."

"The same promise?"

"Precisely." He leaned toward her. "Make no mistake, Kate, for good or ill, I will find you."

Chapter 6

*H*e did hope she wasn't married.

Oliver sat at the end of the long dining table, his mother to one side, Kate to the other. He had studied her throughout dinner as surreptitiously as possible. Not an easy task in such a small gathering. Still, as subtle as he had tried to be, he was hard pressed to tear his gaze away. There was something about the woman . . .

"Now then, Kate," his mother began, "tell me what you know of literature."

"I'm afraid, Lady Norcroft, the problem of my memory does not seem to be resolved as directly as that," Kate explained for perhaps the third time since the start of the meal. An explanation his mother seemed determined to ignore. Still, Kate did not make his mother feel foolish for her endless but well-intentioned suggestions. Whatever else she might or might not be, it struck him that Kate was a genuinely kind person.

And apparently much more patient than he. "I believe she has mentioned this before, Mother."

"I know that, Oliver, there is nothing wrong with *my* memory. But given the manner in which memories are returning to her, it does not seem ill-advised to venture queries in a repetitive fashion. Some morsel of information might occur to her at any moment." She cast her son a chastising glance. "I should think any attempt to assist Kate to recover is well worth the effort. Don't you agree, Kate?"

"I am exceedingly grateful for any and all help," Kate said with a pleasant smile.

Diplomatic as well as kind. Not necessarily qualities of a lady—he knew many well-bred ladies who weren't the least bit kind or diplomatic—but good to know nonetheless.

She ate with an effortless grace, never hesitating over which piece of cutlery to use. This meant she'd been shown from the time she could pick up a fork exactly which one was correct. If she was an actress, and this was some sort of deception on her part, she had obviously trained for the role.

"You say that when you looked at the wall, you knew all about it?" Mother asked.

Kate nodded. "I can't tell you how I knew, the

facts were simply there in my head. I have as well discovered certain things about myself that have come to me without particular effort." She wrinkled her nose. "Character flaws for the most part."

"Flaws are what make us human, my dear, as well as interesting. Perfect people aren't the least bit interesting." Mother shook her head. "Why, Oliver has any number of flaws and he is most interesting."

Oliver ignored her and directed his attention to Kate. "What kind of character flaws?"

"Pride for one. Vanity for another." Kate picked up her glass of wine and took a sip. "I dislike wearing someone else's clothing." She glanced at his mother. "I am grateful but I find I don't like being completely dependent on strangers."

"I, however, am optimistic that while we have never met directly, we are not precisely strangers," Lady Norcroft said firmly.

"I haven't discovered a sense of optimism yet." Kate thought for a moment. "Although I don't seem to feel especially pessimistic either. And given the precarious nature of my situation, one would think pessimism is definitely called for." She shrugged. "Perhaps I am an optimistic person. Or possibly merely hopeful that all will be well in the end. Still, it does seem to me that I am also a sensible sort. It's all most confusing."

What if she was married? She wore no ring, although that might or might not be significant. Not that it really mattered, he was simply curious.

Surely a woman as lovely as she would have been married by her age. In spite of the fact that he really didn't care, the idea that Kate was a married woman was not a pleasant one. Still, she could be a widow. His spirits lifted at the thought. That would explain why she was traveling by herself. If, of course, she wasn't part of a larger group of brigands scheming to hoodwink kind, trusting ladies like his mother out of . . . out of what? A few gowns belonging to his cousin? A few nights at a country house? *Why* when it came to Kate was as big a question as *who*.

"Oliver, after dinner I suggest you show our guest the library. Perhaps a favorite book might spur some recollections." Mother smiled at Kate. "I know my favorites always bring back fond memories. I remember the first time I read *Emma*. I was just a girl and had a rather romantic nature, as most girls of that age do. I thought how lovely and thoughtful of Emma to want to see her friends happily wed. It's a feeling that has remained with me to this day. I like to think I assisted my niece Fiona in finding the perfect match." She signaled to a servant to remove the plates in advance of the next course. "Did I mention that Oliver is not married?"

He groaned to himself. "Mother."

"No, I don't believe you did." Kate cast him a polite smile but there was laughter in her eyes.

"Nor are his affections engaged." She looked at her son. "They aren't, are they?"

"No," he said coolly. "When that day comes you shall be the first person to whom I will reveal the joyous news. Although I daresay you will probably know before I do."

"There's no need for sarcasm, Oliver." She sniffed. "It's most unbecoming." She leaned toward Kate in a confidential manner. "His inability to find a suitable wife is an ongoing topic of discussion between us."

He snorted. "A discussion that is decidedly one-sided."

She continued as if he hadn't said a word. "In spite of his sense of responsibility, he has yet to fulfill his duty to his family in this respect. And he is very nearly in his thirty-third year."

"Really?" Kate's eyes widened and she looked at him. "As old as that."

"And growing older every minute," he said, his tone resigned. He had long ago realized trying to steer his mother away from the subject that was near and dear to her heart was futile. It did no good and she would simply ignore him anyway. Still, it was worth an attempt. "Regardless, Mother, I'm quite sure Kate doesn't want to hear about my failure to wed."

"Oh no, my lord, I find it fascinating." Blast it all, the woman could barely keep from laughing aloud. "Lady Norcroft, surely you have some idea why your son has failed in his familial duties."

"Believe me, I have given it a great deal of consideration and I don't understand it. Oliver has quite a lot to commend himself. His title is old and distinguished. The family fortune is sound." She glanced at him. He nodded. "Admittedly, he has no sense of adventure."

"Define adventure," he said wryly.

"But he's quite a fine-looking fellow. Don't you think so, Kate?" Mother asked in an innocent manner that didn't fool anyone.

"Yes, Kate." In for a penny as they say. He leaned slightly toward her. "What do you think?"

"Well," she said slowly, "I can't recall ever meeting a more attractive man."

"Excellent answer." He laughed. "And most diplomatic."

"He has his father's eyes," his mother said. "They were the bluest eyes I had ever seen."

"They are indeed . . ." Kate's gaze met his and for a moment or a lifetime they stared into each other's eyes. And again he had the oddest feeling that he could gaze into those green eyes for the rest of his days. *Inevitable.* She cleared her throat. "Blue. Quite a lovely shade of blue. Very fetching, my lord."

He grinned. "Thank you."

How peculiar that this stranger had this effect on him. Did he have the same effect on her? He rather hoped so. And that too was odd.

"And most modest as well." Lady Norcroft nodded. "I don't know why he hasn't married."

"Perhaps," Kate chose her words with care. "He simply hasn't found the right woman."

"Yes, well, of course that's part of it. But I fear, very possibly, that is I have come to suspect, perhaps . . ." Lady Norcroft hesitated then lowered her voice. "We are cursed."

The oddest expression flashed across Kate's face. So quickly he wasn't sure he had seen anything at all. Not that it wasn't understandable. Even a woman who did have her memory intact might be startled by his mother's comment.

"Cursed?" Kate said, her eyes wide with . . . what? Curiosity? Apprehension?

"That's ridiculous, Mother," he said firmly. "We are no more cursed than we are spotted gazelles. There are no such things as curses."

"Then how do you explain the fact that your father died at such a young age? As well as his sister, his two brothers before him, and your grandfather. Most of whom met their fates in extremely unusual accidents." She huffed. "If we are not cursed, how would you explain it?"

"Life, Mother." He shrugged. "It's all been most unfortunate but there's nothing more to it than that."

"It seems to me," Mother said thoughtfully. "Your grandmother once mentioned something about an old family curse."

"What kind of curse?" Kate's eyes lit with interest.

"I don't recall exactly." Mother's brows drew together. "It didn't seem important at the time."

"Nor is it important now. What it is is absurd.

Besides, I've never heard anything about it," Oliver said pointedly. "And I would think, as head of the family, I would have heard something."

"From whom?" Mother asked. "You are the last of your line. Your grandmother died when you were very young. Your father is gone. There is no one left who could tell you of such things. And one should know. Forewarned is forearmed you know." A gleam of determination shone in his mother's eyes. He had seen that look before. It did not bode well. "There are trunks full of old family papers in the attic . . ."

"But then people tend not to, do they?" Kate said abruptly. "Hear about things like family curses that is. Everything is going along quite nicely until one day, it rears its head and changes everything you had always understood about the world and much of what you have always accepted as true and rational. And sends your life spinning in a direction you never would have dreamed and never would have chosen had it not been for family responsibility and duty and . . . and . . ."

Oliver and his mother stared at her. Kate glanced from one to another, drew a deep breath and picked up her wine glass.

"I have no idea where that came from," Kate said under her breath and took a long swallow of wine.

"Nonetheless, it was most interesting," Mother murmured.

"Perhaps you are not as practical as you thought," Oliver added, studying her carefully. She appeared as startled by her comments as they were. He did hope she had only lost her memory and not her mind.

"Apparently you are a believer in such things." A casual note sounded in his mother's voice although her gaze on Kate was intense. Oliver grimaced to himself. If there was one thing in recent years that caught his mother's attention nearly as much as her son's marital state, it was all things of a magical nature. Which now appeared to include curses.

"I don't know what I believe, Lady Norcroft." The tiniest hint of unease shaded Kate's green eyes and her smile was weak. "I wish I did."

"I do hope you know how to dance although I can't imagine that you don't. We should probably determine that for certain. After all, the Harvest Ball will be upon us in no time."

Oliver stared at his mother. It was not like her to abruptly change a subject she relished. Still, he was more than willing to discuss anything that was not magical nonsense or his failure to wed.

"It's still nearly a week away," Oliver said. "It's more than likely Kate will no longer be with us by then." The moment he said the words, he realized he hoped he was wrong.

"Rubbish. Why, even if we know her real name by then, we shall insist she remain as our guest until after the ball."

"I can't imagine that I wouldn't want to stay. I can't recall ever having been to a Harvest Ball, or any ball for that matter, but it does sound like a grand time." Kate glanced at him. "If you will have me, of course."

"I will have you, of course," Oliver said at once then realized what he'd said. "What I mean to say is we will have you. As our guest that is. It will be our pleasure."

"You are most gracious, my lord." Amusement danced in Kate's green eyes.

"Now that that's settled, we will need to do something about a gown. You simply can't wear one of Genevieve's. Besides, I always say there is nothing like a new gown to raise a girl's spirits." Mother thought for a moment. "I doubt if there is anyone in the village up to the task of creating an appropriate gown. We shall have to send for Madame DuBois to come from London."

Kate shook her head. "I couldn't possibly—"

"Nonsense. You could and you shall. Madame DuBois will no doubt jump at the chance to leave the city for a few days."

"And the chance to charge us an outrageous amount for her holiday in the country," Oliver said in a dry manner. Not that the idea of seeing Kate in one of Madame DuBois's creations didn't have a great deal of appeal. He knew nothing about fashion but the gowns the Frenchwoman had created for his cousins had transformed each of them from merely pretty to enchanting.

"Quality, Oliver, always has a price." Mother waved off his comment then directed her attention to Kate. "I think shades of green would be lovely with your hair and eyes. The color of sea foam perhaps or . . ."

Kate would be exquisite in green although he would wager she would be remarkable in very nearly any color. Definitely enchanting, completely seductive, and very nearly irresistible.

Irresistible? Shock coursed through him and he scarcely noticed the fig pudding a servant set before him and fig pudding was one of his favorites. What was he thinking? He knew practically nothing about this woman. Not her name, not her purpose. She seemed both honest and kind. The more he thought about it, the more it seemed likely that she had indeed lost her memory. Even so, he had nothing but her admittedly charming nature to base his assessment on.

Seductive? Good God, the woman was seducing him! She was subtle, but he knew a seduction when he saw one. So much for keeping his wits about him.

His mother chatted on about fabrics and plans for the Harvest Ball. Kate responded with nothing personal whatsoever. Oh, she was good, whomever she was. Why, it wasn't enough to seduce him, she was seducing his mother as well!

Well, he wouldn't allow it. No one seduced the Earl of Norcroft without his willing participation. Of course, now that he thought about it, no one had ever seduced him at all. He had always been the one to seduce, to pursue, to capture. No, he wouldn't stand for being seduced.

And why not?

The thought pulled him up short. He narrowed his gaze and watched his guest. She was certainly lovely enough and he was already falling under whatever spell she wove. If she was intent upon seducing him, why not let her? Why not play along with whatever game she played if indeed she played any game at all. If she was exactly as she appeared to be, there would be no harm in it. If not . . . he shrugged to himself. He would no doubt know soon enough one way or the other.

As long as he kept a clear head, he would be fine.

"Did you say something?" his mother interrupted his thoughts.

Kate looked at him expectantly.

"I was just wondering if Kate was ready to join me in the library," he said smoothly.

"I fear I find I am quite exhausted." Kate shook her head. "It's been an unusual day to say the least and in spite of the vast amount of sleep I've had I find I should like nothing better than to retire for the night. Would you mind terribly if we waited until morning? After breakfast perhaps?"

Yes! "Not at all."

She rose to her feet and he stood at once. "I cannot tell you how grateful I am for your kindness."

"Think nothing of it, my dear," his mother said.

"Until the morning then, my lord." Kate cast him a brilliant smile and his heart shifted in his chest.

"Until morning." He nodded and realized the threat posed here had nothing to do with his head.

The risk might well be to his heart.

Chapter 7

"Good morning, Oliver." Kate stepped into the library.

From his perch atop a tall, wheeled ladder that rested against book-laden shelves, Oliver smiled down at her. "Good morning."

The morning light through tall floor-to-ceiling windows flooded the room and she shaded her eyes to peer up at him. "What are you doing up there?"

"Gathering books that may help determine who you are."

"With information about loss of memory?"

"I'm afraid not."

"What a shame," she said more to herself than to him. She had wondered last night that if a blow to the head had caused her problems, a blow might be able to reverse it. As much as it did make sense, she was not at all willing to throw herself off a train platform or anything else on the possibility it would restore her memory.

Oliver started down the rungs, several volumes tucked under one arm, using only one hand to cling to the ladder and guide himself down.

Her heart caught. "Do be careful. I should hate to see you fall."

He flashed her a cocky grin. "I should hate to see that myself."

Three rungs from the bottom, Oliver slipped and Kate held her breath. He dropped to the floor with a thud but no apparent ill effects. "How are you this morning?"

"Perhaps a more pertinent question might be who am I this morning."

"Very well then." He strolled across the room to a long, narrow table and set the books alongside others already arrayed. She trailed after him. "Who are you this morning?"

"As important as the question is, it still has no answer," she said with a sigh. "I am still Kate as far as I know. I had hoped I would awaken today with full knowledge as to my name and where I'm from and all the myriad details of life that one takes for granted until they have vanished."

"No interesting dreams that might provide insight?"

"Not even one." She shook her head. "My sleep

was remarkably undisturbed." Still, in spite of her fatigue, there were several hours before she could get to sleep when she'd tossed and turned and tried to think of something—anything—that would provide a clue to her identity. When she'd tried, with just as little success, not to think about the dashing earl with blue eyes and wicked smile, who had taken up permanent residence in her head. That alone made her wonder if her presence here had to do with him and was far more than mere happenstance. Besides, there was something about the man. "Not a single dream that I can recall, which in and of itself strikes me as odd. One would think someone in a situation like mine would have all sort of dreams."

"Indeed one would."

"Instead, I slept quite soundly." She thought for a moment. "As if I hadn't a responsibility or care in the world which I suppose, at the moment, I don't. It's rather like being on holiday from myself. You should try it, Oliver."

"I suspect there are better ways to begin a holiday than by falling off a train platform."

"Probably." She watched him arrange the books he had deposited on the table. "Still, it's remarkably relaxing. I have the distinct feeling I have any number of worries and concerns that prevent me from having the kind of refreshing slumber that I enjoyed last night."

"I understand Dr. Miller was here earlier this morning."

"He seems very competent."

"And?"

"And he pronounced me fit." She grimaced. "Although how someone who has lost her memory could be called fit makes no sense to me."

"At least he didn't pronounce you mad."

"That is something I suppose." Dr. Miller had been pleasant enough, and he did seem knowledgeable but he'd admitted he'd had no experience with cases like Kate's. "He said my head was fine but he had no idea what to do to restore my memory save wait, although he did seem confident it would return eventually."

"Perhaps there is more we can do than wait." Oliver glanced at her. "If you're willing."

"Yes, of course." Still, as much as she wanted to know who she was, she wasn't at all sure the knowledge would be good. What kind of woman had concerns and responsibilities so pressing as to keep her from sleep? Good Lord—who was she? "I gather, looking at all this, you have some sort of plan."

"Not a plan really, just an idea." He waved at the display of books. "These are the kinds of subjects a properly educated person would be familiar with." He studied the books with a skeptical air. "Although I admit they are probably more representative of the studies of a young man rather than a girl. I have no sisters and I'm not at all familiar with what studies might comprise a girl's education."

"Probably nothing of any significance," she said under her breath and wondered where that thought had come from. "It certainly couldn't hurt. Let us see if anything is familiar."

"This." He picked up a book and handed it to her. "Is Latin grammar."

"So it is." She paged through it. *"Epicuri de grege porcus.* Something about a hog I think or a good meal. It seems vaguely familiar but not at all interesting."

"Then apparently you have studied Latin," he said wryly. "Perhaps we should turn to poetry or literature." He picked up a book and paged through it. "Who wrote 'Ode on a Grecian Urn'?"

"John Keats," she said without thinking.

" 'Love's Philosophy'?"

She grinned. This was easy. Just as with his wall, she had no idea how she knew the correct answers, but she did. "Percy Bysshe Shelley."

"And who is Samuel Coleridge?"

This answer too came to mind without effort. "He wrote 'The Rime of the Ancient Mariner,' of course."

"Robert Burns?"

"As fair as thou, my bonnie lass, so deep in love am I," she said without pause. The words were simply there in her head. *"And I will love thee still, my dear, till all the seas gang dry."* She smiled at him. "It's beautiful, isn't it?"

" 'A Red, Red Rose.' Very good." He smiled. "It is indeed beautiful and most romantic."

"I must be a romantic sort of person. I think it's one of my favorites." Excitement washed through her. "It is one of my favorites! I know that, Oliver. Isn't that lovely?"

"Lovely perhaps but not overly useful especially as we are fairly certain you're from Scotland and Robert Burns is considered one of Scotland's greatest poets."

"Still, it's something more than I knew about myself a few minutes ago." Why wasn't he as pleased as she was? Certainly, she was no closer to knowing her own name but knowing what she liked could surely be considered a step in the right direction. His attitude was most annoying.

"Enough of poetry. Let us determine what you know of geography or history."

"Goodness, Oliver." Impatience edged her voice. "As much as I appreciate the effort you've shown, I do know what country I'm in and I daresay if you showed me a map I could fairly well identify the rest of the world. As for history, Victoria is the current queen and has been since 1837. Rome once ruled a great empire and before the Romans, Alexander of Macedonia, a Greek, conquered most of the civilized world. And on that map, I can certainly show you where Greece and Rome are located." She huffed. "My apologies, but this seems pointless. Any knowledge of history or geography doesn't seem to have the least bit to do with knowing about me."

"I'm simply trying to ascertain your level of

education," he said in a lofty manner. "In order to determine . . ."

"In order to determine what?" An awful suspicion occurred to her.

"It just seems to me . . ." Unease sounded in his voice. "If we know how educated you are—"

"Then we would know my place in society? Whether or not I properly belong at Lord Norcroft's table?" She narrowed her eyes. "Or in his kitchens."

"No, of course not." He scoffed, belying the guilty look in his eye, and took a step backward. "One can tell just by looking at you—"

"One can tell what?" She moved toward him.

"That you are . . ." He took another step back and hit the table.

"That I am what?"

Caught between the library table and Kate, he had the look of a rat in a trap. "Could you move back?"

"No."

He glanced from side to side as if looking for escape. "This is extraordinarily uncomfortable."

"Good."

"See here now, Kate," he began in his best Earl of Norcroft voice.

"That I am what, my lord?" She glared at him. "Finish what you started to say."

He shook his head. "On further consideration, I don't think—"

"Apparently you don't think! That I am what?"

She ground out the words through clenched teeth.

"Well bred," he said with a wince. "A proper lady."

Anger choked her words. "A proper lady?"

"There are certain things a lady is expected to know," he muttered. "It seemed to me, given the circumstances, and as you are living in my home—"

"You wanted to make certain I wasn't going to steal the silver?"

"No." He scoffed then paused to consider the question. "No," he said again firmly.

Oh, the man was infuriating. "You're testing me, aren't you?"

"I don't know that I'd call it—"

"I don't care what you call it, it's a test." She stared at him. "A trial of . . . of . . . I don't know what but a trial nonetheless." She crossed her arms over her chest. "I am torn between laughing aloud and slapping you across the face."

His expression brightened. The rat had spotted a way out. "If I might offer some advice—"

She ignored him. "On one hand, you are utterly absurd and unworthy of any response save laughter."

He nodded. "Laughter is always good. One should be able to laugh at the foibles of—"

"On the other hand, your actions are offensive and insulting and certainly deserve to be responded to in a manner appropriate."

"Still, appropriate often depends—"

Without thinking, she drew her hand back and smacked him across the face.

"Ouch!" His eyes widened and he clapped his hand to his face. "That hurt!"

Shock turned her stomach and she stared in horror. "I can't believe I did that."

"Neither can I." He rubbed his face.

She stepped back and twisted her hands together. "I would wager I have never struck anyone before."

"If it helps you remember—"

"No, no, it's just a feeling but it's a very strong feeling."

"I must say you did it remarkably well for someone who does not strike others."

"Thank you," she murmured. "I was inspired."

He glared at her. "It was not intended as a compliment."

"I must tell you I am as surprised by my action as you are. I didn't think I was the type of person who would resort to violence, even when provoked. Although," she drew a deep breath, "I do feel better."

"I'm glad I could be of service."

"Even so, it's most distressing." She turned away from him and paced the room. "To discover you are the kind of person who could do bodily harm—"

"I did provoke you."

"Yes." She stopped and pinned him with a firm look. "You did indeed."

"I was a cad. A beast. A—"

"A lord." She sighed. "An earl with numerous responsibilities. One can hardly blame you for your suspicions. For doing what you feel you must to determine the truth."

He cast her a relieved smile. "Which just confirms our previous conclusion that you are indeed a rational, practical sort."

"And yet, somehow," her gaze narrowed, "I do blame you."

"My apologies. My intent was not to upset you."

"I feel rather dreadful as well. Guilt, I suppose." She pressed her hands against her midsection. "My stomach positively turned when I struck you. The sound of my hand hitting your cheek. The sting of the blow."

"It was no better from my perspective."

She studied her palm then shook her hand. "It still stings a bit."

"Again," he said in a dry manner. "My apologies."

"Accepted," she said absently then looked at him. "Obviously I feel a certain amount of remorse. Does that help?"

"No."

"Come now, it should help a wee bit. Apparently I have a conscience, which is good to know."

"I know I'm pleased," he said, again rubbing his face.

"Perhaps you should consider it yet another test."

"It's not on my list."

"There's no need for sarcasm, Oliver," she said in a fair imitation of his mother, then paused. "You've written a list?"

"Don't be absurd." He shrugged. "It's in my head."

"It must be a very short list then."

His eyes narrowed. "It's getting longer."

"Regardless of your actions, it was unforgivable of me to have allowed my emotions to get the better of me. I believe I am a better person than that. And I am sorry to have caused you pain." Impulsively she moved to him and rested her hand on his cheek. "Does it hurt terribly?"

He grabbed her hand. "Not terribly." He kissed her palm.

She jerked her hand away. "Why did you do that?"

"I don't know, it seemed the thing to do." He grinned in an unrepentant manner and her anger faded.

"You're being charming again."

He leaned toward her. "I do it well."

"I can see that." Her heart sped up in her chest. He was a scant few inches away, his lips a mere breath from her own.

"I consider it one of my finest accomplishments." His gaze slipped from her eyes to her lips. Dear Lord, was he going to kiss her? Here? Now?

"Do you?" Even worse, what if he had no intention of kissing her?

"Would you care to know of my other accomplishments?" His voice was low with promise. Enticing and seductive.

Seductive? Good Lord, the man was trying to seduce her! In his library no less!

"Kate?"

At once she realized she wouldn't hesitate to allow such a seduction, which was as distressing as knowing that she wouldn't—she hadn't—hesitate to strike him. Not only was she a tart, she was an overly emotional tart with a tendency toward violence!

No. Resolve washed through her and she straightened her shoulders. "Very well then, let's get on with it."

"You don't mind?" he said cautiously.

"Why should I mind?" She shrugged. "You think it's necessary and I daresay, in your situation, I too might well think it's necessary."

"I'm not sure I think it's necessary." He cast her a devilish smile that, at another time, would have melted her resistance. Or any other woman's. "Delightful perhaps but not necessary."

"I may not know who I am, Oliver, but I am fairly certain I know what I am. I am not a thief. I am not attempting to corrupt the morals of an older woman or her idiot son."

His brows drew together. "Being the idiot son in question I'm not sure I under—"

"And I am not—" she leaned close enough to brush her lips across his and steeled herself against the thrill that shot through her at the bare touch—"a tart that you may seduce at will."

He stared at her for a long moment then a wicked grin creased his lips. "Pity."

She stepped back. "You are incorrigible, my lord."

"Nonsense. I am entirely," he searched for a word, "corrigible."

She snorted. "I doubt that. Your intentions are—"

"My dear Kate, as I said yesterday, when I intend to kiss you, you will know it." He paused, then shrugged and without warning pulled her into his arms and pressed his lips hard to hers for an infinite, searing moment. Shock shot through her and with it desire. She wanted him with an all encompassing, inexplicable need that spread from his touch through her blood to curl her toes. And it scarcely mattered if she were a tart or if this was her very first kiss.

He raised his head and grinned down at her. "Did I leave any doubt in your mind?"

"No." She pushed out of his arms.

"And when I intend to seduce you—"

She struggled to catch her breath and tried as well not to let him see what effect one mere kiss had had. "I might well be married, you know."

"That too would be a pity."

"Your standards preclude seduction of a married woman?"

"Thus far."

She stared at him and said the first thing that came into her head. "Then we can only hope I am not wed." Before he could reply she drew a deep breath. "What's next, Oliver?"

He chuckled. "Usually, at this point—"

"No, I mean what's next on your list of ways to determine my position in life?" She studied him closely. "Dare I ask how I am doing thus far?"

"Quite well actually." He ticked the points off on his fingers. "Obviously, you are well educated. You speak French. You know which fork to use."

She glared at him. "You watched me eat?"

"I *observed*," he said in a superior tone. "It's an entirely different matter than merely watching."

"It's exactly the same. Well." She tapped her foot impatiently. "What do you intend to *observe* now?"

"You needn't take that tone. It's not at all easy to determine if a woman is a lady." He frowned. "Under these circumstances that is."

"My apologies if this is awkward for you. Now then." She squared her shoulders. "We have determined that I am well educated and that I can properly eat a meal. What else should a lady know."

"Needlework?" he said hopefully.

"Nonsense." She waved off his suggestion. "I daresay a woman of any station would be skillful with a needle and I am not about to waste my time by embroidering a clever saying on a pillow for you."

He chuckled. "I can well imagine what that saying might be at the moment."

"Oh, I don't think you can." She drew a deep breath. "Anything else?"

"There is more on the list." He considered the question. "Perhaps we should continue this out of doors? With activities appropriate for a lady."

She cast him her sweetest smile. "I can scarcely wait."

"Sarcasm is not becoming in a lady," he said firmly.

She stared at him for a moment then laughed. "You sound like a governess."

He had the good grace to look embarrassed. "I must have heard that somewhere."

She took pity on him. "What kind of appropriate activities?"

"We should determine if you can properly sit a horse. I suspect that would be very telling. If you are familiar with croquet—it's quite popular, you know."

"Croquet," she said slowly. "Yes, that does sound familiar. And golf. I believe I know how to play golf."

"Women don't generally play golf, Kate," he said in a gentle manner that was meant to be kind but was most condescending nonetheless. She felt as if she were a small child and he was patting her on the head.

"Regardless, I believe I do." She thought for a moment. "And archery. Is that on your list of acceptable pursuits for a lady?"

"My mother won a number of competitions in her youth. She was quite good as I recall."

"As, I suspect, am I." She nodded and started toward the door. "I noticed a target yesterday, shall we find out?"

"I'm not at all certain it's wise to arm you with any weapon whatsoever," he said under his breath.

She smiled but held her tongue.

"Kate." He followed a step behind her. "I do hope you realize I am just trying to help you find out who you are."

"And whether I am worthy of being your guest or your servant."

"Kate." He blew an exasperated breath.

"Oliver." She turned on her heel to face him. "I accept that in your place I would no doubt continue to harbor a certain amount of suspicion as to who I really am and what I might want. I realize that in your charming but extremely infuriating and even insulting way you are indeed trying to be of assistance. And I understand as well that you have as little idea about how to do that as I do."

He huffed. "I think I've done exceptionally well, given that I've never tried to ascertain someone's identity before."

She raised a brow.

"Well, I haven't succeeded as of yet."

"But you are trying and one should receive credit for that." She bit back a smile. The man could indeed be endearing and it was extremely difficult to maintain a proper amount of anger at him for very long. She headed for the door. "Come along. I am eager to find out how I feel with a bow in my hand."

"As are we all," he muttered from behind her.

"Perhaps it will bring back all sorts of memories."

"With any luck."

"Queen Mary of Scotland played golf you know," she said over her shoulder to hide the fact that she wasn't at all sure how to get from the library in the manor to the outdoors.

"I didn't know that."

"Apparently I do." As much as she did seem well versed in history, that fact struck her as more than a little obscure. Still it was something.

"She did not end well." A warning sounded in his voice.

"I have no doubt, Oliver, that my own ending shall be much better," she said with a confidence she didn't quite feel.

Kate could be lighthearted and amused with Oliver and she could certainly be angry with him but she would prefer he not know how very frightened she was. It struck her that she was the kind of person who didn't let anyone know when she was afraid.

And she didn't know if that was good or very, very bad.

Chapter 8

*O*liver preferred not to think of himself as his mother's idiot son but today, with his brilliant idea of how to determine Kate's position in life, he may well have earned that title. It was absurd of course. One could tell just by spending a few minutes in her presence that she was indeed a proper lady.

Kate examined the bow given her by Hollinger who had fetched Lady Norcroft's archery equipment and now stood ready to assist Kate in whatever manner she might need. Oliver would prefer Hollinger return to the house but he suspected the long-time family retainer would gnaw off one of his own appendages rather than miss whatever was going to transpire next.

Oliver was quite certain that the entire houseful of servants *and* his own mother hadn't missed a thing. Hollinger and Lady Norcroft were often co-conspirators. Since the butler had appeared with bow and quiver before Oliver had the chance to request them, it was clear that someone had been listening at the library door.

His mother was convinced Kate's origins were legitimate, a point she had pressed after Kate had retired last night. While she hadn't said it in so many words, it was obvious that she thought Kate was the answer to her prayers for a match for her son. Under other circumstances, she might be right.

Kate rested the end of the bow on the ground, braced it against her foot, and strung it in an efficient manner then turned her attention to the quiver of arrows Hollinger presented. Unless she was a very, very good actress Oliver was now fairly confident she had indeed lost her memory. Every now and again there was a look in her eye, the look of someone frightened and lost. In spite of his intentions, that brief, fleeting shadow in her green eyes tugged at his heart.

As to her station in life, one might be able to bluff one's way through a meal but the knowledge she had effortlessly displayed in the library bespoke of a quality education. Too accomplished for a female perhaps, but an education that could only be provided by wealth and position. No matter what else Kate might or might not be, it was obvious she was a lady.

But was she a married lady?

He tried to push the thought out of his head. It scarcely mattered at the moment. Still, it might well matter eventually. Oliver couldn't deny that he liked her. Quite a lot actually. Given the short amount of time he had known her and the fact that he didn't really know her at all, it was most curious. Perhaps it was easier to truly know someone when they were not shackled by all the bits and pieces of life people dragged around with them. It could be that her circumstances simply appealed to his romantic nature and there was nothing more to it than that.

Admittedly, there was something quite compelling about a beautiful woman of mystery. Add to that her obvious intelligence and her innate courage—Oliver was confident that if he had awakened to find himself surrounded by strangers without knowing his own name he'd be a blithering fool by now. Coupled with her willingness to understand, if not completely accept, the basis for his suspicions one might well have a woman one could spend the rest of one's days with.

If, of course, one knew her name.

Kate selected an arrow and glanced at him. "This is all in remarkably good repair. I had the impression it was scarcely used, that your mother no longer pursued archery."

He nodded. "She doesn't."

"Beg pardon, my lord," Hollinger said. "Lady Norcroft regularly practices with her bow."

Oliver drew his brows together. "Really? I had no idea."

Hollinger wisely said nothing.

"But she no longer competes." He glanced at Hollinger. "Does she?"

"Lady Norcroft feels, as she is currently the only Lady Norcroft, her time is better spent attending to the duties of her position." Hollinger paused. "She also says she would prefer to rest on her past triumphs rather than prove a point she believes has already been proved."

"I see." Oliver thought for a moment. "Does she regret it?"

Hollinger hesitated. "I couldn't say, sir."

"I had no idea." Here was yet another thing he didn't know about his mother.

"What a good son you are, Oliver," Kate murmured and selected an arrow.

"Indeed I am." He was, wasn't he? He provided for his mother and kept her from harm exactly as his father had instructed. And if he hadn't known of her desire for adventure or her regrets at sacrificing a pastime she had once enjoyed, it certainly wasn't deliberate. After all, he was a grown man and he had his own life to lead. Besides, he had always assumed his mother did precisely as she pleased. "I am a good son," he repeated in a firmer manner than before.

"Of course you are." Kate cast him a blinding smile and his heart tripped. Blasted woman.

She nocked the arrow and assumed what looked like the proper position. He had never had any particular interest in archery but he remembered watching his mother practice in this very spot when he was a boy. Now, he realized that had ended when his father had died, although she had certainly gone on with her life. At least he'd always *thought* she had.

Kate took aim and let the arrow fly. It hit the outer white circle with a familiar twang.

"You are good at this," he said with a smile.

She wrinkled her nose. "Not at the moment." She took another arrow, determination in the very line of her body. "But I will be."

He chuckled. "I daresay I couldn't have hit the target at all."

"I'm sure you have all sorts of other skills, Oliver," she murmured, sighted the target, and shot. This arrow struck a few inches closer to the center gold circle than the first. She nodded. "Better."

She plucked another arrow from the quiver, her concentration entirely on the task at hand. Oliver realized it scarcely mattered if he were here or not.

Hollinger cleared his throat. "If you would excuse me, sir, I have matters to attend to in the manor."

"Yes, of course." Oliver accepted the quiver of arrows and the butler took his leave. Odd, he would have wagered Hollinger intended to linger as long as possible—unless he had instructions to leave the two of them alone, which wouldn't have surprised Oliver one bit.

The third arrow hit the target's inner white circle and Kate nodded with satisfaction. "There, that's much better."

"It's excellent." He handed her another arrow. "Does this bring back any memories?"

"I'm afraid not." She nocked the arrow and prepared to shoot again. "Apparently, I know how to do this but I don't know how I know. It's as natural as breathing. I do it without thought." She drew back and released the arrow and it struck the red circle.

"You make it look effortless. This is not a skill one acquires overnight."

"Probably not."

"It might well be something you first learned as a girl."

"Possibly."

"Perhaps this is how you came to be here," Oliver said thoughtfully.

"What?" She reached for another arrow and smiled ruefully. "Shot through the air until I landed at the train platform?"

"That would be entirely too easy an explanation." He smiled and passed her an arrow. "If, by some bizarre twist of all that is logical in this world, my mother's theory that you are related to an acquaintance of hers is correct, it could be someone she knew through her involvement in archery."

"Yes, I suppose it could." She nocked the arrow and drew it back.

"Possibly whomever taught you to shoot. Your mother perhaps."

"My mother is dead," she said absently, let the arrow fly, then turned sharply. "My mother is dead! Oliver, I remember that!"

At once he realized there were any number of memories she might not wish to remember. "Kate, I am sorry—"

"No, no." She waved off his apology. "It's quite all right. There's no . . ." Her brow furrowed as if she were searching for the right word. "No *immediate* sorrow attached to it. It is sad, of course, but I have the feeling my mother's death was a very long time ago. My father's as well." Her eyes widened. "Good Lord, I'm an orphan!"

"But are you a widow?" he said without thinking.

"For heaven's sakes, Oliver, now is not the time to concern yourself with my marital status." She thrust the bow at him. He grabbed it, juggling quiver and bow. Kate clasped her hands behind her back and paced to and fro. "We have more important matters to consider."

"I can't think of anything more important than the question of your marital status," he said under his breath.

She ignored him. "What do we know about me thus far?" She glanced at him. "Oh, have I now passed your test?"

He nodded. "I would say without hesitation that

you are indeed a properly raised lady and I suspect one of means as well."

"Why?"

"Accomplishment with a bow these days takes a commitment of leisure time those without money rarely have. Your education is obviously extensive, especially for a female. Such education does not come cheaply. While your accent is Scottish, it indicates as well that you were educated in England, at least according to my mother. Again an indication of wealth."

"Very well then. I am a lady of means and an orphan." She thought for a moment. "Although it does seem to me, even if I do not have parents, I have family."

He nodded. "You said something last night about family responsibility that implied as much."

"Perhaps I have aunts or uncles or grandparents or—"

"A husband or children."

"No, I don't have children," she said firmly. "I am confident of that."

"How can you be so certain?"

She stopped and stared at him. "Goodness, Oliver, I think if I had children I would know."

"You don't know your own name," he said as gently as possible.

"Nonetheless, even if one has lost one's memory, I can't believe one would forget one's own children. You might not remember their names or anything about them but you would know." She pressed her hands to her heart. "Here. I would know."

"And you have no such feeling?"

"No," she said again, a slight wistful note in her voice. "I don't have children."

"What about a husband?" he asked in as casual a tone as he could muster, as though the question wasn't the least bit important. "Wouldn't you have the same sense about a husband?"

"One would think so." The wistful note had vanished and the practical Kate had returned. "But I feel nothing regarding a husband whatsoever."

Oliver shifted the bow. "Perhaps you don't like him?"

She scoffed. "Then I can't imagine I would have married him."

"People marry for any number of reasons aside from affection. For duty or honor or necessity."

"I suppose you're right." She glanced at him. "Would you?"

"I am fortunate enough never to have been in the position where I have had to discover the answer to that." He shrugged. "My father married for love as did my grandfather. I have always assumed I would do so as well. Indeed, I intend to do so." Even as he said the words he realized this was one area in which his familial responsibilities would play no part. As much as he had no reluctance to marry, he would not do so to satisfy any sort of obligation. He had no need to wed for wealth or position; his fortune was sound, his title secure. It struck him that he was extraordinarily lucky to be able to follow his heart when the time came.

She took the bow from him. "Why haven't you married?"

"Just as you said last night, I have not yet found the right woman."

"And when you do?"

"I shall surely marry her at once," he said with a grin. "If only to make my mother happy."

"You are a good son." She laughed and he noted what a lovely laugh it was. Genuine and honest and appealing, the laugh of someone unfettered by day-to-day concerns. He'd never thought a laugh to be particularly significant, but he realized he liked listening to her laugh and he rather hoped that no matter what else might change once they knew the truth about her, regardless of what responsibilities she might have, her laugh would remain as free in spirit as it was now.

Kate shot another few arrows, each landing fairly close to the center of the target. He suspected if a score was being kept she would do quite well.

She glanced at him. "Would you care to give it a try?"

Even though he knew archery was a perfectly acceptable sport for a man, indeed it was more of a man's endeavor than a woman's, he'd never had any particular desire to follow in his mother's footsteps. Still, he had always assumed he could shoot and shoot well if he had wished to. He reached for the bow. "Why not."

"Do you know how to properly stand?" Amusement sparkled in her eye.

"I have been standing much of my life, Kate," he said in a casual manner. "Properly for my needs up to now. However, as a boy I spent long hours watching my mother practice." He planted his feet a comfortable few inches apart, his body at a right angle to the target. "I believe I can do this correctly."

"Very good, Oliver." She handed him an arrow.

"I thought so." He nocked the arrow, raised the bow, and aimed. This was as easy as he had thought it would be. He drew the arrow back and released it. It flew in the general direction of the target but far to the right and entirely too high.

"Nice effort, Oliver." She smiled in a vaguely condescending way.

He drew his brows together in irritation. Obviously he was not concentrating as he should. He shot three more arrows in fast succession, each flying wide and high of the mark.

"You don't like being beaten by a woman, do you?"

Frustration clenched his jaw. "I was not aware this was a competition."

She shrugged.

"I am not being beaten by a woman I am being beaten by my own inadequacy."

"And that's better than being bested by a woman," she said in an altogether too innocent manner.

"Infinitely."

She bit back a smile. "Perhaps if you held the bow more like this." She pantomimed holding the bow. "And drew the arrow back like this."

He gritted his teeth. "That's exactly what I was doing."

"No, that's not what you were doing." She rolled her gaze toward the sky. "You were holding the bow—here, let me show you." She adjusted the bow in his hands then furrowed her brow. "This is most awkward. It's like trying to do it in a mirror. Here." She took the bow. "Stand behind me."

He moved to her back.

"Now, put your arms over mine."

"With pleasure," he murmured and wrapped his arms around her.

She ignored him. "Do you understand what I'm doing? The placement of my arms? The position of my body?"

"Oh, I do, Kate, I do indeed." His chest was flat against her back, her head coming just to his nose. She was quite a perfect height for him. Most convenient if he wished to kiss her again or explore the length of her lovely neck.

She stilled. "What are you doing?"

He shifted his head slightly to nuzzle the side of her neck. She smelled fresh and alive and reminiscent of spring. He drew a deep breath. "I'm learning to shoot an arrow."

"There are many things I do not recall, Oliver," she said slowly. "But I am fairly certain that is not what you are doing."

"I never was much of a scholar," he murmured against the warmth of her skin and she shivered beneath his touch.

She lowered the bow. "This is not a scholarly pursuit."

"Nonetheless, I find it remarkably difficult to concentrate."

"As do I." She sighed and relaxed against him. "Oliver?"

"Hmmm?"

"Does this strike you as unusual?"

"This strikes me as delightful."

"But does it seem entirely too fast?"

"It seems entirely too perfect."

"It strikes me as . . ." She hesitated. "Right."

He paused. He was hard pressed to deny it. Still, deny it he must. There was too much about her he didn't know. Too much she didn't know. He released her and stepped back. "My apologies, Kate. I lost my head. I have no right to—"

She whirled to face him. "And yet you kissed me. Not more than an hour ago."

He drew a deep breath. "That might have been a mistake."

"Was it Oliver?" Her gaze bored into his. "Was it a mistake?"

"Yes. No. I don't know." Surrender, sweet and misguided and inevitable washed through him. A voice in the back of his head screamed too soon, too fast, too uncertain. He ignored it. Oliver took the bow and tossed it aside then pulled her into his arms. "I don't seem to know anything when it comes to you."

"And I don't know anything save how to shoot an arrow and that my parents are dead and . . ." She swallowed hard. "And how I feel when I am in your arms."

He pulled her closer against him. "It is very probably a mistake you know."

"I do know that." Still she made no effort to pull away.

"One of us should keep his wits about him," he said and realized he had no idea how to go about doing so. He'd never been an impulsive sort and his behavior now was as foreign to him as the feelings he had for the stranger in his arms.

"We both should keep our wits about us." She blew a long breath. "This is probably no more than my need for comfort and your need for . . ."

"Adventure." He nodded.

She paused. "Adventure?"

He chuckled. "You have to admit a beautiful woman who has no knowledge as to who she is, appearing from who knows where is certainly an adventure of a sort."

She shrugged off his arms and stepped back. "I have no desire to be any man's *adventure*."

He stared at her. "I did not mean to offend you. I simply meant—"

"Yes, my lord." She crossed her arms over her chest. "What did you mean?"

"Well, I meant . . ." What did he mean? He ran his hand through his hair. "I'm not sure what I meant but I certainly did not intend to insult you."

"What did you intend?" Her eyes narrowed. "Simply because I have misplaced certain facts about my life—"

"Misplaced?" He stared in disbelief. "I would scarce use the word misplaced. You don't know your name!"

"You needn't keep saying that, I am well aware of it. Regardless, that does not give you the right to toy with my affections."

"I'm not toying with your affections. I'm . . ."

"You're what?"

"I'm not sure exactly but I'm not toying." He folded his arms over his chest, a mirror image of her own stance. "Perhaps you're the one toying with my affections. After all, I don't know anything about you."

She snorted. "I don't know anything about you."

"You know my name. My title. My position. I daresay anything else anyone wishes to know about me is easy to determine."

"I know you are annoying and infuriating and arrogant."

"And I know that you are stubborn and outspoken and, and, and I don't know what else."

"And therein lies the problem, my lord."

He raised a brow. "Just one?"

"One of many," she snapped, swiveled away from him and picked up the bow. "If you will excuse me, my lord, I should like to resume shooting."

"One never knows when such a skill will come in handy," he said in a grim manner.

"No." She met his gaze directly. "One doesn't. Go away, Oliver, before I shoot you."

"Indeed, a woman who would slap a man might not hesitate to shoot him."

"It's a chance you might not wish to take."

He leaned closer and wondered if he was indeed taking his life in his hands. "I suspect it's a chance worth taking for the right woman." He straightened. "Good day then." He nodded, turned and strode back toward the house.

The woman was impossible. Charming and vulnerable and altogether delicious one moment and prickly and distrustful and infuriating the next. One minute he wished to thrash her and the next take her in his arms. And that too was annoying.

He had to admit he had never felt this strongly about any woman before and certainly not as quickly as this. It was almost as if forces beyond his control were at work. Fate perhaps or destiny or . . . or what? Magic? That was it. His jaw clenched. She had bewitched him. Cast some sort of Scottish spell over him. Enchanted him when he wasn't looking.

His step slowed. What utter nonsense. How could he possibly even consider such a thing? It was no more than his mother's silly talk about curses that had put the idea in his head in the first place.

Still, magic made just about as much sense as any other answer to explain his feelings. It certainly wasn't anything as absurd as love at first sight. Not that he didn't suspect such things existed. And yes, he had always thought he would know the very moment he met the woman he would spend the rest of his life with. But when he had first seen Kate she had been unconscious, which scarcely counted. It wasn't until he had looked into her eyes that he had felt . . . desire? Yes, of course. Discovered the pull of attraction? Without question. Experienced curiosity? Who wouldn't be curious?

Glimpsed his future?

No, that was ridiculous. He absolutely refused to so much as consider the possibility. He would accept desire and attraction but anything more was absurd. He would help Kate recover her memory but that would be that. What he was feeling was nothing more than the kind of ordinary *lust* any man would feel for a lovely, mysterious woman and there was nothing to be done about it. Given all that he didn't know about her, all that she didn't know about herself, it would be wrong, morally, ethically wrong to pursue her in any manner whatsoever. Utterly irresponsible on his part. Not at all the sort of thing he would do.

And why not?

The thought pulled him up short. Why, he had always done everything expected of him. He more than lived up to the responsibilities of his title, of caring for his mother and his tenants. He was cautious and practical and sane—especially when compared to his friends. Friends who had always looked to him for rational advice, assistance, and occasional rescue. Wasn't it time he did something completely irresponsible that might well require rescue? Didn't he now and again deserve to *not* think about the consequences of his actions, to throw caution to the winds?

Didn't he deserve an adventure?

As for Kate, she was certainly not a child and her character was obviously anything but weak. He didn't have a doubt in his mind that she would never allow anything to happen between them that she didn't wish to happen. But seduction simmered in the air and had since the moment she had opened her eyes. She was as cognizant of it as he. It was as powerful a lure as adventure.

Oliver would pursue Kate as he did any woman that he wanted. No, he would pursue her as he had never pursued any woman before. And if that pursuit led ultimately to seduction—hers or his—so be it.

Kate would be his adventure even if he never again mentioned the word to her. And if he, well, if he lost his heart in the process, wasn't that the risk one ran for adventure?

It was however, disconcerting to realize that the thought of his heart had reared its head at all.

Chapter 9

As much as Kate wanted to know everything about herself, some discoveries weren't as comforting as others. It was gratifying to learn she was skilled with a bow and not at all pleasant to realize she had a somewhat quick temper, an impatient nature and she found men who acted as if she did not exist most annoying. Certainly one could argue that a man who feared he might well end up with an arrow imbedded in a vulnerable part of his body would be wise to avoid the woman in question. Still, the fact that his avoidance was prudent made it no less irritating. Kate sat across the dinner table from Oliver and tried not to glare at him.

From the moment he had left her two days ago, Oliver had been polite and cordial, the perfect host, but if he was not actually avoiding her presence he was doing nothing to be in her company either. She had the oddest feeling he was not merely staying away from her but somehow biding his time, considering his options, even devising a plan of battle which made no sense at all and was probably no more than her imagination run amok.

Kate was equally polite and every bit as cordial, but for the moment, she too kept her distance. She told herself she preferred her own company to his, but if truth were told the man scared her. Oh, not that Oliver was frightening in and of himself, but her feelings when she was in his presence were anything but cordial, cool, and aloof.

It was odd that he was not married by now. The man was amusing and clever, generous and kind. The type of man who would give coins to a stranger on the street simply because it looked as if she would need them whereas Oliver did not. He insisted they had never met but Kate felt more and more certain that somehow she knew him.

"And then there is Dr. Miller, charming man, but of course you have met him," Lady Norcroft continued apparently unaware that neither Kate nor Oliver was responding with more than cursory interest.

It had been remarkably easy to avoid each other. Oliver had spent much of the last two days visiting with tenants. Today he had met with his estate manager and then had spent the rest of the day riding. Kate would have liked to have felt a horse beneath her—she suspected she rode well—but he had not invited her to join him and she had not invited herself. No, it was better not to be alone with him.

Kate had used her time in exploration of the greenhouse and the library. She'd found Lady Norcroft had a passion for filling her home with the flowers of spring. Her gardeners were skilled at forcing the blooms of tulips, daffodils, and a profusion of other flowers, as well as growing a variety of small fruit trees kept in pots. The greenhouse smelled of spring and hope and provided a fresh and delightful escape.

In the library, she had discovered she was indeed well read. She had found copies of *Jane Eyre* and *Wuthering Heights*—Lady Norcroft's no doubt—and it was as though she had discovered old friends. Indeed, while she had intended simply to page through *Jane Eyre,* she had soon found herself immersed in the familiar story of the passionate governess. Jane's turbulent life took Kate's mind off her own precarious situation.

As did archery. Kate had spent hours with bow and arrow yesterday afternoon and again today. The concentration required to aim and shoot accurately eased her mind and provided a respite from both dwelling on Oliver and trying to recall anything pertinent about her life. Unfortunately she had had no new revelations since realizing her parents were dead although she had discovered she was not an especially patient person. Surely there was something she should be doing to recover her lost memory other than waiting.

"Oliver, I should think you would . . ."

Dinner tonight was no less awkward than last night or the night before. Kate was grateful to Lady Norcroft, who carried the conversation, oblivious to the tension in the air whenever her son and her guest were in the same room. Kate certainly felt it and was sure Oliver felt it as well. On his part it might well be that his suspicions about her had not abated although she had thought they had. She would catch him looking at her, studying her as if by doing so he could learn the truth. Her jaw clenched in impatience. She hoped he would and soon. As comfortable and pleasant as Norcroft Manor was, it was not her home and she did long to know where home was. Where she belonged.

And the sooner that happened, the better. The growing attraction she felt for Oliver was as irresistible as it was impossible. She had no right to feel anything whatsoever for the man. No right to lie awake at night thinking about the feel of his lips on hers. And certainly no right to wonder what course their relationship might have taken if they had met under normal circumstances.

"And then I said to her . . ."

Lady Norcroft had sent off a flurry of letters

apparently to anyone she had ever met in an effort to learn Kate's identity. It was too early for them to have produced results but Lady Norcroft was confident they would. She had also sent for Madame DuBois to come from London. The seamstress was expected tomorrow. Kate had protested once again, given the no doubt exorbitant cost involved but Lady Norcroft had waved aside her objections. In this, even Oliver had agreed with his mother.

Lady Norcroft's nieces were expected tomorrow as well, and with more guests in the house it would be next to impossible to be alone with Oliver. Which was, of course, for the best.

"Excellent suggestion, Mother," Oliver said with enthusiasm. "What do you say, Kate?"

Oliver's voice jerked her attention back to the table. "Well, yes, certainly, if Lady Norcroft thinks it's a good idea." She smiled weakly.

"As it was my idea, I think it's excellent." Lady Norcroft beamed. "Oliver, I suggest you precede us and make certain everything is prepared."

He laughed. "I don't see that any particular preparation is necessary but as you so obviously wish to speak to Kate alone, I shall take my leave." He rose to his feet then stepped behind Kate's chair, leaned close, and lowered his voice. "Dancing, Kate. My mother thinks it's a good idea if we make certain you are proficient on the dance floor. Although I have no fears in that quarter, practice is always beneficial." His breath was warm against her ear and she shivered with delight and sheer desire. The man simply melted something inside her. "And I can think of nothing I'd rather do than have you in my arms."

Oliver straightened. "I shall meet you in the ballroom then." He cast his mother a firm glance. "Do not take too long. I am looking forward to this."

"I am certain you are." Lady Norcroft favored her son with an affectionate smile. Her gaze followed him from the room. "He is a good man, Kate. Not perfect by any means, but a good man."

Kate smiled but said nothing. Oliver did seem to be a good man, which made everything all the more difficult.

"Might I ask where your thoughts were this evening? They were certainly not here."

"My apologies." Kate grimaced. "My thoughts are where they always are. On a hundred unanswered questions. A thousand unknown possibilities." And one annoying man.

Lady Norcroft studied her for a long moment. "This is difficult for you, isn't it?"

"I imagine it would be difficult for anyone."

"But most especially for someone like you."

Kate pulled her brows together. "What do you mean, someone like me?"

"My dear Kate, it is obvious to me that you are a very strong and intelligent woman. The kind of female who never doubts her purpose, her place in the world, who accepts the responsibilities life hands her without fail."

Kate stared. "That is obvious to you?"

The older woman laughed. "It is indeed." She paused. "You should know I was not always the frivolous creature you see now."

"I don't think you're at all frivolous," Kate said staunchly.

"Oh, but I am and I quite enjoy being frivolous. I have earned it," she said firmly. "When Oliver's father died, a great deal of responsibility fell upon my shoulders. We had no other family to speak of. Charles left it to me to take care of our son and his future. I ran the estate, I managed the family finances and I made certain when Oliver was old enough to take over the responsibilities of his position there would be something left to take over. So you see my dear I am well aware of the strength inherent in women. Enough so to recognize it when I see it."

Kate stared.

Sympathy shone in Lady Norcroft's blue eyes. "I am sorry this is so hard for you."

Impulsively Kate reached over and laid her hand on the older woman's. "Thank you for being so kind."

"It's I who should thank you." Lady Norcroft shook her head. "I don't believe I have ever seen Oliver quite so taken with a woman before."

"Taken?" Kate scoffed. "I think he's more inconvenienced and annoyed than taken."

"Nonsense." Lady Norcroft waved off Kate's comment. "The inconvenience is temporary and I daresay any annoyance is more with the situation than with you. Besides, annoying a man is an excellent way to begin. Why, I annoyed my husband no end when we first met."

"Yes, but he knew your name." Kate shook her head. "Oliver knows nothing about me. Regardless of how he might feel, or think he feels, it's nothing more than the . . . *adventure*, if you will, of the circumstances."

"Do not discount the benefit of adventure. It can be quite," a wicked light sparked in Lady Norcroft's eye, "stimulating and most romantic."

Kate choked back a gasp.

"Oliver always has had a romantic side," his mother said more to herself than to Kate. "And he could certainly use an adventure—"

"I beg your pardon, Lady Norcroft, but this is not an adventure for me. It is an ordeal. As for your son, we are in an impossible situation." Kate stared at the older woman. "I have no right to feel anything at all until I know who I am nor does Lord Norcroft."

"Quite right, my dear. I expected nothing less from you." Lady Norcroft smiled with satisfaction and rose to her feet. "Now then, shall we join my son?"

Lady Norcroft led the way from the dining room, down the corridor into the ballroom chattering all the while about the upcoming ball, leaving Kate entirely to her own thoughts.

So his mother thought Oliver was taken with

her. It was, as Kate had said, an impossible situation yet the idea that he was as drawn to her as she was to him warmed her heart. Dear Lord, she hoped she was free but until she knew there should be—there could be—no more double entendres or stolen kisses or longings deep in the night for something she might never have. Lady Norcroft thought Kate was a strong woman. She drew a deep breath and resolved to draw on that strength.

Lady Norcroft left Kate at the top of a short flight of steps to take her place at the piano. The steps led down to the ballroom and to Oliver, waiting below. He smiled up at her and her breath caught. She stared down at him, and wondered how anyone could make her feel this way and wondered as well if anyone ever had. She started down the steps and scarcely noticed the first strains of a waltz played on a piano drifting from somewhere above her.

She moved into his arms as if she were meant to be there. His gaze locked with hers and without a word they began to dance. He led her around the ballroom with an easy grace and she followed his every step without effort as if they had danced together before or always. For this one moment, here in his arms, she could forget all that she didn't know and revel in the feel of his body close to hers, the music washing through her soul and the overwhelming sensation that this was indeed where she was supposed to be.

"I knew you could dance." He grinned and the spell was broken.

"As did I," she said in a lofty manner that belied her relief. If she wasn't careful, she could easily fall in love with this man if she hadn't already. She brushed the thought away. Strength, she reminded herself, strength would see her through.

"I have been giving the question of you and I a great deal of thought, Kate," Oliver began.

"I didn't realize there was a you and I," she said lightly but her pulse raced nonetheless.

"Oh but there is and you know it as well as I," he said firmly.

"If indeed there is a you and I, and I don't see how there can be given the circumstances, should we be discussing this in front of your mother?"

He laughed. "First of all, my mother would be delighted at the very thought of a you and I. She quite likes you, you know. Secondly, as she is not dancing between us but is at the keys of the piano, she can't hear a word we say."

"Where is the piano?" Kate glanced around the ballroom.

"Above us." He nodded at a mezzanine that wrapped around three sides of the ballroom and overlooked the dance floor below. Lady Norcroft sat at a grand piano tucked into an alcove suitable for a large group of musicians. "So you see we are practically alone." Oliver executed a complicated turn and she followed his lead smoothly. "I think we have a great deal in common, Kate."

"Do we, Oliver?"

"I think you have as much a sense of responsibility as I do."

"How can you possibly think so?"

"I am an astute judge of human nature," he said firmly.

She laughed. "Thus far I have seen no evidence of that."

"I hide it admirably." He grinned then sobered. "It's some of the things you've said unexpectedly. There is as well a presence about you that reminds me, regrettably, of myself."

"Oh dear."

"I think as well that you are as sadly lacking in adventures as I am."

She stared into his blue eyes. "Why on earth would you think that?"

"I'm not sure." He shrugged. "It's no more than a feeling but it's a very strong feeling."

"Feelings can be misleading," she said primly. "And certainly should not be acted upon in a rash and impetuous manner."

"I have never acted in a rash and impetuous manner, not once that I can recall, but I think it might well be past time that I do." He nodded. "Furthermore, I have a confession to make to you."

"My, that is rash and impetuous," she teased but her heart skipped a beat.

"I want you, Kate."

"You . . ." It was all she could do not to stumble over her own feet. "I . . . I don't know what to say."

He chuckled. "Come now, Kate. I find that hard to believe."

"I suppose your comment is not completely un-expected." She chose her words with care. "But I never imagined you to be so blunt."

"I never have been. I am usually quite subtle, even restrained." He paused. "I hope I have not offended you."

"I haven't decided yet." She shook her head. "I suppose it depends on whether your . . . desire?"

He nodded. "Definitely desire."

"Desire it is then. Whether said desire is because you think I am the kind of woman who would indiscriminately surrender to desire."

"No, absolutely not," he said staunchly and heaven help her she believed him. "I don't think you would indiscriminately surrender to any emotion let alone desire."

"I see." She certainly should be offended if not by his declaration of desire then by his conviction that she would not be swayed by emotion. It was rather unflattering as if she were cold and heartless although he obviously didn't mean it that way. Regardless, offense would be the proper and appropriate reaction to his comments. Still, it would be much more interesting to see exactly what he intended to do now. "I thought you were not given to the seduction of married women?"

"Ah, but we don't know whether or not you are married." He flashed a wicked smile. "Therefore it would be an act of ignorance which would surely be forgiven."

"But never forgotten."

"No." His brow furrowed. "That is a problem."

"Once done some things can never be undone."

"Yes, I realize that."

She tilted her head and studied him. "Then what are you to do, Oliver?"

"Alas, Kate." He heaved a heartfelt sigh. "Nothing. Nothing at all."

She stumbled to a halt and stared at him. "Nothing?"

"Of course not." He smiled in an annoyingly casual manner as if he declared his desire for a possibly married woman who didn't know if indeed she was married every day. "It wouldn't be the least bit honorable."

"Then why say anything at all if you did not intend to do something about it?"

"Well, I did want to know what your response might be."

She raised a brow. "I hope you were not disappointed?"

"As you did not run screaming into the night nor did you slap my face again, I would say I was not in the least disappointed. Now then shall we continue the dance?"

"I'm not sure dancing with you is wise," she murmured but stepped into his arms once again.

"I'm not sure having anything whatsoever to do with you is wise."

"Probably not."

"I still don't understand why you would say something like that to me if you did not intend to do anything about it."

"I do not intend to do anything about it." He paused. "At the moment."

"You didn't say that."

"My apologies. It must have slipped my mind. It simply seems to me, Kate, that it might be weeks or even months before you recover your memory and there is a distinct possibility you might never recover it at all."

"I hadn't thought of that." It was not a pleasant thought.

"I fully intend to wait for you."

"My, that is romantic."

"But not forever."

"So much for romantic."

He stared into her eyes. "There is something about you that calls to something in me. I don't know if it's a similarity of character or something as yet undefined but it is . . . inevitable."

A delightful chill ran up her spine. "Inevitable?"

"You have haunted my thoughts since your arrival in my life. You have lingered in my dreams." His blue eyes bored into hers. "Call it fate or destiny or forces beyond our control but I have come to wonder if your presence here is not an accident."

She swallowed hard. "You have?"

"And I think you feel it too." He pulled her slightly closer than was proper for the dance. His voice was low and seductive. "Do you lay awake at night thinking of me? Do you close your eyes only to see my face? Do you relive the moment that our lips touched over and over in your mind until you think you will go mad until we kiss again?"

Yes! "No, of course not."

He smiled a slow, knowing smile. "You're lying my dear. And in spite of my earlier suspicions, I do not think you do it well."

"It's the adventure, Oliver," she said, forcing a no-nonsense tone to her voice. It would not do to allow the longing to wrap her arms around him and press her lips firmly to his to show. It would not be wise to let him know she shared his desire. "The mystery if you will. You know nothing about me and that is what you find intriguing."

"Oh, but I know a great deal about you."

"Certainly you know I can shoot an arrow properly and I am well educated—"

"I know you wrinkle your nose when you're annoyed with yourself. I know your laugh is honest and unfettered. I know you straighten your shoulders when you are determined."

"Merely observances. I scarcely think—"

He stopped in mid step and pulled her closer against him, her hand in his trapped against his chest. "I know you are too kind to rebuke an older woman who might be overly interfering. I know when you think no one is looking your eyes show how frightened you are and I know you have the courage to go on nonetheless." His hand tightened around hers. "And I know when your lips meet mine I feel as though I have never been kissed before."

"Oh my." The words were little more than a sigh.

"And I know if you had never come into my life I would spend the rest of my days knowing there was something I had missed."

"Oliver." Did it matter so much who she was or whether she was free to return his feelings? Did anything matter save the look in his eyes and the yearning in her heart? Could something that felt so very right possibly be wrong?

"Kate, mysterious Kate," he murmured and lowered his lips to hers.

"Oliver!" A female voice rang out across the ballroom. "We're here!"

Chapter 10

*O*liver winced, released Kate, then stepped back.

Kate drew a calming breath, at once grateful and more than a little disappointed. After all, one never knew when the opportunity to fully abandon one's rational nature and give in to desire would occur again. She was apparently around thirty years of age and as far as she could remember had only been kissed once. If indeed she was a tart she was—at least at the moment—a fairly frustrated one. Still, nothing of significance would have happened with Oliver's mother somewhere above them like a heavenly orchestra so the interruption scarcely mattered. It was probably for the best all things considered. Kate adopted a cordial smile and turned toward the voice that had sounded from the steps leading into the ballroom.

"Aunt Edwina!" A pretty young woman waved at the alcove. Two others, equally pretty, started down the stairs.

"Prepare yourself, Kate," Oliver said out of the side of his mouth. "This should be interesting."

"Interesting?" Kate kept her gaze on the approaching women. One was slightly taller than the other two and all had dark hair. From this distance, they could have been triplets, the similarity of appearance was so strong. A young man trailed behind them. "They're your cousins aren't they?"

"My darlings!" Lady Norcroft called from above. "You're early. How delightful. I'll be down in a moment. I have a great deal to tell you."

"Cousins in name only," he said dryly. "In truth, since their arrival this past Christmas, they have become the sisters I never had. I find myself in the position of being a responsible brother to three girls in their first season and I must say it's not the least bit enjoyable."

"I don't have a brother," Kate murmured then widened her eyes. "Or a sister either for that matter. Oliver, I remember that!"

He nodded. "Your life is coming back to you."

"I haven't recalled anything new for days. Not since I realized my parents were dead." She shook her head. "Apparently I don't have these revelations unless I am with you."

He grinned. "Then I shall consider it my duty to be with you as much as possible."

"How gallant of you," she said lightly. As beneficial as that might be for her memory, it might not be wise for her heart. A minute ago she had been ready to toss caution aside and surrender to her feelings. Who knew what might happen with more time spent in Oliver's company.

"Oliver!" The tallest girl flung her arms around him followed in quick succession by her sisters in a flurry of hugs and greetings and chatter. Aside from one being a few inches taller than the others, with their dark hair and deep brown eyes, there was no mistaking a family resemblance.

"Gen." Oliver disentangled her arms from around his neck and set her gently aside then turned to Kate. "Kate, may I present my cousins—"

"Cousins by marriage," the taller girl—Gen— said. "Oliver's father's sister was married to our father before he married our mother. Our older sister is Oliver's cousin by blood but there's really no blood connection between the rest of us and Oliver at all."

"And yet we are family all the same," Oliver said firmly and Kate had the distinct feeling that one—if not all—of the girls would have been more than willing to overlook the tenuous family connection in favor of a union with the handsome earl himself. "Kate, this is Miss Genevieve Fairchild. Gen is the oldest."

Genevieve's gaze flicked over Kate in an assessing manner. "Is that my dress?"

"It is and I am most grateful for the loan of it," Kate said quickly. "I find myself in the awkward position of having misplaced my luggage."

"Oh we know about that," one of the other girls said. She and the remaining sister were obviously twins. "Hollinger told us all about you."

A long-suffering expression washed across Oliver's face. "And this is Miss Arabella Fairchild."

"But you may call her Belle," the third girl said. "And I am Sophia, Sophie. I must say that dress looks much better on you than it ever did on Gen. You should keep it."

"Oh, I don't think—" Kate began.

"It is *my* dress," Gen said sharply, then sighed. "But she's right." She cast Kate a half-hearted smile. "It does look lovely on you."

Sophie hooked her arm through Kate's. "We can't tell you how exciting we think this is." She glanced at Oliver. "We're not interrupting are we?"

Oliver slanted Kate an apologetic look. "No, of course not."

"Good." Sophie beamed at Kate. "You must come along now and tell us all about it."

"I don't know that there's much—" Kate started.

"We're beside ourselves with curiosity and we want to know everything. Everything you know that is." Belle linked Kate's other arm and at once she felt surrounded and distinctly outnumbered.

"We think it's all terribly romantic. Like a good novel. A beautiful woman of mystery and a handsome earl who is obviously swept—"

"Hollinger talks a great deal doesn't he?" Oliver interrupted.

Gen grinned. "You'd be surprised at the things Hollinger knows."

"I'd be surprised if there was something he didn't know." He nodded at the younger girls. "There'll be plenty of time to speak to Kate. For now, I suggest you release her."

Reluctantly, the girls let go. Kate smiled. "I promise we shall all have a long talk tomorrow."

"A-hem." The young man Kate had noted earlier cleared his throat. He stood behind the girls, ignored and more than likely forgotten. Fair-haired and handsome, he appeared to be in his mid-twenties and did not look like the kind of man any girl would forget for long.

"Who," Oliver's eyes narrowed. "Are you?"

He stepped forward. "Emerson Berkley, sir."

"He's the youngest son of Viscount Berkley." A note of satisfaction sounded in Gen's voice.

"I believe you know my brother, sir. Marcus Berkley?" Mr. Berkley said hopefully.

"Marcus Berkley." Oliver nodded. "I have made his acquaintance. Good sort if I recall."

Relief washed across the younger Berkley's face. "Thank you, sir."

"Mr. Berkley was in attendance at the Roxborough Ride at Effington Hall." Gen favored the young man with an admiring smile. "He sits a horse exceptionally well."

Mr. Berkley grinned with barely concealed pride.

"The Ride is a steeplechase of sorts," Sophie said to Kate. "A huge crowd of people attends. Festivities go on for days. There are all sorts of parties including a grand ball—"

"And there are lots and lots of dashing young men," Belle added with a twinkle in her eye. "It was quite the most fun we've ever had."

"I invited Mr. Berkley to stay with us." Gen turned a challenging look on her cousin. "I knew Aunt Edwina wouldn't mind."

"I could certainly stay at an inn, sir," Mr. Berkley said quickly.

"I suppose we can make room for him in the stables," Oliver muttered.

"Don't be absurd." Lady Norcroft joined them. "There is more than enough room in the manor. Besides, with all these women in the house, it will be good for you to have a male ally."

"Aunt Edwina!" The girls threw themselves into the older woman's arms and there was a repeat of their greeting of Oliver with even more enthusiasm if possible and all four ladies talking at once. Poor Mr. Berkley was left to look on with an awkward smile on his face.

Oliver pulled Kate a few steps away, leaned close to her ear, and spoke in a low voice. "I don't like this."

Kate laughed. "Why on earth not? He seems a nice enough young man."

"Gen is only nineteen," Oliver said in a grim manner. "She has an excellent dowry and would be a prime target for any unscrupulous man looking for an heiress."

"He doesn't appear to be impoverished."

"No, as far as I know his family's fortune is sound."

Kate raised a brow. "Are his relations disreputable then? Was their fortune gained through nefarious and unscrupulous means?"

"Quite the contrary." Reluctance sounded in Oliver's voice.

"Have you heard gossip about the young man that leads you to believe he is a dishonorable sort?"

"No. I'm not sure I've ever heard his name before."

Kate studied Mr. Berkley now being introduced to Oliver's mother. "Then do you consider nineteen too young to wed?"

He clenched his teeth. "Probably not."

"Perhaps you do not like the gentleman himself." The young man kissed Lady Norcroft's hand in a most gallant manner. "He seems quite charming and he's certainly handsome enough."

"Too handsome," Oliver said darkly as if the fact of his handsome face was not a gift from God but rather a calculated means by which to seduce young, impressionable girls.

"Certainly as their guardian you have every right—"

"Oh, I'm not their guardian. Actually as Gen is nineteen and the twins are eighteen they are all of age. But their sister, Fiona, she's the future Duchess of Roxborough, is in control of their inheritance—dowries really—until they wed. However, they live in my home and as the head of this family, assuring their well-being and more importantly, their futures, is dependent upon me," he said staunchly.

"I see." So even though Oliver had no true obligation to the Fairchild girls he considered them his responsibility. His mother was right. He was a good man. "I think, Oliver, I shall retire for the evening and leave you to enjoy this reunion without me."

"So soon?" He gazed down at her. "But we haven't . . ."

"We haven't what?"

He paused for a moment then grimaced. "Our dance. We haven't finished our dance."

"That's exactly what I was thinking." She offered her hand and he raised it to his lips. "Perhaps tomorrow."

"Until tomorrow then." His gaze met hers. "Remember, we should be together as much as possible."

She nodded. "To help restore my memory."

He grinned in an altogether unrepentant manner. "That too." His lips brushed across her hand and it was all she could do not to wrap her arms around him and kiss him in a thorough and passionate manner. And be kissed quite thoroughly in return. A mistake, no doubt, but a glorious one.

Kate bid the rest of the gathering good evening and although it was difficult to extricate herself from their overly enthusiastic inclusion, finally managed to escape to the calm of her rooms.

All in all, it had been a most illuminating evening. She had realized she had no brothers or sisters. She had seen firsthand Oliver's sense of responsibility and generosity. And she had very nearly lost her head which certainly could not happen again. If she were married—and surely as she had remembered her lack of parents and siblings she should by now remember something as important as a husband—she knew enough about herself now and enough about Oliver to understand betrayal would be one thing neither of them could forgive. She had said it earlier—once done some things could never be undone. It bore repeating.

Still, as she settled into bed his words lingered in her head like a song she could not forget.

Do you relive the moment that our lips touched over and over in your mind until you think you will go mad until we kiss again?

Nonsense. Certainly the kiss they had shared was quite nice. More than merely nice but it was simply a kiss after all. The denial of which would not lead to insanity.

Do you close your eyes only to see my face?

Only because she was thinking about seeing his

face. It was exactly like when one was told not to think about elephants and then the only thing one could think about was elephants.

Do you lay awake at night thinking of me?

She clenched her fists by her side and tried to think of anything but him. And in the long hours that she tossed and turned and waited for sleep her one satisfaction was in the sure and certain knowledge that, more than likely, Oliver would sleep no better than she.

Chapter 11

$\mathcal{A}$ worried frown creased Lady Norcroft's forehead. "And you're certain it can be finished in time?"

From the expression of disdain on Madame DuBois's face one might have thought Lady Norcroft had questioned the honor of France itself. "But of course, my lady, precisely why we have come here to you."

Madame DuBois had arrived far earlier than expected. Before Kate was scarcely out of bed, Ellen, one of the family's maids, had whisked her to Lady Norcroft's parlor. She now stood on a stool in front of a cheval mirror wearing her chemise and petticoats, swathed in lengths of rainbow-colored silks and satins and surrounded by Lady Norcroft, the dressmaker, two of her seamstresses, and a rather effeminate-looking, haughty young man who had been introduced as Madame's assistant. One by one Belle, Sophie, and Gen had wandered in and now provided a rapt audience willing to volunteer their opinions. Kate found herself the focus of all eyes and it was more than a little disconcerting.

"You are fortunate that I am not overly busy at this time of year," Madame said in a vaguely chastising manner.

"I am most grateful that you were able to make the trip from London." Lady Norcroft smiled at the Frenchwoman and Kate had the distinct impression that this was some sort of game played with respect on both sides by the two women.

With her three nieces and her willingness to pay generously for what she wanted, as well as her connection to the future Duchess of Roxborough, Lady Norcroft was obviously a valuable client. Yet Madame's skill, reputation, even nationality decreed that while she might not be on a social footing with the countess, she certainly considered herself her equal. "You have a workroom prepared for us, no?"

"Of course." Lady Norcroft nodded. "And sleeping rooms as well."

"Excellent." Madame smiled with satisfaction.

Obviously there was no need for further discussion. Kate assumed—as no doubt did the Frenchwoman—that her entourage would be accommodated near a workroom in close proximity to the servants' quarters while Madame herself would have one of the less desirable, but still respectable, rooms reserved for guests. It was how arrangements like this worked. Kate had no idea how she knew that but she did.

"Well?" Madame turned to the sisters. "You have not been reluctant thus far to express your opinions. What color do you think is best for her?"

"The pink," Sophie, or it might have been Belle, said. "It brings out the blush in her cheeks."

"It's entirely too pale." Belle, or possibly Sophie, shook her head. "The rose is much better on her."

"Nonsense." Gen scoffed. "The bronze goes with her hair."

"Kate." Lady Norcroft fingered a length of fabric. "I believe this blue-green satin is most flattering."

"I think—" Kate started.

"Excellent." Madame nodded and gestured to one of the seamstresses to rearrange the fabrics draped around Kate and position Lady Norcroft's choice nearer to her face. It was indeed a lovely fabric, intense and almost iridescent, blue or green depending on how the light struck it. It deepened the color of her eyes and cast a warm glow on her skin. "It does indeed suit her well."

Kate stared into the mirror. "I have always looked good in blues and greens."

The three Fairchild girls traded glances.

"Kate," Lady Norcroft said gently. "Do you remember that?"

"Yes. No." She shook her head. "I'm not sure I remember it as much as I know it."

"One look and it is obvious. It does not seem to me a revelation of memory as much as a fact displayed in the mirror." Madame signaled to her staff and without question they removed the other fabrics and bustled around Kate, pinning and measuring and doing all sorts of things that went into the creation of a new gown. Surely Kate had been through all this before, still, she did wonder if it was always so tiresome. Madame glanced at Lady Norcroft. "You say she remembers nothing?"

Lady Norcroft shrugged. "Nothing of significance."

Madame thought for a moment. "And she has been here how long now?"

"Nearly a week," Lady Norcroft said.

"A week? And no one has come looking for her?" Madame shook her head. "It is most odd. One would think someone would have noticed her missing by now."

"Oh, she has no parents," one of the twins said. "And no brothers or sisters." Kate really needed to determine a way to tell Belle from Sophie. "She does know that. But she doesn't know whether or not she has a husband." She cast an apologetic look at Kate. "Oliver told us."

"I would say there is no husband then," Madame said with a decisive nod. "A husband worth the name would have come to find her by now."

"That's quite what I think. You haven't heard anything, have you?" Lady Norcroft's tone was deceptively off-hand. "About anyone who might have mislaid a wife?" At once Kate wondered if Madame's true purpose here was as much for her knowledge of current gossip as for her fashion sense.

"Nothing at all." Madame's brow furrowed. "But then most of my clients do not return to the city from their country homes until later in the year." Madame nodded to her staff and her assistant offered his hand to help Kate off the stool.

One of the twins leaned toward Kate. "Madame knows everything about everyone in London."

The slightest hint of a knowing smile quirked the lips of Madame's assistant and Kate wondered if the frills on the young man's cuff and manner were due more to his position than any personal preference on his part.

"And you have not had any response thus far from the letters you sent?" Madame had already been told Lady Norcroft's theory that Kate was the daughter of someone she might have known as well as everything else Oliver's mother knew about their guest.

Lady Norcroft shook her head. "It's entirely too soon but I am optimistic."

"I shall be happy to make inquiries when I return to London," Madame said. "Discreetly, of course."

Lady Norcroft grinned. "I expected no less. Now then." She started for the door, Madame a step behind her. "I'll have Hollinger show you to your rooms. Have you any ideas for Kate's gown?"

"I have some thoughts I should like to discuss." Madame cast one last critical look at Kate then left the room after Lady Norcroft. "She has an excellent waist, very small, but the bosom, well, there are ways . . ."

Kate tried and failed to resist glancing down at her bosom. It wasn't especially large but it wasn't particularly small either.

"Madame makes us all feel wanting in some respect," Gen said coolly. "But she is quite brilliant and cleverly manages to hide any number of flaws. Why, she can make *anyone* look exquisite."

"I wasn't aware I had that many flaws," Kate said under her breath. Ellen helped her into her day dress—or rather Gen's day dress—and immediately took her leave. "Does she always talk about you as if you weren't there?"

"Always." One of the younger girls nodded. "Why she quite crushed poor Belle the first time we had a fitting with her."

"It was most disheartening." Belle sniffed and Kate made a mental note of the dress she was wearing. There really seemed to be no other way to tell the twins apart. "She thought I had any number of flaws whereas Sophie did not. And as we are exactly the same—"

"Except for the flaws." Sophie grinned.

Belle ignored her. "It wasn't the least bit fair." Her eyes narrowed. "I think she just doesn't like me although I can't see why. Monsieur Harvey seems to like me quite a lot."

"Monsieur Harvey?" Kate asked.

Sophie nodded toward the door. "Madame's assistant."

"Utter nonsense." Gen rolled her eyes at the ceiling. "It's obvious that Monsieur Harvey doesn't like, well, girls. Madame certainly would never allow him in a fitting room otherwise."

"No, of course not," Belle said under her breath and once again Kate wondered as to the true likes and dislikes of Monsieur Harvey.

"Now that we're alone." Gen's eyes narrowed. "We were wondering what your intentions are."

Kate raised a brow. "My intentions? I don't particularly have any intentions other than to learn who I am."

"It's rather farfetched, don't you think?" Gen said. "This nonsense about losing your memory. I've never heard of anything so absurd."

"I may have read something about this sort of thing once," Belle murmured.

"Gen doesn't believe you," Sophie said.

"I see." Kate's gaze moved from one twin to the next. "Do you?"

"We really don't know," Sophie said quickly. "We don't know what to think."

"We are exceptionally fond of Aunt Edwina and Oliver," Belle said in an apologetic manner. "They took us in and made us part of their family in spite of the vague nature of our connection. They are both very kind and generous and we would hate to see them . . . misled in any way."

Kate bristled. "That is not my purpose."

Gen leaned forward. "What is your purpose?"

"I don't have a purpose." Kate's tone was sharper than she had intended. She drew a deep breath. "My apologies. The circumstances I find myself in are both confusing and distressing."

"Of course it would be," Sophie said quickly. "We don't mean to upset you but—"

"We don't trust you," Gen said.

"*She* doesn't trust you," Belle added.

"Let me ask you a question." Kate chose her words with care. "If I am deceiving Lady Norcroft and her son, to what end? What could I possibly gain by a charade like this?"

"That's what I wondered." Sophie looked at her older sister. "Well?"

"Oliver." Gen shrugged. "She wants Oliver."

Belle nudged her twin. "And Oliver apparently wants her."

Kate stared. "Why do you say that?"

"If you don't know you've lost more than your memory," Gen muttered. "It's apparent to even the most dull-witted observer that he is attracted to you. Hollinger said so and he is never wrong. And Oliver was most evasive when we asked about you."

"When we arrived last night it was obvious that he was about to kiss you." Sophie smirked. "Practically under the nose of his mother.

"It's been my experience that if a man is willing to kiss you with his mother very nearly in the same room . . ." All eyes turned toward Belle and she winced. "Not that I truly have any experience, mind you."

"Oliver is extremely wealthy," Gen said.

Belle nodded. "And quite handsome."

"And an earl," Sophie added. "Why the man is one of the most eligible bachelors in the country."

"And you are." Gen's gaze flickered over Kate. "*Old.* And probably desperate."

Kate gasped. "I am not old."

"She didn't mean old." Belle cast a sharp look at her older sister. "She meant *older.* Than we are, that is."

Kate crossed her arms over her chest. "And I am certainly not desperate."

Gen smirked. "But you *say* you don't know."

Kate clenched her teeth. "I suspect I would know if I were desperate."

Gen shrugged in a disparaging manner.

"But allow me to tell you a few things about my situation." Kate ticked the points off on her fingers. "One, if my true purpose here was to trap a husband, no doubt there are easier ways to do so than to pretend not to know who I am. Two, I more than likely have wealth of my own as, from what we have been able to gather, I appear to be well educated. A characteristic, I might add, that would be remarkably difficult to feign."

"You're right, such a charade would not be easy to maintain for long." A determined glint sparked in Gen's eye. "Dedicated observers might well be able to catch a mistake."

"And three." Kate fixed her gaze hard on Gen. "If I were involved in some kind of convoluted scheme, it would be the height of stupidity to attempt it without my own clothes. While the gowns Lady Norcroft has leant me are flattering if a bit too large," she met Gen's gaze, "they are also somewhat immature."

Belle gasped.

"Childlike," Kate added.

Sophie winced.

"And entirely without so much as a modicum of . . ." Kate paused for emphasis. "Sophistication."

Gen got to her feet, anger sparked in her eyes. Excellent. Kate was in the mood for a good fight. She really should work on that tendency toward violence she had discovered but not now.

Gen glared. "I can certainly understand why you think my dresses are entirely too youthful for someone of your advanced years."

"I say, am I interrupting?" Oliver poked his head in the door.

"Not yet," Belle said under her breath.

"I was just telling Kate that I intend to be much more observant in the future." Gen said, her gaze still locked with Kate's.

"And I was just saying to your cousins that astute observation is an excellent quality for a young woman to develop." Kate's voice rang cool and controlled. "Among others that will only come with maturity."

"And we are most grateful for the advice." Sophie cast Oliver an innocent smile.

"No doubt." Oliver studied his cousins, suspicion in his blue eyes, then glanced at Kate. "I was sent to fetch you, if you are finished here?"

"I daresay I am more than finished." Kate nodded at the sisters. "Ladies." She turned and swept from the room in a vaguely grand exit but then why not? She was certainly old enough for a grand exit.

A moment later Oliver joined her. "I gather you and my cousins were getting on well together."

"We were certainly getting on."

He chuckled. "I suspected as much. They interrogated me last night."

"You could have warned me."

He cast her an unrepentant grin. "And where would be the fun in that?"

She slanted him an annoyed look.

"I know, I know, I am incorrigible."

She stopped and studied him. "Who sent you to fetch me and where are we going?"

"You shall see."

He steered her through the corridors of the manor and out of doors.

"I should like to know where we are going, Oliver." She huffed.

He grinned but held his tongue.

"Very well then don't tell me," she said sharply and regretted it the moment the words were out of her mouth.

He wasn't the one she was annoyed with after all. It was his cousin. Or perhaps it was herself she was annoyed with. As irritating as Gen's charges were, Kate wasn't at all sure they didn't contain at least a morsel of truth. It was a bothersome thought.

They reached the stretch of lawn that hosted the archery target. There on the grass stood a table covered in a fine white tablecloth and two chairs. On the table was a teapot, two cups, and a platter of pastries.

"Oliver!" She stared in surprise. "Are you responsible for this?"

He grinned. "I knew you wouldn't have time for a proper breakfast. I arranged for Ellen to let me know when you were finished." He held out a chair for her. "It is all right then?"

"It's perfect Oliver. And most romantic." She poured the tea and offered him a cup.

"I have heard a session with Madame DuBois can be quite draining. Add to that the presence of my mother and cousins and I thought you would be in need of a relaxing moment. From what I heard." He nodded at the bow and quiver on the ground a few feet away from the table. "You might wish a bit of practice as well. I have noticed it has a calming influence."

"You can be quite thoughtful," she murmured. "I do appreciate it."

"I am nothing if not thoughtful."

"Oliver." She took a sip of tea. "Do you think I'm desperate?"

He choked on his tea. "Desperate?"

"Yes." She set down her cup and stared at him. "Desperate."

"I should think you are somewhat desperate to find out who you are."

"Well, yes, that of course." Still, there was a gnawing sense inside her that felt very much like a desperation that had nothing to do with her identity. The absolutely certain feeling that there was something important she had to do. "Your cousins think I'm desperate to find a husband. That I am pretending to have lost my memory to ensnare you."

"Really?" He grinned.

She drew her brows together. "And you find this amusing?"

"Not amusing as much as flattering." He cast her a wicked grin. "I am extremely flattered."

She stared at him. "Do you agree with them?"

"Admittedly, when you first awoke and claimed to have lost your memory I had doubts as to the

quite dismiss the sense of desperation Genevieve's charge had triggered. Nor could she ignore the growing feeling that there was something important, something critical, she had to accomplish.

As well as the increasing belief it had everything to do with the future and the past and most of all, the Earl of Norcroft.

liver was going to have to kill them. One at a time or possibly all three together. And why not? A man could only hang once.

"Don't you think so, Oliver?" Gen fluttered her lashes at him and he muttered an incoherent response.

A jury of his peers—men with sisters or interfering female cousins—would certainly understand. They might not even convict him.

Gen turned her attention to a more receptive quarter. "Mr. Berkley?"

"Oh, I quite agree, Miss Fairchild." Berkley nodded with the kind of enthusiasm only a young man eager to work his way into the affections of a

Oliver had never been involved with a married woman. Nor, he was confident, was Kate the type of woman who would betray a husband whether she liked him or not. No, she would be an excellent wife.

Sophie nodded. "It's the first time, you know, that anything of this nature has occurred."

Kind and loyal and . . . bloody hell, every day she was here she was that much harder to resist. He had never been good at resisting anything tempting. And he wasn't sure he had ever met anyone as tempting as Kate.

"Not that we didn't think it would eventually," Belle added quickly. "And we do think it's most romantic."

What would he do when she was gone?

Belle glanced at him. "Well, what do you say?"

"I told you the night you arrived that I am not going to discuss Kate with the three of you. You know everything you need to know. Anything beyond that is quite frankly none of your business."

"Oliver," Belle said.

"I don't care what Hollinger says, I don't know how I feel about her or what my intentions are."

"Oliver, we—" Sophie started.

"It's damnably hard to determine how you feel about a woman when you don't know her blasted name. And yes, admittedly there are . . . feelings."

"Oliver," Belle tried again.

He ran his hand through his hair. "But I have no right, no right at all. There," he snapped. "Are the two of you happy now? Have you learned what you wanted to know?"

The girls exchanged glances.

"Oliver," Belle said carefully. "We were asking what you thought of Mr. Berkley."

"Not what you think of Kate." Sophie grinned. "But it was most interesting nonetheless."

"And we have certainly been wondering." Belle's smile matched her sister's. "But we never imagined you'd tell us."

"Yes, and I shouldn't have but what's done is done." He drew a deep breath. "Now, what about Mr. Berkley?"

"What is your opinion of him?" Sophie asked.

"He seems adequate enough. But he's entirely too young for anything of a permanent nature. As is Gen," Oliver added firmly.

"Don't be absurd." Belle scoffed. "Gen is a full year older than we are and women our age are married all the time."

Oliver stopped in mid-stride. "Is it that serious then?"

Sophie shrugged. "We're not entirely sure. The three of us have always shared everything but Gen has been remarkably reticent to say anything at all about Mr. Berkley."

"Almost as much as you have been about Kate," Belle said in an overly innocent manner.

"But we do have our suspicions. We're fairly confident that Gen invited Mr. Berkley here to get your

the words, he realized they were true. He had been remiss up to now. He was the protector of these young women and protect them he would. "Especially as you are now out in society and you have learned so much about"—he cleared his throat—"men. We are a wicked, unscrupulous lot and certainly not to be trusted when it comes to lovely young women. There is a great deal I should warn you about the ways of men. I assure you, I will no longer shirk my responsibilities in that respect."

Oh, this was fun. Not that he didn't mean every word. Still, the expressions on their faces were most amusing. Both girls appeared stricken, as if they had just been confronted with their worst fear.

They traded glances. Oliver could practically see the gears and wheels of their minds spinning. It was at moments like this when he wondered if each twin knew what the other was thinking without saying a word.

"I'm famished," Sophie said abruptly. "Perhaps we should go back to the manor?"

"There's nothing like a long walk to make one hungry." Belle nodded far more eagerly than was necessary given the subject. "Oliver, isn't it almost time for tea?"

"Call your sister and Mr. Berkley and we'll start back." It was obvious the girls needed to discuss his newfound determination to watch their every move with each other and probably Gen as well. He could scarcely keep from laughing aloud. It served them right.

They had been watching Kate's every move since their arrival. It was obvious that they—or at least Gen—didn't believe Kate had truly lost her memory and now hoped to catch her in a lie. It was obvious as well that they wished to keep Kate and Oliver apart. While annoying, he could reluctantly forgive them for that. After all, they only wanted to keep him from harm just as he wanted to protect them.

Oliver pulled out his pocket watch and flipped it open. "I hadn't realized it was so late. It's already half past three."

Kate's eyes fluttered open. Good Lord, how long had she slept? She hadn't intended to do more than close her eyes but without warning exhaustion had slammed into her. She glanced at the clock on the mantel. She'd slept for more than an hour. It was already half past three.

Was it only a week ago that she and Hannah had taken the train—

Hannah!

Kate bolted upright. She remembered Hannah! She remembered it all! She wasn't Kate, only one person had ever called her Kate—her husband. Her *dead* husband. Dear Lord how could she have forgotten Kenneth? How could she have forgotten everything?

She slid off the bed and paced the room. She was Lady Kathleen MacDavid. Widow of Sir Kenneth. Granddaughter of the Countess of Dumleavy,

murmured something else Kathleen hadn't caught and the next thing Kathleen knew she'd been falling the scant three feet or so off the platform. She remembered as well hitting the ground and noting it wasn't a bad fall. Why, she hadn't been the least bit injured.

Damnation, Hannah hadn't touched her!

In her aunt's fifty-some years of life Kathleen would wager Hannah had never cast a spell that had worked. Until, perhaps, now. It certainly explained the fall, her loss of consciousness as well as losing her memory. No, it was impossible. Her mind was obviously befuddled for her even to consider something so farfetched. She might be willing to believe in a family curse but *magic*—as well as the idea that Hannah had mastered such a craft—was another matter entirely. Somehow, Hannah had pushed her and Kathleen had hit her head and lost her memory. Yes, that was the answer. After all, Hannah certainly wouldn't hesitate to do such a thing. Extreme ills and all that. Still . . .

A *pretense* of amnesia on Kathleen's part had been Hannah's plan all along. Kathleen drew a deep breath. It was entirely too much of a coincidence that it had simply happened of its own accord, and had lasted a full week, nearly to the hour. But to accept that this was all Hannah's doing was to accept, well, magic and Kathleen wasn't at all certain she was prepared to do that. Still, she was a rational person and magic, no matter how irrational it sounded, was, under these circumstances, the only rational answer. Regardless, the spell, if that's what it was, had run its course.

She knew her name, she knew why she was here and more importantly, she knew she was free. Free to be with the man she loved.

The man she loved? Kathleen sank down on the bed. The last thing she needed at the moment was another revelation. But as much as she'd tried to resist it, she had fallen in love with Oliver. Love that had nothing to do with a curse or fate or any kind of magic save that which occurred between a man and a woman. She loved him because he was kind and generous and thoughtful. Because he carried his responsibilities with grace and humor. And because when he kissed her, it was as if she had never been kissed before. Certainly she had loved her husband and nothing would ever change that. But her brief marriage was a very long time ago and what she had found with Oliver was right for today and tomorrow and the rest of her life. And that had nothing to do with any curse. He was what she wanted, what she needed, now and forever.

And with any luck, what he wanted was her.

She rose to her feet and started toward the door. She had to tell him she knew who she was. Her step faltered. Exactly what did she intend to say? She couldn't just blurt out the truth. A man as sensible as Oliver would be hard pressed to accept magic as an explanation for anything. And if he didn't believe that—and what rational person would?—he would wonder whether she had indeed ever lost her memory at all. As for the curse . . . she cringed. When his mother had brought up the suggestion of a curse he had sensibly rejected the idea as nonsense. She distinctly recalled having had much the same reaction when she was first told about it.

No, she had to find the right words or she could well lose Oliver forever. Her heart caught at the thought. She couldn't just come out with something like this. Kathleen twisted her hands together in desperation. How could she tell him? What could she say?

She moved to stand before the cheval mirror in the corner of her room. Absently she noted that it was rather nice to look into a mirror and recognize your own face. Still, that scarcely mattered at the moment. She clasped her hands together, ignored the queasy feeling in the pit of her stomach and drew a deep breath.

"Oliver," she began. That was good. Forthright, honest, direct.

"Oliver," she said again. "I have something to tell you." Yes, so far, very good.

"I have news." Better. Who didn't like news?

"Good news." Better yet.

"I know who I am." And then? "And . . . and . . ." She raised her chin. "And my purpose here is to convince you to marry me as both our families are under a curse and only our marriage will break the curse." She cast her most brilliant smile at the image in the mirror. "Fortunately, I am fairly certain I have fallen in love with you." Dear God, she looked like an idiot. "Which is quite fortuitous as this is a match five hundred years in the making." Even worse, she sounded like one.

This was going to require serious thought and until she had determined the best way to tell Oliver everything, it might be wise not to tell him anything at all.

Perhaps it would be best if she didn't remember her entire life at once. Perhaps she should lead him by the hand and ease his way into the truth, one fact at a time. She could start by telling him she had remembered she was a widow. Yes, he'd like that. Or perhaps she should simply flee, borrow a carriage and find her aunt, who probably couldn't undo what she had done anyway.

Right now, Kathleen could certainly do with a bracing cup of tea. And perhaps a small glass of brandy. Or good Scottish whisky.

She cast one last glance at the mirror and shook her head. Wringing Hannah's neck wouldn't solve Kathleen's dilemma, although it had a great deal of appeal. Hannah had taken any decision out of her niece's hands and had placed her in a situation where she risked losing everything. She had taken Kathleen's memory and left her alone.

And damn the woman, she had taken her clothes.

Chapter 13

"Good morning, Oliver." Kate stepped into the library and closed the door behind her. Oliver rose to his feet behind his desk. "Kate, what a pleasant surprise." He grinned. "I feared we would never see one another alone again."

"I had hoped to speak with you yesterday afternoon. Or evening." Her jaw clenched. "Your cousins seem to have appointed themselves my constant companions. They're pleasant enough about it but I cannot seem to get away from them. Not only do they suspect me of deceit but I think they wish to keep you and I apart. They're very protective of you, you know."

He chuckled. "They are probably taking turns watching your bedroom door at night."

"Or yours," she said wryly but in spite of the amusement in her voice there was something different about Kate today.

He wasn't sure what it was but he had first noticed it yesterday afternoon at tea and again at dinner. Kate had been unusually quiet, preoccupied he had thought, but there was more. It struck him that she moved differently than she had before. Her carriage had always been excellent but her shoulders seemed somewhat straighter. There was as well a subtle air of resolve about her as if she were determined to go forward. And the lost look in her eyes was gone. He couldn't help but wonder if she had given up. His heart twisted for her. Kate was the type of woman who would never be happy to live with unanswered questions. But perhaps now her courage was failing.

"Kate," he said gently. "Is something amiss?"

She raised a brow. "Something new you mean?"

He chuckled. "Yes, I suppose so." He paused. "You seem . . . different today."

"Do I?" She wandered to a bookshelf and perused the offered spines but Oliver had the distinct feeling she wasn't seeing the books. "In what manner do I seem different?"

"I'm not sure." He moved to her side, leaned his back against the shelves and crossed his arms.

Her gaze stayed on the books but she directed her words to him. "Why are you staring at me?"

"I'm trying to answer your question." He studied her for a long moment. "Let me see. Your appearance has not changed. Your nose is still disturbingly pert."

The corner of her mouth quirked upwards. "Disturbingly?"

"I find myself quite disturbed by it. It is among the many things about you I cannot get out of my head."

"Ah yes. You close your eyes only to see my face."

"I don't believe I ever actually said that." He grinned. "Although it's true. And then there are your eyes."

"Part of my face."

"And yet worthy of comment on their own."

"Are they disturbing as well?"

"Nothing disturbs me more. As for the rest of you." His gaze slid over her and his stomach tightened. Had he ever wanted any woman more? "Your form, your figure is quite disturbing. And I suspect your legs might well be my undoing."

She slanted him an amused glance. "You're flirting with me, Oliver. In a most outrageous and completely improper way."

"Indeed, I am." He grinned in an unrepentant manner.

"To what end?"

He laughed. "I must confess, while I have been accused of flirting any number of times, I have never been asked my intention in doing so before."

"What are your intentions?"

"Well, my *desire* is to take you in my arms and kiss you quite thoroughly until the two of us are reduced to a quivering puddle of delight. Then my desire would be to carry you to the sofa in front of the fireplace and make love to you in a mad and passionate manner until the very earth beneath us explodes with the intensity of our union."

She gasped in feigned shock. "Here in the library?"

He nodded. "Right here in front of Browning and Wordsworth."

She stared at him for a moment then laughed.

"Not precisely the response a man wants to hear when he issues declarations of this nature." He clasped his hand over his heart. "You wound me deeply."

"Nonsense, Oliver." She scoffed. "You're not the least bit wounded. Besides the question was about your intentions not your desires."

"Ah well, intentions, that's another matter entirely. My *intention* always is to take you in my arms and—"

"Yes, I believe you mentioned that." She bit back a smile.

"Unfortunately, as I suspect our moments alone together are fleeting and any minute now one, or all, of my cousins shall burst through the door with an excuse that sounds quite plausible but is ridiculous nonetheless, that particular intention will have to wait. Therefore, at the moment, my intention." He met her gaze. "Is simply to make you smile."

A genuine smile curved her lips. "You have succeeded admirably. Should I ever find myself the least bit downhearted I shall think of your desires in the library and I shall surely never be melancholy again."

"Are you melancholy?"

"No." She stepped away, wandered slowly along the bookshelves, trailing her long, slender fingers over the volumes. "I am . . . reflective. Pensive perhaps. I have been doing a great deal of thinking."

He shook his head in a mournful manner. "That's never good."

She stopped and stared at him. "Why on earth not?"

"It's been my experience that when an intelligent woman thinks too much, no good can come of it."

Her gaze narrowed. "Are you trying to make me smile again?"

"No." He grinned. "I was being entirely forthright. There is nothing I find more terrifying than the end result of the thinking of a clever woman. However, I am a brave sort." He squared his shoulders. "Tell me straight off, what have you been thinking?"

"I have been wondering . . ." She continued along the shelves and he found himself the tiniest bit jealous of the books who were at this moment knowing Kate's lingering touch. "What will happen when I recover my memory?"

"I would say that very much depends on what you remember. Who you are, where you are from." He shrugged. "All of it."

"Yes, I realize that." A hint of impatience sounded in her voice. "What I meant was"—she paused and met his gaze directly—"what will happen between you and I?"

"That too depends. My hope is that you are free and you and I—"

"Yes?"

He stared at her for a moment. *You and I what?* Oliver drew a deep breath, then plunged ahead. "You and I can look toward a future together."

"How lovely." She smiled but her green eyes were somber. Apparently his answer wasn't entirely right. "Regardless?"

"What do you mean regardless," he said slowly.

"I mean there are all sorts of things that might preclude a future together."

He drew his brows together. "Other than your being married I can't think of anything that would preclude a future together."

"What if I was . . ." She thought for a moment. "Poor?"

"I have more than enough money."

"What if my family was . . . disreputable?"

"Then we shan't invite them for dinner."

"What if they were odd? Or unusual?"

He laughed. "Then I would say they would fit in splendidly."

"What if your family and mine are . . . are mortal enemies?"

"My family has no mortal enemies. We are quite an unassuming lot, we very rarely annoy anyone. At least, not all of us at once. But if we did have mortal enemies, then you and I shall be Romeo and Juliet."

"They did not end well." A warning sounded in her voice.

"We will end better," he said firmly.

"What if . . ." She searched for the right words. "What if I am not the type of person you think I am?"

"No, Kate. That is one eventuality I have every confidence will not occur. No." He shook his head. "My feelings won't change because your name does."

She considered him for a long moment. "Very well then." She drew a deep breath. "Oliver, I have something to tell you."

"Go on."

"I have . . . news."

"How very intriguing."

"I have remembered . . ." The most awful look of apprehension flashed through her eye. Bloody hell, she *was* married. A heavy weight settled in the pit of his stomach. "A few things," she said weakly. "A house, a face, that sort of thing."

"The face perhaps of a husband?"

"Of a grandmother I believe."

Relief washed through him. "Well, that's very good. Very good indeed. Anything else? Names? That sort of thing?"

She stared at him. "No," she said at last. "Not yet but bits and pieces are starting to return to me. Hopefully, it will all become clear any day now."

"Excellent." He moved to her and took her hands. "With any luck we shall soon be able to put all this behind us." Voices sounded in the corridor; obviously his cousins were preparing for invasion. He leaned forward, quickly brushed his lips across hers and ignored the pressing need for more than a mere kiss. "Until then."

She gazed up at him, uncertainty in her green eyes. What did she fear she would remember that was so dreadful? "I have another fitting. I should go before . . ." She nodded at the door.

"I should hate to provide a bad example for them." He chuckled. "If I were to find Gen in the arms of Mr. Berkley in the library, I would have to take the young man to task as well as demand to know if his intentions are honorable."

"How very brotherly of you."

"Indeed it is and I don't mind telling you it's quite a daunting responsibility. One I should have understood long before now. If my cousins were to catch you in my arms they would no doubt charge me with hypocrisy and I would be forced to explain the differences in behavior expected of young ladies in their first season and those of us considerably more experienced."

She raised a brow. "More experienced?"

"By virtue of age," he said quickly. "I meant experienced in . . . in life. Nothing more than that."

She laughed lightly. "You needn't look so concerned. I am not the least bit offended. I am well aware of my age if not, at the moment, my experiences." She turned toward the door then turned back. "Oliver, are your intentions honorable?"

"As previously stated, my intentions, for the moment, are the epitome of honor." He grinned in a wicked manner. "My desires are another matter entirely."

She met his gaze boldly. "As are mine." She nodded, opened the door and stepped into the corridor. The sound of feminine chatter drifted into the room.

As annoying as it was to be constantly chaperoned by young women barely out of the schoolroom, he was right. He and Kate did need to set an example. Why if Oliver so much as suspected Mr. Berkley of having the same type of lascivious thoughts about Gen that Oliver had about Kate, Oliver would indeed be forced to thrash him thoroughly in defense of the young woman's honor. Although it wouldn't be at all fair to thrash a man simply for his thoughts. Good Lord, neither Oliver nor any of his friends would have survived their younger days if they'd been taken to task for idle lusting. No, Oliver would simply have to make certain young Berkley, and Gen as well, did not act on those desires. Still, as long as she and her sisters were busy watching he and Kate, he grinned with satisfaction, Gen would have no time for Berkley.

As for Kate, his smile faded, her concern was obvious. It was, no doubt, fear of the unknown and nothing more significant than that. He had meant what he'd said. He couldn't imagine anything that would be so dreadful as to keep them apart.

Kathleen never imagined she'd be grateful for the interference of the Fairchild sisters but their efforts to keep her and Oliver apart had a decided benefit. If she couldn't be alone with him she certainly couldn't tell him the truth. And she still had no idea how to do that.

She paced to and fro in her sitting room. She had fully intended to tell him yesterday that her memory had returned but had had no opportunity thanks to the girls. Today in the library she had started to confess everything but her courage had failed her. It was most annoying as she had always considered herself to be quite courageous. Why, hadn't she come to England in the first place to marry a man she'd never met? Still, her courage at the moment was obviously contingent on the right words and the right words evaded her. Nor could she shake the terror that gripped her at the thought of his reaction. She couldn't recall ever knowing fear like this before. She had always been in control of her life and her emotions. Fear was foreign to her but then she'd never had so much to lose before.

Blast it all, she needed somebody besides herself to talk to about all this. She simply couldn't work it out by herself. It was entirely too convoluted and confusing. As angry as she was at Hannah, she now wished Hannah was here. At least Hannah would come up with some sort of plan. It would probably be absurd with no hope of success but it would be better than nothing and nothing was precisely what Kathleen had at the moment.

A knock sounded at her door.

The girls had no doubt tracked her down although she had assumed she was safe alone in her room. They probably wanted to make certain Oliver wasn't with her. She resisted the urge to snap. "Yes?"

The door opened and Lady Norcroft poked her head in. "I wondered where you had gone off to. Whatever are you doing here alone?"

"I am simply trying to sort out . . ." Kathleen paused. Sort out what? "Everything."

Lady Norcroft stepped into the room and closed the door behind her. "Everything about my son you mean."

Kathleen nodded. "For the most part."

Lady Norcroft settled into a chair and studied Kathleen. "What do you intend to do now?"

"That's very much the problem. I have no idea what to do now."

"You need a plan."

Kathleen uttered a short laugh. "Indeed I do. Pity I don't have one."

"On the other hand a plan is probably pointless until your memory returns."

"Yes, of course," Kate murmured.

"However, one should be prepared for any eventuality." Lady Norcroft shook her head. "I would hate to see the two of you lose what you have found."

Kathleen sank onto the chaise. "Lose what we have found?"

"You needn't deny it. Why, he nearly kissed you in the ballroom, right under the nose of his mother. Oliver has never been known to be that impulsive or that improper. No." She met Kathleen's gaze directly. "Whenever the two of you are in the same room, the very air is thick with something quite remarkable. I feel as if I am witness to the convergence of fate."

"Fate?"

"Or destiny perhaps." A knowing smile curved Lady Norcroft's lips. "Or even a match five hundred years in the making."

Kathleen stared. Surely Lady Norcroft didn't know the truth? She couldn't possibly know. "I don't understand."

"Of course you understand. Do remember that I am full of surprises as well as secrets. And I do so love keeping them, I'm very good at that." Lady Norcroft's smile widened. "I not only know who you are but I know precisely why you are here."

Kathleen tried not to let the panic surging within her show on her face. This was not the moment to panic. There would be time enough for that later. Besides, if Lady Norcroft knew who Kathleen was then it did sound as though she would be an ally. "Perhaps you would be so good as to share that with me."

"As to who you are, you, my dear, are the answer to my prayers."

"Your prayers?" Kathleen said slowly.

"Absolutely. I cannot tell you how long I have waited for my son to look at a woman the way he looks at you."

"But you said a match five hundred years in the making."

"Did I?" The older woman waved off the comment. "How very clever of me. It was an exaggeration of course. One of those things one says, the first thing that popped into my head. I must have heard it somewhere. I could have as easily said thousands of years in the making or centuries in the making or eons in the making."

Kathleen released a small breath of relief. That Lady Norcroft had used the same phrase her grandmother had used over and over again was no more than a coincidence. An odd coincidence but surely a coincidence nonetheless.

"There are no coincidences you know," the older woman said as if she had read Kathleen's thoughts. "In truth, it's been no more than the last few years that I have been waiting for Oliver to find the right match. It simply seems longer. And now, from out of nowhere, here you are. It's enough to make one believe in, well, magic."

Kathleen swallowed hard. "Magic?"

"Magic." Lady Norcroft nodded firmly. "Do you believe in magic my dear?

"Do I—"

"No, never mind. What a silly thing for me to ask and I believe this is the second time I've asked. It must be on my mind, I have no idea why. You couldn't possibly remember something like that. It's not one of those things that is readily apparent like the color of your hair or that you have resided in Scotland."

"No, of course not."

"I know you are worried about what might happen when you regain your memory. You needn't be." Lady Norcroft rose to her feet. "There are all sorts of magic in the world to believe in, Kate. Much of it is utter nonsense although most amusing nonetheless. Spells and curses and the like. But the magic to be found between a man and a woman, that magic, my dear, is real."

Kathleen stood. "How can it be if it's predicated on deceit?"

"There are as many kinds of deceit as there are magic. Why, it's not at all uncommon to lie to a loved one to keep them safe or protected. Then there is"—she thought for a moment—"unintended deceit."

Kathleen drew her brows together. "Unintended deceit."

"Yes indeed. You can't deceive someone if you don't know that you are deceiving them."

"You can't?"

"Intent, my dear, it all comes down to intent."

"The distinction is rather fine isn't it?"

"But is a distinction nonetheless. Aside from that, there are times when one has to do wrong in order to accomplish a greater good. Sometimes one has to do what one must." Lady Norcroft paused, then chose her words with care. "If Oliver is truly what you want, and I am confident he feels the same about you, then you must do whatever you think is necessary. As women we have any number of excellent methods of doing just that."

Kathleen widened her eyes. "Do we?"

Lady Norcroft chuckled. "We do indeed." She started toward the door then paused and reached into a pocket in her skirt. "My apologies." She pulled Kathleen's bracelet out of her pocket. "I forgot to return this to you. I found the charm most interesting." She put the bracelet in Kathleen's hand and closed the younger woman's hand around it. "It took me a while to decipher it. It was quite enlightening and most appropriate." She opened the door. "Will you be joining us?"

"I'll be right down." Kathleen met the older woman's gaze. "I cannot tell you how grateful I am for, well, you."

"It is I who am grateful." Lady Norcroft smiled and took her leave.

Kathleen stared at the door. Surely she was mistaken but it very much sounded as though Oliver's mother had just given her permission to pursue her son with whatever means necessary. Not that she actually had means. She didn't even have her own clothes. And it wasn't as if she could seduce him into marriage. While she hadn't been with a man since her husband's death, she was certainly not an innocent whose family could demand marriage after seduction.

Oliver might well want nothing to do with her when he knew the truth. Certainly, she hadn't deceived him up until now but would he believe that? If the situation was reversed, she would be hard pressed to believe him. Besides, while she was confident of her feelings for him, his feelings might well have more to do with the mystery surrounding her, the adventure of her situation, than anything else. Add to that the fact that she was forbidden fruit given their uncertainty about her marital state and whatever feelings Oliver might now have could well vanish with the truth. Men very often only wanted that which they couldn't have.

Very well then. Without thinking, she squared her shoulders. She had no idea what might happen once Oliver knew everything but she was not about to spend the rest of her days wondering what might have been. She had fallen in love with him when she couldn't remember the curse or her own name. Love had not been her intention. Indeed, she had never given it so much as a second thought. She would be a fool if she passed up the chance to once again know the touch of a man she loved. Finding love once was hard enough, twice in one lifetime was something of a miracle. And love might well never come again.

Oliver was not the sort of man to agree to anything as permanent as marriage to satisfy a barely remembered curse. But he was the sort of man to give into his desires, to accept something freely offered.

Her hand tightened around the bracelet and its circular charm dug into her palm. She didn't need to read it to know what was engraved on its face. And, God help her, while she had never especially accepted it in the past she did now.

Extremis malis, extrema remedia.

Chapter 14

*T*his was absurd.

Oliver threw off the bedcovers and slid out of bed. If he wasn't going to sleep, it was pointless to lay here hour after hour staring into the dark. Tossing and turning. Wanting Kate.

He stumbled across the room, fumbled for a match and lit the lamp. This wasn't the first night since her arrival that Oliver had been unable to sleep but tonight was the worst. It was nearly dawn and he hadn't so much as closed his eyes. He found his dressing gown and shrugged it on over his nightshirt.

He was going mad and there didn't seem to be anything he could do to prevent it. His mother, and the rest of the household, was busy with preparations for tomorrow's ball which meant his newfound realization of his responsibilities in regards to his cousins had effectively halted any effort on his part to be alone with Kate. After all, if he managed to be alone with her, it was more than likely Gen would manage to be alone with Berkley. And Berkley reminded him far too much of himself and his friends at that age to be trusted.

He and Kate hadn't been alone since she had joined him in the library yesterday morning and, blast it all, he missed her. Not that he hadn't been in her company along with everyone else. But exchanging glances with her over the dinner table or watching her listen to the twins play the piano last night or hearing her laugh during a rousing game of croquet this afternoon had been more frustrating than satisfying. And only increased his longing to take her in his arms.

Damn it all, things like this were not supposed to happen to him. Never had he felt so helpless, so at the hands of forces beyond his control. His life had always been . . . expected. Yes, that was the right word for it. He expected that certain things would happen at certain times. He expected that his estate manager would do a good job. That Hollinger, his valet, Cook and the rest of the staff would perform their duties with efficiency and a minimum of fuss. That his friends would have adventures that he would not. And he had always expected that someday he would meet the right woman in an entirely expected manner.

He certainly never expected that she would arrive unconscious without knowing so much as her own name.

Not that he was sure Kate was the right woman. How could he possibly be sure at this point? But there had been something inevitable about her from the moment she'd first opened her eyes. Still, he'd reserve that decision until he knew if a life with her was possible. If his heart hadn't already made the decision for him. Admittedly, it was fear that held him back. Fear, more than likely, of the unexpected.

He had to do something, take action of some sort. He was not at all used to not doing anything when a situation arose. This waiting for her memory to come back, or worse, a husband to show up, was driving him mad.

He crossed the room to a conveniently placed decanter of brandy. It had first appeared in his room the night his cousins had arrived. He had to remember to thank Hollinger for that but then again, he expected Hollinger to know what he needed before he knew himself. Oliver poured a glass and took a long swallow.

What could he do? It hadn't appeared necessary at first to do anything at all. Even the doctor had said Kate's memory could return at any minute. But one day had become two and then four and now more than a week had passed. A week in which he found himself growing closer and closer to a woman he knew hardly anything about.

No, that wasn't entirely true. He sipped at the brandy. He knew a great deal about her, about the kind of woman she was. What he didn't know were the details of her life. Those significant as well as inconsequential details that make a person who she is. He might not know the details but he had every confidence he knew the woman.

He tossed back the rest of his drink, refilled his glass and sat down at the secretary he occasionally used for middle-of-the-night correspondence. He grabbed a piece of stationery, pen and ink. He'd write to his solicitor and direct him to hire an investigator to find out who Kate was. He should have done this when she'd first arrived but it hadn't seemed as urgent as it was now. Admittedly, it wasn't much but it was the only thing he could think of to do and he was bloody well tired of not doing anything.

A soft tapping sounded at his door.

Who on earth would be at his room in the middle of the night? He pushed away from the desk, strode to the door and pulled it open.

Kate stood in the doorway, her fist poised to knock again. "I saw your light under the door. May I come in?"

Her dark red hair was loose and disheveled and hung past her shoulders. She looked like a vision in the night. Something from his dreams. His heart thudded in his chest and he resisted the urge to pull her into his arms. Instead he stepped back. "Yes, of course."

She walked into his room and he closed the door behind her. It wouldn't do to have anyone else who might be awake wander past his open door and see Kate. It would be most improper and nothing short of scandalous. And a very bad example.

"I find I am far too restless to sleep." Her gaze moved from his bed to the secretary. "I gather you couldn't sleep either?"

"I haven't slept well in days," he muttered.

She raised a brow.

"Nearly a week."

"We seem to share a common ailment." She glanced at the brandy decanter. "Only one glass?"

"I was not expecting visitors."

"Good." She cast him a private sort of smile and his heart tripped. "I would hate to be expected."

Nothing about you is expected. "I could call for another glass," he said quickly and moved toward the bell pull in the corner.

"At this hour? Don't be silly. That would be most inconvenient for your staff. Besides, it might well awaken other members of the household, which would be terribly rude and not the least bit appreciated."

"I hadn't thought of that." Nor could he think of anything the least bit sensible at the moment but what man could? He crossed the room as much to avoid staring at her as to pick up his glass.

Kate wore a wrapper over nightclothes obviously borrowed from Gen. Eminently proper and unquestionably virginal, they were fashioned from yards of a fine white material. The sleeves were full and flowing and reached past her wrists, the neck of the nightgown beneath the wrapper stretched to just under her chin. There was not so much as an indiscreet hint of skin exposed. Even so, when she passed in front of the light, there was little left unrevealed. He grabbed his glass and tossed back the contents. "What are you doing here?"

Her brow furrowed. "That's not exactly the greeting I expected."

"One doesn't always get what one expects," he muttered.

Her eyes widened. "Am I not welcome then?"

"Always." He refilled his glass. "But you haven't answered my question. Why are you here?"

She shrugged in a casual manner as if they were at a public gathering and not the intimate setting of his private rooms. "I have missed you, Oliver."

"Nonsense." He scoffed. "You have seen me every day."

"I've missed sharing a private word with you then." She meandered around the perimeter of his room. "Are you not pleased to see me?"

In a moment, it would be obvious just how glad to see her he was. "I am always pleased to see you."

She moved to him, took his glass from his hand,

and took a long sip of the brandy. "This is very good."

"It's quite potent." He stared down at her and tried to ignore how close to him she stood. Entirely improper, and damn near irresistible. "And extremely dangerous."

"Dangerous?" She gazed up at him in an altogether too seductive way. "I rather like that."

"Brandy muddles the mind," he said staunchly then winced to himself at the stuffy tone of his voice.

She bit back a smile. "And yet my mind is clear." She took another sip. "Extremely clear." She put the glass back in his hand. "I quite know what I'm doing."

He narrowed his eyes. "What are you doing?"

She laughed. "Goodness, Oliver, I should think that would be obvious."

"Not entirely," he said under his breath, moved away from her and again filled his glass. "What is obvious to me is that you shouldn't be here at this time of night. Alone. Dressed like that."

"This is what all proper young ladies wear." She glanced down at her gown. "Although your cousins would tell you I am not especially young and I suspect I am not overly proper."

"You're not?"

"Not at the moment." Her gaze met his. She untied her wrapper, shrugged it off, and let it fall to the floor.

There may well have been fabric covering every

inch of her but he could see the outlines of her nipples and the dark shadow at the juncture of her thighs. Kate enveloped in acres of virginal white might well be the most exciting thing he had ever seen. He took a bracing pull of the brandy.

Her glaze slid down his body. "My, you are glad to see me."

"You should know, Kate . . ."

"What?" She took his glass, downed the contents, then placed the empty glass on a chest of drawers.

"I have never been good at . . ."

"I suspect." She moved close, rested her hands on his chest and gazed up at him. "There are any number of things that you are very good at."

"Yes, well, of course. What I was trying to say . . ." It was bloody hard to say anything at all with her hands now wandering to the knotted sash at his waist. Her deft fingers untied the sash and his dressing gown opened to reveal his nightshirt. "I'm not very good at resisting temptation."

"No?" She leaned forward and kissed the base of his throat. "Yet another thing we have in common." One hand trailed over his stomach and lower. Her fingers brushed across his erection.

He shuddered and grabbed her hand. "Have you any idea what you're doing?"

"I haven't done it for a very long time but I'm certain I remember how."

He stared at her. "Are you seducing me?"

Amusement shone in her eye. "Well, I am trying. I suspect I can be quite seductive."

"I can assure you that suspicion is accurate. Nonetheless." He shook his head. "This is not a good idea."

"On the contrary, Oliver." She pulled her hand free from his and wrapped her arms around his neck. "I think it's an excellent idea."

Her breasts pressed against his chest and it was all he could do to form a coherent word. "But you and I—"

"We are both adults. I want you and there isn't a doubt in my mind that"—she shifted her hips against his and he gasped—"you want me."

"I should warn you, Kate." His arms slipped around her as if of their own accord. "I am a weak man. My character is not as strong as it may appear."

"Good." Her lips brushed across the line of his jaw.

"Nor do the moral considerations regarding your marital state seem especially important at the moment." No, what was important was the curve of the small of her back beneath his hands.

"Excellent." She kissed the corner of his mouth. "Moral considerations can be dreadfully inhibiting."

"Kate." He groaned. "What are you doing to me?"

"I thought we had agreed that I am seducing you."

"And a fine job you are doing too in spite of . . ." He paused and pulled away and stared at her.

"What did you mean when you said that you haven't done it for a very long time?"

She laughed. "I think the statement speaks for itself."

"Kate." He chose his words with care. "How would you know?"

"I knew there was something I wished to tell you." She pulled him closer. "I've remembered something else. I was married once and now I am a widow." She reached up and spoke softly into his ear. "And my marriage was a very long time ago."

He removed her arms from around his neck and stepped back. "You could have mentioned this earlier."

She shrugged. "I could have but that wouldn't have been nearly as much fun."

He stared at her. He'd been resisting her from the moment she'd walked in the door when he could have been—"You've been toying with me."

She smiled wickedly.

"Is that all you've remembered? You still don't know your name or anything else?"

She paused. "No."

He studied her for a long minute. "That is a pity." He heaved an overly dramatic sigh. "I would never take carnal advantage of a woman who did not know her own name. It would be morally reprehensible."

"Not at all." She shook her head firmly. "Naughty perhaps but not reprehensible."

"Ethically wrong."

"Oh, perhaps a mistake in judgment but certainly not wrong," she said quickly.

"And utterly unforgivable."

"No, no, don't be absurd." She scoffed. "I could
forgive you. I do forgive you. Why, you haven't
even done anything yet and I forgive you."

"Are you certain?"

"Absolutely."

"Still, I'm not sure—"

"Oliver!"

"Very well then." He moved closer and yanked
her into his arms. "You should have told me
sooner."

"But this was so much fun."

He lowered his head and nibbled at a lovely
spot where her neck met her shoulder. "Oh but we
could have been having so much more."

"We shall simply have to make up for it then."
She pushed his dressing gown off his shoulders
and it fell to the floor. She wrapped her arms around
his neck and he pulled her tighter against him, the
heat of her body searing him through the layers of
her clothes and his. His lips met hers and she tasted
of brandy and mystery and forever. Need, urgent
and unyielding, gripped him and dashed away any
reservations.

He caressed the small of her back and the lus-
cious curves of her derrière. Her fingers tunneled
through his hair and her mouth opened to his,
with a hunger and greed he shared. He pulled her

tighter against him and slanted his mouth over hers again and again. She ground her hips against his and he groaned aloud with the pleasure of it and the promise of pleasure to come.

Kate gathered the fabric of his nightshirt in her hand until her fingers rested on the bare flesh of his leg. Oliver shuddered, drew a deep breath and stepped back. He pulled his shirt off and let it fall.

Her gaze slid down his body, "Oh my, you are very pleased to see me."

"Not as pleased as I will be." He started toward her.

She held out her hand to stop him, then pulled her nightdress over her head and tossed it aside. She brushed her hair away from her face and straightened her shoulders. For a long moment he could do nothing but stare at her. Her ivory skin was aglow with the light from the gas lamp and flushed with desire. Her breasts were full and round, her waist narrow, her hips lush and inviting.

"Oliver." She swallowed hard. "If you don't find me or you don't want or—"

"Kate." There was an odd, tremulous feeling deep inside him and he knew it was more than mere desire. "I have wanted you forever." He scooped her into his arms and carried her to the bed. "I have waited for you forever."

"Five hundred years," she murmured.

He chuckled softly. "At least."

He laid her on the bed and she pulled him down

beside her. He nuzzled the hollow of her throat and trailed kisses between her breasts. He cupped one perfect breast with his hand and took her nipple into his mouth. She gasped, her fingers running restlessly over his shoulders and his back. He teased the hard, erect point with teeth and tongue until her breath came fast and then shifted his attention to her other breast. His hand roamed over the flat of her stomach and drifted lower to caress the curve of her hips and her leg.

She threw one leg over his and shifted to straddle him, his erection behind her. She sat up and stared down at him.

"I believe I was seducing you, Oliver." Kate leaned forward, her hair falling around her face, and trailed light kisses along his jaw and neck. Her tongue teased the base of his throat and her hands explored the planes of his chest. She took his nipple between her teeth and flicked it with her tongue and he sucked in a sharp breath.

She stretched out on top of him and delicious shock at the press of flesh to flesh coursed through him. His arousal nestled between her legs and she nibbled at the lobes of his ears then moved her lips to his. His tongue danced and dueled with hers. Heat pulsed in his veins. Her body rocked against him. He could feel the wet evidence of her desire. And his own excitement increased.

"And now, Kate." He locked his leg around hers and in one quick motion, turned until she lay beneath him. "I am doing the seducing."

He positioned himself between her legs, and got to his knees. She stared up at him, her green eyes dark with passion. He leaned over her and ran his tongue in a measured and teasing manner around one nipple and then the next. Her hands clutched at the bed and it was all he could do to restrain himself from taking her right now. He traced slow, lazy circles on her stomach with his tongue and felt her muscles tighten beneath his touch.

His fingers toyed with the curls at the meeting of her thighs then he slipped his hand between her legs. She gasped and arched upward. She was wet and slick and hot. His fingers stroked the heated folds of flesh and the hard point of her passion, over and over in an ever-increasing rhythm and he watched her respond to the pleasure he provoked. Her eyes were glazed, her skin flushed and her breath came faster. He wanted her to enjoy, to revel in the sensations he caused. His own need, hard and aching, grew with every breath she took. Every moan that broke from her lips reverberated deep inside him in a hot pool of desire.

He could feel the tension in her body building and knew with unquestioned instinct when she could take no more. When he could bear no more.

She gasped. "Oliver."

"Kate." He leaned in to nuzzle her neck and his chest grazed the hardened peaks of her breast. "Mysterious, wonderful Kate."

He straddled her and braced himself with one arm. Then guided his member into her, slowly with a restraint he didn't know he possessed, he slid into her tight, wet fire. His breath caught with the sheer sensation that swept from her body through his. He pushed deeply into her and paused, then withdrew in a deliberate manner. She wrapped her legs around him and he thrust deeply again and again until a primal urge as old as man gripped him. And he knew nothing but the throbbing pleasure of being one with her. And existed only as a creature of sensation, ruled by passion, fueled by desire.

Faster and harder he thrust into her. She met him stroke for stroke and arched against him. Blood pounded in his ears and he felt her convulse around him in a long, explosive climax that roared through his veins and seared his soul. She cried out and her legs tightened around him. He shuddered hard with his own endless release and wondered that he wouldn't shatter with the glory of it. And die a happy, happy man.

They collapsed together and lay with heaving breath still joined for long moments. He didn't want to pull out of her, didn't want to end his body being one with hers. In truth, he wasn't sure he had the strength.

At last he drew a deep breath, braced himself on his forearms and lifted up to stare down at her.

She smiled at him, the dreamy sort of smile of a woman well satisfied, a woman well loved, and his heart skipped a beat.

"I knew there were any number of things you were good at." Her voice was low and sultry.

He chuckled, shifted to lay by her side and took her in his arms. "I'm glad you were not disappointed."

"Oh, Oliver." Her gaze met his. "You are more than I could have hoped for."

"As are you." He brushed his lips across hers and realized he could be content to lay like this, with her in his arms for the rest of his days.

"I should probably go before the servants are up."

"Kate." He smiled. "I'm glad you came."

"As am I, Oliver." Her lips whispered against him. "As am I."

Kathleen stretched her arms over her head and grinned at the coffered ceiling in her bedroom. What a lovely ceiling it was. What a glorious day this would be. And what a wonderful night last night had been.

A man didn't make love to a woman like Oliver had if he didn't care for her, if he didn't love her. Certainly, as she'd only ever shared the bed of one other man her experience in this regard was limited. Still, there were things that didn't rely on experience or memory, things a woman simply knew. Neither Oliver nor she had actually said the words, but she knew.

She scrambled out of bed and moved to the mirror. She stared at her image. She looked as different as she felt today. It struck her that she was happy, truly happy. Why, she positively glowed. She had the look of a woman well loved. It had been a very long time since she'd been well loved. And a very long time since she'd been happy.

Kathleen clasped her hands in front of her and drew a deep breath.

"Oliver, I have remembered everything. I am Kathleen MacDavid and I am indeed nearly thirty years of age. My husband died nine years ago and until last night, I had never been with another man. My family dabbles in magic, generally without success although recent developments may prove me wrong. Your family and mine were cursed five hundred years ago and unless you and I join in marriage both families will come to an end and dreadful things will happen to all of us." She cast her image a bright smile. "And, oh yes, I believe I have fallen in love with you." She laughed aloud. She still sounded like something of an idiot but it scarcely mattered. She certainly wouldn't love Oliver any less if he sounded like an idiot.

She would tell him tonight at the ball, in his arms under the stars. It would be the perfect place and time. She would tell him everything. Who she was, why she was here and that she'd fallen in love with him.

Certainly, he might be somewhat . . . bothered by her revelations. She had come to England with the explicit purpose of marrying him after all, but she hadn't had any sort of plan. Her loss of memory—if not caused by Hannah—was certainly not intentional. At least not on her part.

No, Oliver was a rational, sensible man, if something of a romantic, and was not averse to marriage. He might be unwilling to marry to break a centuries old curse but he would marry for love.

She ignored the thought that just possibly he might not see it that way.

Chapter 15

$\mathcal{I}$t was a perfect night. Rain had threatened all day but now the skies had cleared and stars shone between the clouds. The terrace and the gardens were set with tents and fluttering banners in the colors of the season. Miniature lanterns echoed the starlight and everywhere lights twinkled. Kathleen had helped Lady Norcroft, her nieces, Mr. Berkley, and an assortment of footmen in decorating the grounds, but she'd had no idea the result would be so enchanting. The day had been chaotic. At one point Lady Norcroft had claimed a last-minute errand in the village and had vanished for a few hours. Now, the ball was drawing to a close and Kathleen had the satisfying feeling of a job well done.

She was rather pleased with herself as well. Even though they had agreed on the color and the fabric, Kathleen had never imagined Madame DuBois could create a gown that was nothing less than perfect. Indeed, when she had gazed in the mirror tonight, even knowing who she was, she had scarcely recognized herself. The style was the latest in fashion, revealing and provocative without being scandalous and Kathleen looked perfect in it. Madame's skills could truly be called magic.

Now, Kathleen stood to one side of the terrace, watching the dancers, a glass of punch in her hand, Oliver by her side. As he had done all evening, he scanned the crowd, keeping a close eye on his cousins and Mr. Berkley.

In Kathleen's experience, it was an unusual ball. Everyone in attendance was wearing their best but there was scarcely a diamond brooch or emerald bracelet in sight. Guests were not limited to landed or wealthy families. Villagers were invited as were tenants and neighboring families. This was, Lady Norcroft had explained, how the Harvest Ball had always been and how it would always be. The tradition of inviting everyone in the county had begun long before she had become the countess of Norcroft and, she assured Kathleen, it would continue well after she was gone. For one and all on this night, the grounds of Norcroft Manor had become a place of welcome and magic where anything could happen.

"Anything," Kathleen said softly.

Oliver glanced at her. "Did you say something?"

She smiled with the sheer delight of the evening. "I was just noting how very magical this is tonight."

He chuckled. "It's remarkable what a few lights and music will do."

"I don't think it's the lights and the music."

"It's the feel in the air then." He leaned against the balustrade and watched the dancers. "I always feel it at this time of year. There is a sense of anticipation. The feeling that something is about to happen. Something quite remarkable."

She raised a brow. "Winter?"

"That too." He laughed. "It's quite a fanciful notion I suppose and probably makes no sense at all."

"No, I know exactly what you mean. On a night like this, one feels that almost anything is possible."

He flashed her a suggestive grin. "Indeed one does."

"Oliver Leighton." She took a sip of her punch. "You are a wicked, wicked man."

"Only when it comes to you."

"I like it."

"You are a mysterious woman, Kate."

"Am I?" She forced a light laugh. "I should think after last night there is little mystery left. I have no more secrets."

He chuckled. "Other than your life, which remains a secret for both of us, I suspect you have any number of private secrets I shall quite enjoy discovering." He paused for a moment. "Kate, I have been meaning to discuss that with you."

"Private secrets? Here? My goodness, Oliver, you are an adventurer."

"I certainly would be if that was what I meant. I have decided it's time, past time really, to take matters in hand."

"It did seem to me you took matters quite admirably in hand last night," she murmured.

"Indeed I did." He leaned closer to her. "And I have every intention of doing so again." He straightened and his tone sobered. "However I decided last night—"

"When did you find the time?"

He choked back a laugh. "Last night before I was interrupted—"

"My apologies."

"Not accepted and I shall certainly expect you to make amends."

She sipped her drink. "Tonight perhaps?"

"I was thinking the same thing. What a remarkable coincidence."

"We have a great deal in common, Oliver."

"Indeed we do. Now, as I was saying, I intend to have my solicitor engage the services of an investigator to find out who you are."

"Do you?" The tiniest hint of panic touched her, but she brushed it away. There was no need to be concerned. Oliver would have his answers long before he could write, much less send, a letter.

Kathleen fully intended to tell him everything at the end of the evening. Or perhaps later tonight when she was in his bed. Or possibly tomorrow. The right moment had simply not yet presented itself, nor had the right words. It was important to tell him everything in the proper way. And important as well that she be the one to do the telling. "Somehow, I doubt that will be necessary."

"Kate." His tone was gentle as if she were a fragile, delicate creature and guilt washed through her. "I know you have remembered a few facts about your life—"

"I am remembering more every day."

He cast her a sympathetic look. "Are you content to wait? For an answer that might never come?" He shook his head. "I have never considered myself an impatient man but I confess my patience has grown thin." He nodded at the gathering. "The guests here tonight, whether they are from neighboring estates or the village, very nearly every family here has been connected in some way with my family and Norcroft Manor for generations. I like that. I like the sense of continuation, of the past, that is ever present here. And never is it as strong as it is during this Harvest Ball." He slanted her a quick glance. "Do I sound absurd?"

"No. You sound quite like an earl should."

He laughed. "That's something I suppose." He paused to choose his words. "And this particular earl would like nothing better than to introduce you to these people with a name that is truly yours."

Her heart fluttered and she realized how very lucky she was to have found this man. Whether the curse was real or not it had led her to him and for that she would be forever grateful. "That's the loveliest thing anyone has ever said to me."

"That you can recall," he said wryly. For a long moment he watched the dancers. "What I'm trying to say is that without a solid basis in the past, life cannot go on toward the future. And I would very much like to look toward the future."

"I see." She considered him thoughtfully. This wasn't how she had envisioned it, but perhaps this was the right time to tell him she knew all about her past. She drew a deep breath. "Oliver."

"Yes?"

She set her glass on the balustrade and clasped her hands in front of her. "I have something to tell you."

He grinned wickedly. "Something about making amends perhaps?"

"Probably not." Blast it all, the words still wouldn't come. This was absurd. An honest, forthright approach would be best. She should just tell him. Very well then. "Oliver." She shifted her gaze from his as if to find the right words lingering in the air somewhere just past his shoulder. "I remember . . ."

"Yes?"

On the other side of the terrace, a tall, distinguished older man was kissing Lady Norcroft's hand. Even from this distance there was an air about him, something in the way he stood perhaps, that said he was the type of man a wise woman should be wary of but would not be nonetheless. He turned to lead Lady Norcroft into the dance and Kathleen caught a glimpse of his face. She sucked in a hard breath.

"You remember what?" Oliver prompted.

What on earth was he doing here? Good Lord, he would ruin everything.

"Kate? What is it?"

"The music, Oliver," she said quickly. She had to speak to the newcomer before he spoke to anyone else. "This waltz, it's my favorite."

"Well, that is important to remember." He grinned and offered his arm. "Shall we then?"

"Excellent idea." Dancing would bring her closer to Lady Norcroft and her partner. Then what?

Oliver led her onto the floor and for the first time tonight, being in his arms was not uppermost in her mind.

"Are you remembering something else?"

"No," she said absently, trying to find Oliver's mother and her escort amidst the other swirling couples. It was very nearly impossible.

"You seem somewhat preoccupied."

"Not at all." Where were they?

"I often find a particular work of music brings back all sorts of memories."

"Do you?" She scanned the crowd.

"Of where I heard it first or last. Of a person or a place."

"How nice for you." She craned her neck to see past him.

"Perhaps if I were to be quiet." His tone was dry, she scarcely noticed. "Something would occur to you."

"Perhaps." Even though the ball was nearing an end, the floor and the grounds remained crowded. Soon, guests would begin to leave for home and finding anyone would be much easier. But that might well be too late.

The music drew to a close and Oliver steered her to the edge of the dance floor. Concern shone in his eyes. "Are you all right?"

"Yes, I'm fine." She favored him with a bright smile. "Really quite fine."

His brow furrowed. "You don't seem fine."

"I am rather . . . parched. Yes, that's it. If you would be so good as to fetch me another glass of punch."

He studied her for a moment then nodded. "Of course."

Oliver headed toward the refreshment tables and the music started again. Where was he?

"May I have the pleasure of this dance," a deep, familiar voice sounded behind her.

She whirled around. "What are you doing here?"

He raised a brow. "Not the greeting I was expecting."

"Well, I was not expecting to greet you!"

"I gather we have a great deal to talk about." He chuckled. "Shall we talk while we dance?"

"Don't be absurd, we're not going to dance." She glanced toward Oliver. He had stopped to speak with someone and wouldn't notice her absence for a few minutes. "We need to speak privately. There's a great deal I should tell you. Come along." She started off.

He trailed after her and she could hear the grin in his voice. "You always have been a demanding sort."

She led him across the ballroom, down a corridor and fairly shoved him into the parlor. "Now then, Uncle, what are you doing here?"

Uncle Malcolm, the Earl of Dumleavy, grinned. "I have come to rescue you, lass."

She stared in disbelief. "What do you mean rescue me? I don't need rescuing. I have everything completely under control."

He wandered across the room to the fireplace and studied the portrait over the mantel. "That's not what I hear."

"What precisely have you heard?" She narrowed her gaze. "And more to the point, from whom?"

"The problem was we didn't hear anything at first, from you or my sister either." Malcolm cast her a chastising look. "I didn't think sending the two of you off alone was a good idea right from the start. I should have come with you in the first place."

"So Grandmother sent you?"

"Your grandmother and I discussed it. We knew you wouldn't want me to interfere, but—"

"But you came anyway."

He ignored her. "It's been more than a fortnight since you left Scotland. When we didn't receive so much as a cursory note, we decided I should come to London as well. Imagine my surprise when I discovered neither you nor Hannah was where you were supposed to be."

"I can see where that might have been a surprise," she muttered. "It was not my doing."

"I am well aware of that. It wasn't hard to determine where my sister had gone," he said with a wry smile. "So from London I traveled to Lord Darlington's estate."

She widened her eyes. "You saw Hannah? What did she tell you?"

Malcolm leaned against the mantel, crossed his arms over his chest, and studied his niece thoughtfully, exactly as he had when she was a little girl and had done something she shouldn't have. "An absurd tale about a ridiculous plan her devious mind had come up with. And how you refused to go along with it so she had taken matters into her own hands."

"How?" Kathleen demanded.

"How?"

"Yes, how?" She resisted the urge to stamp her foot as she might have when she was a child. "How did she take matters into her own hands?"

He shook his head. "You're not going to like it."

"I already don't like it." She braced herself. "Tell me the truth, Uncle."

He grimaced. "Magic."

"No, I don't believe that. I won't believe that." She wrapped her arms around herself and paced the room. "It's absurd."

"So you'll believe in a curse but not in magic?"

"Yes," she snapped. "It's an entirely different thing altogether. Everything that has happened to me, to you, to the entire family and now I realize to Oliver's family as well, has convinced me that I have to believe in it because someone has to do something and that someone is me."

"So." Malcolm said slowly. "You'll believe in something as far-fetched as a curse but the fact that your mad aunt had a plan that requires you to pretend to lose your memory—"

"Which I refused to go along with."

"And then you do in fact lose your memory, that is . . . a coincidence?"

"Stranger things have happened in this world," she said staunchly.

He snorted. "Not very likely."

"Call it whatever you want but the fact remains—" She pulled up short and stared at him. "How did you know about my loss of memory? Hannah left before I woke up."

"And yet she knew." He shrugged. "As she would if she had—"

Kathleen held out her hand to stop him. "Don't say it."

"As you wish." He paused. "The spell has run its course then?"

"There was no spell." She clenched her teeth.

She certainly was not going to tell him her loss of memory had lasted exactly one week. "I recovered my memory that was no doubt lost due to a blow to the head. It was a simple medical matter, nothing magical about it."

"That is neither here nor there at the moment I suppose. At any rate, Hannah told me where you were. By the way, she sent along your bags."

"The least she could do."

"I arrived in the village this morning and sent a note to Lady Norcroft."

Kathleen narrowed her eyes. "Why?"

"I thought it best to find out what you had gotten yourself into before I suddenly appeared. Lady Norcroft met me at the inn."

"Did she?"

"She did indeed." He chuckled. "She's a fine figure of a woman, lass, with a spirit to match."

Kathleen groaned. She had seen that look in his eye before. "Uncle."

Malcolm grinned. "Are you not glad to see me, Kathleen?"

"Glad?" At once the aching sense of being lost that had gripped her every minute that she hadn't known her name swept through her and vanquished any annoyance she felt at his arrival. "Glad?" She could barely choke out the word.

She threw herself into his embrace and she was a little girl again seeking comfort from the one man who had always been there to heal her hurts. "I have never been happier to see anyone in my life."

He stroked her hair. "It's been hard for you, Kathleen?"

"You have no idea." She sniffed against his chest. "I didn't know who I was, where I was from. I didn't remember you or Grandmother or Hannah or Kenneth or anything. I didn't know my name or what I was going to do. It's been horrible."

His arms tightened around her. "My sister will have to be taken to task for this."

"For magic?" She choked back a giggle. "Not that I believe it, of course, but for the one time her magic might have worked?" She raised her head and gazed up at him. "I daresay grandmother will be thrilled."

"Your grandmother will be furious," he said firmly and kissed the tip of her nose. "As am I."

"I do hope I'm not interrupting." Oliver's voice sounded from the doorway. "Kate?"

Malcolm raised a brow. "You allow him to call you Kate?"

Kathleen wrinkled her nose and stepped out of her uncle's arms. "Oliver, I have something to tell you."

"I can see that." Oliver stared, confusion and concern on his face. "Please God, don't tell me this is your husband."

"Her husband? Don't be absurd, lad." Malcolm laughed. "I'm her uncle."

Chapter 16

*O*liver stared at the tall, rugged-looking man with the graying hair who had held Kate in his arms a moment ago. "Your uncle?"

"I did tell you I had remembered I wasn't married," Kate said quickly. "May I introduce my uncle, the Earl of Dumleavy, Malcolm Armstrong. Uncle, this is Oliver, Lord Norcroft, the Earl of Norcroft."

Shock coursed through Oliver. His gaze jerked to Kate's. "Your uncle?"

Dumleavy inclined his head toward Kate. "If that's all he can say, lass, you've made a bad bargain of it."

"She hasn't made any bargain of it," Oliver said sharply. "This is your uncle?"

Dumleavy snorted.

"Yes," Kate said firmly.

Oliver narrowed his eyes. "You remember him?"

She nodded. "I do."

"Then your memory has returned?" Oliver said slowly.

Kate smiled. "It has."

Oliver stared.

"Oliver?" Unease sounded in her voice.

"I have to admit, I'm somewhat taken aback. Of course, we knew or rather we hoped . . ." Oliver shook his head to clear it. "This is"—a slow grin spread across his face with the realization of exactly what this meant—"bloody marvelous. Kate, you must be pleased."

"I am," she said with a relieved sigh.

"When did you remember?"

"A few days ago."

"A few days? Then it was before . . ." His grin widened and he stepped toward her. Dumleavy's brow furrowed in a forbidding manner and Oliver thought better of it. "Why didn't you tell me?"

"I did try," she said. "I told you some of it."

He chuckled. "Indeed you did."

"Here you are, Oliver." His mother sailed blithely into the room. "I see everyone has met."

"Not entirely." Oliver caught Kate's gaze. "I still have not had the pleasure."

"I'm not sure that's quite accurate," Kate said under her breath.

Dumleavy's gaze slid from Kate to Oliver and he narrowed his eyes suspiciously. If the man wasn't her uncle he certainly acted like one.

"Nonetheless, Oliver, guests are leaving and we should bid them good evening." Mother started toward the door.

"Mother, Kate has recovered her memory."

"How lovely, dear." She favored Kate with a warm smile. "While I confess to a great deal of curiosity, this will have to wait. For now, Oliver, we have obligations to attend to."

"Damnation." She was right of course, but the last thing he wanted to do at the moment was take care of the social niceties that were as much a part of the tradition of the ball as everything else. What he wanted was to find out every detail about the woman who had worked her way into his affections. Still, he did know the most important thing and he supposed all else could wait. After all, they had the rest of their lives. "Very well then." He met Kate's gaze firmly. "Wait for me here."

"We won't take a step outside this room," Dumleavy said. "However, if you could see your way clear to send someone with a bit of refreshment, a wee draught of something tasty would be most welcome."

"My apologies, Lord Dumleavy. We are not usually so inhospitable. I'm afraid everyone's attentions are focused on the out-of-doors festivities. I shall have something sent round at once." Mother cast him a smile that, if Oliver didn't know better, he would call flirtatious. "We have some excellent Scottish whisky. Will that do?"

Dumleavy smiled in a slow and decidedly seductive manner. "Indeed it will, my lady. Indeed it will."

Oliver stared at the older man. What did he think he was doing?

"Oliver?" His mother raised a brow. And what was she doing? "Are you coming?"

"Yes, of course." He paused at the doorway and looked back at Kate. "By the way, what is your name?"

"Kathleen."

"Kathleen." He thought for a moment. "It suits you." He grinned and took his leave.

Behind him Dumleavy said in a low voice. "I'd say that went well."

"That, Uncle, is just the beginning." Kate—now Kathleen—sighed. "Until I tell him the . . ."

Tell him what? Tell him everything of course.

For the next endless hour or so Oliver smiled and nodded and made all sorts of polite, appropriate comments. It was difficult to keep his mind on the task at hand even though he had always liked this part of the evening. As he had told Kate—or rather Kathleen—it was all part and parcel of the continuation of life surrounding the manor and his family. While it was next to impossible to greet every guest upon arrival, given the less than formal nature of the ball and its setting, it had always been considered essential for the current earl, and or countess, to bid good evening to each guest and wish them well until next year. In reality, it was a small enough gesture but it made every person in attendance, be they wealthy landowner or tenant, feel valued and respected. His father and his grandfather before him and every title holder for as long as there had been an Earl of Norcroft had bid farewell to each and every guest at the end of the ball and Oliver was confident every earl to come would do so as well.

Still, try as he might to ignore them, a hundred unanswered questions filled his head and de-manded attention. Now at least he knew her name—Kathleen—and it did indeed suit her. And he knew her uncle was titled if indeed he was her uncle. Oliver would have to have some assurances on that score, not that he was suspicious but cer-tainly caution was advisable. In spite of his earlier skepticism as to Kate—Kathleen's—veracity, he had come to accept her situation. Now, he was willing to accept that this man was indeed her relation but it was only reasonable to expect, well, proof. Admittedly, Dumleavy's obviously protective attitude was an indication as to his position. Beyond that, Oliver wanted to know everything there was to know about her.

The moment the last guest had taken his leave and his cousins retired for the evening, Oliver made certain Berkley was escorted to his rooms. In spite of his eagerness to return to Kate—Kathleen, he trusted Berkley no more than he did any young man when it came to the girls. Finally, Oliver and his mother headed back to the parlor.

"I must say this is exciting," his mother said in a casual manner that belied her words. "I do hope you will keep an open mind."

"An open mind?" He drew his brows together. "What do you mean?"

"Nothing really." Mother shrugged. "It's simply that, on occasion, you tend to be somewhat inflexible when it comes to anything of an . . . an unforeseen nature."

"Nonsense." He scoffed. "I am completely open to the unexpected."

"We shall see," she murmured.

The low hum of agitated voices sounded from the parlor. Oliver waved his mother ahead of him into the room, abruptly ending the conversation. Kate—Kathleen's cheeks were flushed and a distinct note of tension hung in the air. Oliver wondered if they had had words and if so about what? Both uncle and niece stood near the fireplace and each had a glass of whisky in hand. And not, he suspected, their first.

Again it struck him how very beautiful she was in the gown Madame DuBois had created. The color of the fabric reflected the green of her eyes and heightened the creamy color of her skin. The garment itself fit as though it was a part of her, caressing the curves of her body like a second skin. Lucky gown.

His gaze met Kate's—Kathleen's. He should try

to think of her as Kathleen but Kate was the woman he had come to know. "Are you all right?"

She slanted a quick glance at her uncle, then nodded. "Quite."

"How lovely, all of us here together." Mother beamed at the guests. "Oliver, do be a dear and fetch me a glass of whatever it is they're drinking."

"Whisky, I suspect." Oliver crossed the room to where a crystal decanter that matched the one in his room sat on a tray amid several additional glasses. Hollinger, once again, had anticipated what would be needed.

"Do allow me, Lady Norcroft." Dumleavy smoothly stepped around Oliver, poured a glass, then presented it to Oliver's mother with a slight bow. "I should warn you, it's not for the faint of heart."

"Excellent." Mother gazed into the older man's eyes. "Neither am I."

"Mother!" Surprise sharpened Oliver's tone.

Dumleavy chuckled in a decidedly wicked manner. Apparently, young Berkley wasn't the only one Oliver would have to keep an eye on.

"Do pour yourself something to drink, Oliver," his mother said firmly. "Kathleen has a great deal to tell us."

He smiled at Kate. "And I am most impatient to hear it."

"As are we all," Mother said brightly. She seated herself on the sofa and patted the spot next to her. "Kathleen?"

"Thank you but I think I'd prefer to stand." Kate was decidedly nervous. It was absurd, of course. What could she possibly have remembered that would make her this apprehensive? At once he realized she was not the only one.

Oliver filled a glass for himself and thoughtfully took a sip. His gaze slid from Kate to Dumleavy to his mother. It could well be attributed to the odd nature of the situation they found themselves in but he had the distinct impression the others knew something he did not. And, as that impression included his mother, it did not bode well.

"I'm not sure where to begin." Kate twisted her hands in front of her.

"The beginning?" Mother suggested.

"Your name would be nice," Oliver said.

"Certainly, my name, I should have . . ." Kate nodded. "My name is Kathleen MacDavid. Lady Kathleen. My grandmother is the dowager Countess of Dumleavy and you have met my uncle."

Dumleavy raised his glass in a slight salute.

Kate ignored him. "My husband was Sir Kenneth, dead these past nine years."

"My condolences," Oliver murmured.

"It was a very long time ago, but your sympathy is most appreciated nonetheless. However." She glanced at Oliver's mother. "Kenneth's death really is the beginning."

The older woman nodded with satisfaction. "Always the best place to start."

Kate nodded. "It wasn't until after his death that my grandmother told me a . . . a story as it were. I suppose you could call it . . ." She glanced at her uncle. "A legend? A family legend?"

Dumleavy sipped his whisky. "That'll do."

"I have always been fond of legends," Oliver's mother murmured.

Kate continued. "According to the legend, five hundred years ago this very season two border families, one Scottish and one English, were supposed to be joined in marriage to end the years of violence between them. But the marriage never occurred."

"Probably the girl was to blame. English lass." Dumleavy's gaze met Oliver's mother's. "Flighty sort no doubt."

She smiled in a disturbingly provocative manner. "You would be surprised at what might be hiding behind flighty."

Dumleavy chuckled then directed his words to Oliver. "Here's where it becomes interesting." He crossed to the decanter, refilled his glass, then topped off Oliver's. "You're going to need this."

"I can't imagine why," Oliver said staunchly but took a long sip nonetheless. Thus far, Kate's story had indeed been mildly interesting but pointless. Oliver really didn't care about matters that happened five hundred years ago. Still, everyone else seemed intrigued.

"When the marriage did not occur, an old woman—"

"It's always an old woman," Mother said in an aside to Dumleavy.

"This particular old woman had lost everyone she loved to the bloodshed and was furious that it would continue." Kate paused, then chose her words with care. "So she cast a . . . a curse on the families involved. If they didn't join in marriage by the end of five hundred years, both families would cease to exist and terrible, dreadful things would happen."

He stared at her for a moment then laughed. "Terrible, dreadful things? That's rather imprecise. What kind of terrible, dreadful things?"

"I don't know exactly what kind of terrible, dreadful things. The curse was cast a very long time ago. Now, the details are . . . well . . ." Kate glanced at her uncle.

"Lost in the mists of time," Dumleavy offered.

"They always are," Mother said under her breath.

"How convenient." Oliver laughed again. "This is absurd but most amusing although I cannot for the life of me figure out why you're telling this tale in the first place. It doesn't seem to have anything to do with the situation at hand."

"It's not absurd, nor is it amusing." Kate glared at him. "And it has everything to do with the situation at hand."

"Perhaps, lass, he wouldn't think it quite so funny if he knew it all," her uncle said. "You've left out a few pertinent points."

"I was coming to them but I was interrupted," Kate said sharply then drew a deep breath. "The families in question were yours and mine. You and I are the last of our lines." She met Oliver's gaze directly. "We must marry to end the curse."

Oliver resisted the urge to laugh again. "You're mad aren't you?"

Dumleavy chuckled. "Runs in the family."

"Aside from the fact that this is the most ridiculous thing I have ever heard." A smug note sounded in Oliver's voice. "My family has never lived anywhere near Scotland. You have the wrong family."

"Not exactly, dear." His mother shook her head. "Your grandfather's family did indeed once occupy land near the border. It was centuries ago but nonetheless, we are the right family."

"Do you really think we'd go through all of this without being certain we had the right family?" Indignation rang in Kate's voice. "I came to England to marry you."

He stared at her. "You what?"

"I came to England to marry you," she said with a huff, as if he were the one making bizarre claims about curses and his intentions.

"Marry the Englishman, break the curse." Dumleavy shrugged. "Happens all the time."

"Not to this Englishman!" Was Oliver the only one who thought this was the most ridiculous thing he'd ever heard? "I don't believe any of this and I especially don't believe in curses." He turned toward his mother. "You can't tell me you believe this nonsense."

Mother smiled pleasantly. "I can't tell you I don't."

"How long have you known about this?"

"Known about which part, dear?"

"Pick one!" Oliver glared.

"Well, I do recall first hearing of the curse from your grandmother long before you were born. But she wasn't very specific." Mother looked at Dumleavy. "I would think when one needs to impart information about something as formidable as a curse, one would be more precise wouldn't you?"

Dumleavy nodded. "It would seem fair. Forewarned and all."

"Exactly." She smiled at the Scotsman then continued. "Some years ago, oh, seven or eight I think, Lady Dumleavy"—she nodded at Kate—"your grandmother, wrote to me. We exchanged several letters but ultimately I told her I couldn't encourage my son in a match simply to end a curse I didn't believe in."

"You couldn't?" Oliver said slowly.

"I couldn't *then*."

Oliver narrowed his eyes. "But you just said you didn't believe in the curse."

"No, dear, I said I didn't believe in it *then*, although I must say Lady Dumleavy made some excellent arguments in support of its existence. Tragic, unforeseen deaths, that sort of thing." Mother sipped her whisky. "Why, I had barely remembered anything about a curse at all until the other night at dinner when it just popped into my head, which is either quite fortunate or most curious depending on how you wish to view it. Then of course after I realized the truth—"

"What truth?" Suspicion sounded in Oliver's voice.

"What truth?" Kate said slowly.

"Why the truth about Kathleen," Mother said casually.

Oliver drew his brows together. "Are you saying you knew who she was?"

Kate stared in disbelief. "You knew who I was?"

"Your bracelet, dear," Mother said with a shrug. "It has your family's motto on it."

"Extremis malis, extrema remedia," Dumleavy intoned.

"Extremis . . . what?" Oliver stared. This was getting odder and more confusing with every word. And more annoying.

"Extreme remedies for extreme ills." Kate waved off his question in an impatient manner and turned to his mother. "You knew who I was and you didn't tell me?"

"My apologies." Mother cast her a repentant smile. "But it did seem best."

"About her loss of memory—" Oliver began.

Disbelief shone in Kate's eye. "But why?"

"I am sorry, I know how difficult this has been for you. However." His mother met Kate's gaze

firmly. "I thought it would be far better if you and
Oliver had the opportunity to get to know one another without a curse hanging over your heads."

"I don't believe in curses," Oliver said again.

"No one does at first, dear," Mother said. "I certainly didn't."

Dumleavy shook his head. "It took Kathleen
years to accept it."

"You needn't tell him that," Kate said in a lofty
manner. "It's nothing he needs to know and really
none of his business."

"I should think it's all my business and certainly I
should know everything," Oliver said sharply.
"Because all I know thus far is you have come to
England to trap me into marriage—"

Kate gasped. "Trap!"

"Trap is such a harsh word," his mother murmured.

"Yes, trap me into a marriage based, if I were to
believe you which I'm not saying I do, on some
obscure, practically forgotten story, the details of
which are vague—"

Dumleavy nodded. "Lost in the mists of time."

Mother shrugged. "As they always are."

"Would you two stop saying that!" Oliver glared
at the older couple, then turned his attention back
to Kate. "As I was saying, all I know is that you
came here to trap—"

Her eyes narrowed at the word.

"—me into marriage. Obviously feigning a loss
of memory as part of a plan to do just that!" He

tossed back the rest of his drink and smacked the glass down on the table beside the decanter.

"Oh dear," his mother said.

Kate stared at him. "You think I was pretending?"

"I don't know what to think!" Oliver crossed his arms over his chest and studied her. "Thus far this evening you tell me you've recovered your memory and then I learn you were only here in the first place to trick me into marriage. How am I supposed to believe anything that you say?"

"First of all, I had no intention of tricking you or trapping you. As for how—" Kate drew a deep breath and squared her shoulders. Anger sparked in her green eyes. Oliver's stomach twisted and he realized he might have pushed her too far. Not that it mattered. He was angry himself and justifiably so. "I should think the answer to that is because you have come to know me."

"I came to know a woman named Kate, not Lady Kathleen." Even as he said the words he wondered if he was wrong. Regardless of her name, he did know her. At least he had thought he did. But she'd made a fool of him and he was no longer confident as to what he did and didn't know. Or what he felt.

Her gaze met his. "I certainly thought I knew you."

"You'd best tell him the rest, lass," Dumleavy said abruptly. "You can't blame the man for not knowing what to believe."

"I most certainly can." A cold note sounded in Kate's voice.

"There's more?" Oliver huffed and held his hand out for the glass Kate's uncle was currently refilling. "I can hardly wait."

"Sarcasm, Oliver." Mother pressed her lips together. "Is most unbecoming."

"Very well then," Kate said, "the rest is really rather simple. My Aunt Hannah and I traveled to London—"

"Your Aunt Hannah? Yet another character in this farce?"

She nodded. "Lady Fitzgivens."

He narrowed his eyes. "The same Lady Fitzgivens who found you and brought you here?"

Kate rolled her gaze toward the ceiling. "Apparently."

"Ah-hah!" Triumph sounded in Oliver's voice. "There we have it!"

Dumleavy and Oliver's mother exchanged looks. "There we have what, dear?"

"The answer of course." He gestured at Kate. "It was a conspiracy to manipulate me—"

"Trap," Kate snapped. "You said trap before, let's stay with trap, shall we?"

"It seems appropriate!"

"As I was saying, my aunt and I traveled to London to meet you, and I must confess at that point, we had no actual plan for doing so. Then we learned you were here in the country, which did limit opportunities to meet."

"Well, you could have shown up at my door, pretending not to know who you were," Oliver said.

Kate ignored him. "Therefore my aunt suggested we both attend Lord Darlington's party and that we travel to Norcroft by train then take a hired carriage the rest of the way."

"It's much faster that way," Oliver's mother said to Dumleavy.

"After we arrived in Norcroft . . ." Kate paused.

"Go on." Oliver nodded.

"After we arrived in Norcroft," she chose her words with care. "The next thing I knew was waking up in your house."

"Without any knowledge as to your own name." Oliver snorted in disdain. "Hah!"

"That was not intentional." She wrinkled her nose. "On my part."

"On whose part then?"

"My aunt had this absurd idea about pretending to have lost my memory—"

"Ah-hah," he said again.

"If you say ah-hah one more time . . ." Kate closed her eyes as if to pray for patience, then drew a calming breath. "As I was saying, Hannah had a silly plan involving my pretending to have lost my memory but I refused to go along with it." She met his gaze and he could see the truth in her eyes. If he could believe it. "It appears Hannah then took matters into her own hands."

"You're saying your aunt pushed you off the train platform?"

Kate hesitated. "In a manner of speaking."

"And it was sheer coincidence that you lost your memory?"

"Possibly," Kate said slowly.

"I say again ah-hah!"

"Or it might have been . . ." Kate glanced at his mother and her uncle. Thunder rumbled in the distance. She met Oliver's gaze. "Magic."

Chapter 17

liver's brow rose. "Magic?"

Kathleen studied him for a long moment. Regardless of her own disbelief, at this particular second, it was disloyal to her family not to defend what they believed to be real. "Yes, Oliver, magic."

Oliver stared. "What kind of an idiot do you think I am?"

"I don't know." Kathleen crossed her arms over her chest. "What kind of idiot are you?"

"Well I'm certainly not so stupid as to believe in anything as absurd as magic!"

"An open mind, Oliver," Lady Norcroft said in the same tone of chastisement she might have used when he was a boy.

"My mind is open," Oliver snapped. "More than open."

Malcolm snorted.

Kathleen chose her words with care. "Then perhaps, if indeed your mind is open, we can discuss this in a calm and rational manner."

Oliver glared. "I am calm and I am always rational."

"It seems to me, there have been far too many revelations this evening for anyone to remain calm." Lady Norcroft got to her feet. "The hour grows late and it has been a very long day. I suggest we all retire for the evening. We can continue this discussion tomorrow." She turned to Uncle Malcolm. "I shall show you to your rooms, my lord."

"Oh, no." Oliver shook his head. "He's not going to stay here."

"Of course he is, dear. There are plenty of rooms available and I suspect it's going to rain at any minute. We certainly can't send him on his way now."

"I should be most grateful for your hospitality." Malcolm nodded a bow.

"Besides," Lady Norcroft continued, "he is Kathleen's uncle and as such is practically a member of the family."

"He is not a member of this family." Oliver's voice rose. "Nor is she! Furthermore, I have no intention of marrying anyone to satisfy a curse I fully believe is rubbish."

"So much for an open mind," Malcolm said.

"Perhaps you've forgotten our own family's motto, Oliver." Lady Norcroft cast her son a pointed look.

Oliver's jaw clenched. "Veneratio, prosapia, officium."

"English please."

"Honor, family, duty," he muttered.

Lady Norcroft beamed. "How appropriate."

"I'm not marrying her." A warning sounded in his voice.

"Well, certainly not tonight." Lady Norcroft moved to Kathleen and took her hands. "Again, please accept my apologies. It might have been a mistake not to tell you who you were the moment I realized it but I thought it was best. And I must confess, if I had to do it over again," she winced, "I'm afraid I would."

"Lady Norcroft." It was certainly upsetting to learn Kathleen could have had information as to her identity far sooner but she couldn't fault Lady Norcroft's intentions. She squeezed the older woman's hands. "We all do what we think is wise." Kathleen smiled reluctantly. "Whether it is or not."

Lady Norcroft looked firmly into her eyes. "I am confident all will turn out well." She stepped back and nodded at her son. "Good evening, Oliver."

"You don't seem very upset by all this." He glared at his mother. "If you believe this nonsense then you must believe as well that there will be no more Leightons or Earls of Norcroft—"

"Only if you don't marry Kathleen and I must

say, regardless of the curse, I quite approve of the match."

"—and terrible, dreadful things will happen!"

"My dear boy, terrible, dreadful things have already happened." The vaguest suggestion of sorrow flashed through Lady Norcroft's eyes and Kathleen realized, whether or not Oliver's mother truly believed in the curse, she would do whatever was necessary to ensure the safety and security of her family. She always had. "We shall sort all this out tomorrow. Good evening, Oliver."

"Kathleen, it's a relief to see you are well." Malcolm moved closer and brushed a kiss across her cheek. "Watch him, lass. I don't think he's nearly as much of an idiot as he appears."

"I heard that!" Oliver huffed. "And I'm not as much of an idiot as I appear!"

"No one possibly could be," Kathleen said coolly.

Lady Norcroft sighed and turned to Malcolm. "My lord."

He nodded and followed her out of the room.

"Lord Dumleavy, might I ask how you feel about adventures?" Lady Norcroft's voice drifted into the parlor.

Malcolm laughed and Kathleen couldn't hear his response.

"Did you see that?" Indignation rang in Oliver's voice. "That man is—"

She narrowed her eyes. "Careful, Oliver, that man is my uncle."

"And as such is probably not to be trusted."

She raised a brow. "As is his niece?"

Oliver hesitated.

"I thought as much." She swept past him and refilled her glass, noting the shake of her hand echoed the tremulous feeling deep in the pit of her stomach. She took a long sip and stared at the wall in front of her. "Did you mean any of it?"

"Any of what?" he said cautiously.

"Any of those lovely things you said to me. About a future together. About not imagining anything that would preclude a future."

"Well, I certainly didn't expect this."

"This?" She whirled to face him. "What did you expect?"

"Well, I expected, I don't know, something more in the realm of ordinary."

"Ordinary?"

"Yes, you know." He gestured in an aimless manner. "An ordinary family, ordinary circumstances, ordinary answers."

"Adventure, Oliver." She raised her glass to him. "Is never ordinary."

"I wouldn't know. I don't have adventures. Ask my mother, ask anyone." He shook his head. "I am a rational, responsible person who does not have adventures."

"Neither do I." She sighed. "At least I never have before and I too am rational and responsible."

He studied her skeptically. "But you believe in this curse."

She chose her words with care. "I have come to

believe in it. It wasn't something I accepted blindly. As my uncle said it took me a long time."

"But you were married so—"

"My marriage lasted barely a year. I married Kenneth because I loved him. I'm not sure I would have done so if I had known about the curse. I can't help but think he died because he married me and I was always supposed to marry you."

"Rubbish." Oliver scoffed. "People die all the time. It doesn't mean they're cursed."

"How many people do you know who are killed when they walk behind a wagon filled with barrels of whisky, tied together quite securely I might add, that somehow managed to break loose and fall on him?"

"Admittedly that's unusual." Reluctance sounded in his voice.

"Unusual?"

"Quite odd, in fact, but it doesn't mean—"

"That's when my grandmother told me about the curse. Even then I didn't believe in it. But the first gentlemen after Kenneth that I felt any sort of affection for fell off a roof."

"That isn't—"

"In truth, he was blown off the roof."

"Sheer stupidity." Oliver shrugged. "He had no business being on a roof in the first place on a windy day."

"There was neither a cloud in the sky nor a breeze to be had." She drew a deep swallow of the whisky. "The gentleman after that was struck by lightning."

"Certainly that has been known to happen."

"Again, there was not a cloud in the sky." She shook her head. "The next gentleman—"

"How many gentlemen have there been?" he said in a distinctly possessive manner, which was probably a good sign.

"Oliver, I have been a widow for nine years. For nine very long years I have been quite alone." She met his gaze. "Until last night."

He drew a deep breath. "Go on."

"As I was saying, the next gentleman drowned. Slipped on a stone and fell into a stream." She sipped her whisky. "A very shallow stream. It was quite disturbing."

"For him."

"And for me. I am not heartless. At the point at which each gentleman met his untimely death, I had started to care for him and the idea of marriage had been mentioned which apparently sealed each particular suitor's fate. I had begun to suspect forces beyond my control were involved. When William died—"

"The one who drowned?"

She nodded. "I was at last convinced that resistance to the curse would only claim more lives. That the only man I could safely marry was the last remaining member of the family tied to mine by the legend." She aimed her glass at him. "You."

He stared at her. "Still, there's a logical explanation—"

"No, Oliver, there isn't. Even if you can dismiss the deaths of four good men as coincidence there is still compelling evidence." She set her glass down and ticked the points off on her fingers. "One, doesn't it strike you as odd that after five hundred years our families have come down to just you and I? One would think, through the years, a family tree would grow more expansive, not smaller."

"Logically, I suppose—"

"Secondly, my parents as well as your father died unusually young."

Oliver waved off her comment. "Such tragedies happen in life."

"But they have happened to us." She continued. "Third, my aunt's husband died young as well, and she never had children. Nor did I, nor did Malcolm. And I would think of any of us, Malcolm would sire children. As time grows closer to the end of five hundred years, the curse is coming true. Dreadful, terrible things have happened and our families are dying, trickling down to where there will be no one left." She shook her head. "I do not intend to let it end this way."

"So you came to England to marry me."

She nodded.

"And you pretended to have lost your memory—"

"No," she said sharply. "You may believe it or

not, you may call it coincidence that my aunt concocted an insane plan that came to pass or you may call it magic—"

He snorted in disdain.

She gazed heavenward and prayed for patience. He was not going to take this well. "You should know, my family has always believed in magic particularly my aunt and my grandmother and her mother before her and so on. They have, well, dabbled for want of a better word, in the mystic arts. Casting spells, concocting charms, that sort of thing. Never, I might point out, with any success whatsoever until possibly now, so it always seemed quite harmless to me."

"Until possibly now," he muttered.

"But if you believe nothing else, believe this." She met his gaze directly. "I never lied to you about not knowing who I was."

He stared at her for a moment then blew a long breath. "I believe you."

She narrowed her eyes. "Why?"

"I don't know, maybe I am an idiot." He ran his hand through his hair. "But there was something in your eyes, the look of someone lost. I daresay a look like that cannot be feigned."

"Thank you." Relief washed through her. Perhaps there was hope after all.

"I noticed that look had vanished a few days ago, no doubt that was when your memory returned, before . . ." His eyes widened with realization. "Before you seduced me!"

"Before *I* seduced *you*? It seems to me the seduction was mutual."

"I am not the one who came to your room in the middle of the night. If you think I am going to marry you simply because you and I—"

"I don't, nor would I ever. Besides, I am no innocent virgin. I am an adult fully capable of making my own decisions." She aimed an angry finger at him. "I came to your bed because that is where I wanted to be. I would never seduce a man into marriage. Even you!"

"Until now!"

"Although an honorable man would see his seduction of a woman who did not know her own name as not the least bit honorable. As taking unfair advantage of her. An indiscretion that could only be remedied by marriage."

"But you did know your own name!

"But you didn't know that!"

"Regardless, I did not seduce you."

"Very well, Oliver." She clenched her teeth. "I suppose I did indeed seduce you. I certainly couldn't count on you to do it."

He gasped. "I thought you might be married! I was being honorable."

She shrugged. "That didn't stop you from wanting me. From saying you felt as though you had never been kissed before. From speaking of the possibility of a future together."

"A momentary moral transgression on my part," he said in a lofty manner. "It could have happened to anyone."

"As I recall, it was more than momentary," she said under her breath.

"Kate, I—"

"Kathleen," she said without thinking. "I was called Kate as a child and by my husband, only because he knew it annoyed me. Yet another coincidence, I suppose, that your mother would pick that particular name but I prefer Kathleen." She shrugged. "I simply grew out of Kate. It no longer suits."

"No," he said slowly, "I suppose it doesn't."

His gaze caught hers and they stared at one another for a long moment.

"I'm returning to London tomorrow," he said abruptly.

Her heart sank. "Fleeing are we, Oliver? Rather cowardly of you."

"Not at all. I should say it was prudent." His attitude was cool, his demeanor calm, the perfect earl. "You have given me a great deal to consider and I suspect I shall not be able to reach any sensible conclusions here. Between you and my mother and your uncle, and God knows what the girls will think when they learn about this—" he shuddered—"no, I think it's best that I leave."

The last thing she wanted was for him to leave. "We don't have forever. You should know that. We have to marry before the autumnal equinox, which is in three weeks."

"Or?"

"Or dreadful, terrible things will happen," she snapped.

"I shall take the risk."

"What about Mr. Berkley?" she said quickly. "Should you leave while he is still here?"

Oliver thought for a minute. "I shall bring him with me. If his intentions towards Gen are serious, he will no doubt appreciate the opportunity to show me what a fine fellow he is."

She shook her head. "You can't go."

"Why? We are at an impasse. You intend to marry me to satisfy an absurd, ancient legend and I have no intention of marrying for such a ridiculous reason."

She lifted her chin. "And I have no intention of shirking my responsibilities."

"And your responsibility is to marry me? How romantic."

"Your mother is right," she said coolly. "Sarcasm is not the least bit becoming."

"Then I shall take my unbecoming character and retire for the night." He nodded and started toward the door.

"Oliver." She stepped toward him. "May I ask you a question?"

He paused but didn't turn toward her. "What is it?"

"Have you ever been in love?"

He shrugged in an off hand manner. "Once, a long time ago, I thought I was."

"It did not end well?"

"She was in love with someone else."

"I see." She chose her words with care. "Knowing about the curse now—"

"A curse I don't believe in."

"Regardless, simply knowing about it, and knowing of my experiences, four fine, honorable gentlemen now dead, would you take the risk that anyone you cared for would meet with the same fate?"

"I don't believe . . ." Oliver paused and she held her breath. "I don't know. Good evening." He nodded and took his leave.

For a long moment Kathleen stared at the doorway. That went well. She sighed and sank down on the sofa. As well as could be expected.

She couldn't blame Oliver for his skepticism. She certainly would be hard pressed to believe a story as absurd as hers. Oliver was no doubt feeling betrayed as well. She would be. But at least he believed that she hadn't lied to him which was probably more than she had any right to expect.

Oliver had said he had no intention of marrying for a reason as ridiculous as a curse. Very well then, she'd give him a better reason. She hadn't intended for any of this to happen. The more she considered the situation, the more she realized none of this would have happened if not for her amnesia. She would have to remember to thank Hannah before she strangled her.

She heaved a heartfelt sigh. She was in love with

him, which would indeed complicate matters as well as strengthen her resolve. She was fairly certain he was in love with her as well. Now all she had to do was make him realize it. It wasn't going to be easy, but she had fate on her side, and love.

Still, it might well be easier to make him believe in magic.

This was not how he had thought this evening would end. After last night, Oliver had been more than confident Kate would again grace his bed. He never imagined he'd spend the night alone in his rooms, unable to sleep, pacing the floor, trying in vain to sort out a dozen conflicting emotions.

Certainly he was happy that Kate had recovered her memory. And he did indeed believe she had not deceived him in that. He had meant what he had said about the look in her eye. No one could possibly be that good an actress to feign a look that lost. As for the rest of it . . .

A curse on both their families? How very Shakespearean and how utterly absurd. Even if Kate and his mother and everyone else believed it, curses had no place in his well-ordered, practical existence. Kate was certainly convinced and admittedly, given all that had happened in her life, he could see why she might be. Her life had been marred by unexpected tragedy, and perhaps it was easier to blame it on something as ridiculous as a curse rather than accept that there was no rhyme or reason to the bad things in life.

Would you take the risk that anyone you cared for would meet with the same fate?

The question lingered in his mind and he still had no answer. Nor was it necessary to have an answer at the moment. After all, the only person he cared for right now was the one person it would be safe to love. If he believed such rubbish.

It was all nonsense, complete and utter nonsense. And nothing was more preposterous than Kate's claim that her loss of memory had been achieved by magical means. The fact that she seemed to believe it was in direct contrast with everything he had thought he knew about her. With the sort of person he had thought she was. Sensible and, well, sane. Still, he ran his hand through his hair, if one accepted a curse as fact it was no more than another step down the road to absurdity to believe in magic as well.

Magic. He snorted in disdain. He certainly didn't believe in either magic or the curse. Everything that had happened to Kate, up to and including her loss of memory, as well as the tragedies that had occurred in his own life could be explained as nothing more than the twists and turns of life. Coincidences, even as farfetched as a woman coming up with a silly plan that then plays out, happened in this world. It was as simple as that.

He was not about to let superstitious nonsense dictate who and when he married. True, he wanted to marry, wanted to spend the rest of his days with the woman he loved. Still, he had never really come close to marrying anyone and when the question of marriage had surfaced tonight, coupled with the imperative nature of the curse, he had felt something akin to panic. As if he were caught in the claws of a trap, or had a noose tightening around his neck or fingers poised to strangle the breath out of him. As if his life, his very future was no longer in his hands. It was the height of irony that he alone among his friends had never thought of marriage as something to be feared but apparently, fear it he did.

Admittedly, he had already thought about a future with Kate. And yes, he had feelings for her. And perhaps indeed what he felt was love. But that was precisely why it was necessary that he leave all this behind and consider everything in a calm and reasonable manner. How he felt and what he wanted. He was, after all, a calm and rational man.

Kate might be right, he might well be a coward. But he couldn't determine anything here because every time he looked into her green eyes he was lost.

Lost. He blew a long breath. Maybe he was under some sort of spell. Or maybe he was indeed in love. And maybe love was what he feared.

Worst of all, he didn't know exactly who he might be in love with.

Chapter 18

"*Y*ou can't possibly be considering return-ing to London today." His mother swept into the library in a wave of indignation.

"I am not considering it, Mother," Oliver said calmly without looking up from the correspondence spread on the desk before him. Not that in the time he had sat here this morning he had actually seen any of it. Or accomplished anything. Or made any kind of decision. "I intend to leave as soon as the rain eases."

The day had dawned wet and dreary. A steady rain showed no signs of letting up.

"You're running away. Like a frightened rabbit."

"No, Mother, if I was a frightened rabbit I would

be gone by now." He glanced up at her and smiled politely. "I am retreating. Strategically. As any good general would upon finding himself outnumbered with nothing but sanity as his weapon."

"Nonsense, Oliver." His mother seated herself in the chair in front of his desk. "The rest of us are quite sane."

"Sane?" He raised a brow. "My apologies, Mother, but which was the sane part? The curse or the magic?"

"*Most* unbecoming," she said under her breath. "I noticed you did not appear for breakfast."

"As I shall fail to appear for luncheon."

"And dinner?"

He had avoided Kate thus far today but he could not do so forever. Not if he remained here. "I shall be gone by dinner."

"Even if it continues to rain?" She shook her head in a mournful manner. "It's dangerous to travel in the rain, Oliver. The roads are treacherous and anything can happen. Why, I remember when poor Lord Carlton's carriage slid right off the road in the rain and killed him."

Oliver bit back a grin. "If I recall, Lord Carlton died from lung fever."

"A direct result of his carriage going off the road in the rain."

"It was three months later."

"A slow, lingering death." Mother sniffed. "Cut down in the prime of his life, poor man."

"He was in his eighty-third year."

"And might have had a good many years left had he not decided to travel in the rain. However, you must do what you feel necessary." She unfolded a lace trimmed handkerchief hidden in her hand. "Go to London. In the rain. Risk life and limb." She dabbed at her eyes. "I shall fear for your safety every moment you are away."

He stared in disbelief.

"However, I shall try to carry on without you." Her chin wobbled as if she were holding back tears. "Your father would want me to be brave."

She was good. Very good. He'd never realized it before but Edwina Leighton, Countess of Norcroft, might well have had a successful career on the stage if she had so chosen.

"I'm certain my heart can take the strain . . ."

He burst into laugher. "You are mad."

"Not at all," she said indignantly. "I am simply getting older, which means I am increasingly subject to all kinds of ills including those of the heart." She sighed dramatically. "It might well crack with—"

"Enough." He laughed. "I promise not to travel in the rain. Will that make you happy?"

"What will make me happy is for you to stay right here and resolve all of this with Kathleen," she said, all evidence of her previous dismay now vanished.

"There is nothing to resolve." He shook his head. "I have no intention of marrying anyone to satisfy the conditions of a curse that I consider ridiculous."

His mother leaned forward and met his gaze firmly. "Then marry her because you love her."

"What makes you think I love her?"

"What makes you think you don't?"

"This is precisely why I intend to leave." He blew a long breath. "I cannot reach any kind of sensible decision as long as you and everyone else in this household insists on offering up my . . . my freedom on the altar of superstition."

Her forehead furrowed in annoyance. "You are a stubborn, stubborn man, Oliver. As was your father."

"Thank you." He grinned.

She huffed. "It was not intended as a compliment."

"Mother." He paused. "Do you really wish me to enter marriage for the wrong reasons?"

"Of course not. What I really wish is for you to see the reasons that are in front of your very nose."

"I don't know how I feel," he said simply.

"And I don't think you can determine that in London. I think your leaving is a dreadful mistake." She rose to her feet. "Oliver, I have never seen you do anything truly stupid. I do hope I am not seeing you do so now."

"I'm afraid I cannot guarantee that." He chuckled then sobered. "But I shall not let superstitious nonsense dictate my actions. And it is my life and my decision."

"And your responsibility," she said pointedly.

"Well, I have matters of my own to attend to." She started toward the door. "I am off to pray for rain."

"Mother," he called after her, "You do not look anywhere near your age, you know."

"Yes, darling." She flashed him a wicked grin over her shoulder. "I do know." With that she took her leave.

Perhaps it was unwise to return to London with Dumleavy still at the manor and his mother's desire for adventure. He certainly didn't trust Kate's uncle and he wasn't entirely sure he trusted his mother either. Still, he drummed his fingers on the desk, she was just as capable of making her own decisions about her life as he was.

Was she right? Was he fleeing in fear? Afraid of marriage? Afraid of love? Admittedly he had felt the noose of marriage wrapping around his neck since last night which was odd in and of itself. He had never been afraid of marriage, never especially avoided it. And if true love had evaded him thus far, well, that was the way things happened in life. Regardless, if he knew nothing else he knew he couldn't sort out his feelings here.

A knock sounded at the door. Before he could answer, it was flung open and his cousins stormed into the room like the force of nature they were.

"Oliver," Belle started. "You can't possibly be leaving."

"Please, come in," he said in a dry manner.

"You can't go now." Sophie stared at him. "Not now that you know everything."

"We find it all quite romantic." Belle's eyes shone with excitement. "The curse and magic and all of it."

"Even I find it romantic," Gen said with a shrug. "Even though I didn't trust her in the beginning."

Sophie scoffed. "And you trust her now?"

"Mr. Berkley trusts her," Gwen said in a lofty manner. "And I trust Mr. Berkley. He is an excellent judge of character."

Belle crossed her arms over her chest. "Why are you running off, Oliver?"

Sophie shook her head. "It's quite cowardly and not at all what we expected of you."

Gen stared. "Well?"

"Not that it is any of your concern, but I am not running off. I am returning to London to come to some sort of rational decision about what I should do."

"You mean whether or not you should marry Lady Kathleen to end the curse?" Sophie said.

"Yes, I suppose that is indeed what I mean." He shook his head. "I am not about to be herded into marriage because of something as ridiculous as a curse."

Gen studied him. "So if there was no curse, would you marry her?"

"I . . ." It was a question that hadn't occurred to him. "I suppose that's another issue I need to consider."

Gen's eyes widened. "You have to *think* about that?"

All three sisters stared at him as if he were insane.

"Yes, I have to think about it. And, as none of this has anything to do with any of you, this discussion is at an end," he said firmly. "Oh, yes." He looked at Gen. "And I am taking Mr. Berkley with me."

Gen stared at him for a moment then nodded. "What a good idea."

"Really?" Oliver pulled his brows together. "You're not upset that he's leaving?"

"No, no, not at all." Gen waved him off. "Go on, take him."

"I thought you liked him," Oliver said.

"Oh, she does." Belle nodded.

"Quite a lot actually," Sophie added.

"Indeed I do like him. I might well more than like him and I'm finding that rather confusing." Gen sighed. "So it probably is best for him to go."

Oliver narrowed his eyes. "I don't trust you."

"Goodness, Oliver, you are a suspicious sort." Gen shook her head. "I simply think it's unwise to rush into anything as permanent as marriage at my age. I have plenty of time. After all, I am not nearly so old as Lady Kathleen."

"Lady Kathleen is not old," he said sharply.

Gen ignored him. "I am fairly certain I have fallen in love with Mr. Berkley which frankly plays havoc with intelligent thought."

Oliver stared. "That's very . . . sensible of you."

"Thank you," Gen continued, "I don't think a decision this important should rely simply on feelings of the heart. After all, my heart has never been engaged before and I am not at all sure I can trust it."

Oliver raised a brow. "You can't?"

"Of course not." Gen nodded. "I need time and distance as well to determine if Mr. Berkley is truly what I want. I have begun making a list of his good points and his faults. Would you like to see it?"

"Thank you, but no."

"I need to make a well-considered decision about my future and I simply can't do it with Mr. Berkley underfoot," Gen said firmly.

"I can see where that might be difficult," Oliver said slowly.

"Very nearly impossible." Gen sighed. "He is entirely too . . . tempting."

Oliver winced. "Tempting?"

Belle nodded. "Irresistible."

Sophie shrugged. "Utterly delicious."

"Then it is indeed a very good thing that he is leaving. Now then." He waved them toward the door. "If you don't mind, I have things I would like to accomplish before I go."

"We'll leave you be but we think it's a dreadful mistake for you to leave the manor," Sophie said, heading toward the door.

Belle followed a step behind. "We think you should marry Lady Kathleen at once."

"Thus ending the curse." Gen reached the doorway and paused. "You should consider, Oliver, that even though we are not related by blood something as dreadful as a curse might well extend to relatives by marriage. Surely, you can see it's your duty—"

"Enough," he snapped.

"You needn't be rude about it." Gen huffed and closed the door behind her.

Well that was a surprise. Oliver had fully expected Gen to protest Mr. Berkley's departure. He certainly hadn't anticipated her to be quite so sensible. He was obviously having a good influence on his cousins.

He tried to focus his attention on his correspondence but his mind continued to return to the one question he hadn't thought of. Would he marry Kate if there was no curse? For that too, he had no answer.

Once again a knock sounded at his door. He toyed with the idea of not answering but whoever it was would no doubt track him to the ends of the earth to ensure he had yet another opinion as to what he should do next.

"Come in."

The door swung open and Kate swept into the room, a sheaf of paper in her hands. "Do you intend to avoid me all day?"

He rose to his feet. "And a good day to you too."

She sniffed. "It's not the least bit good thus far. Well? Are you going to answer my question?"

"Avoiding you was my intention, yes."

"Why?" There was a distinct wounded look in her eye. Guilt washed through him. Regardless of the circumstances, he didn't wish to hurt her.

"Why?" he said slowly.

"It was not a difficult question."

"I intend to avoid you because I find it difficult to think in a rational manner when you are around."

"Oh." She sank into the chair in front of his desk. "I didn't expect that. That's very nice."

"I can be very nice." He resumed his seat and leaned back. "What did you expect?"

"I'm not entirely sure." She studied him thoughtfully. "More of last night I suppose." She shrugged. "Accusations of trying to trap you into marriage, charges of insanity, anger out of all proportion to the crime."

"Things always look better after one has had a restful night's sleep."

She raised a brow. "And was your sleep restful?"

"Like a small child's without a care in the world." He smiled pleasantly.

She stared at him then laughed. "You're lying. You slept no better than I did."

"Oh?" He adopted an innocent manner. "You did not sleep well?"

"No, I scarcely slept at all. And I slept alone which is not at all what I had . . . *expected*."

"It seems life is full of the unexpected these days."

"Indeed it is. I did not expect . . ." She stared at

him for a long moment. "Do you still plan to return to London?"

"As soon as the rains end."

"I see." She thought for a moment. "It doesn't seem right, that I should chase you out of your home—"

"You're not chasing me."

"That I should frighten you away—"

"I am not the least bit frightened."

"Actually, I feel quite badly about this. I should be the one to leave."

"Well, if you wish—"

"And yet I shall remain. Your mother has invited us to stay until the end of the month." She met his gaze directly. Resolve shone in her eyes. "I will not give up, Oliver. I have found you and I do not intend to lose you."

There it was again. The distinct sense of a trap closing around him. "You don't have me."

"But I should. It's fate, destiny, a match five hundred years in the making."

"You're just as mad as the rest of them."

She laughed. "That's entirely possible."

She was delightful when she laughed. No, she was delightful always. A reluctant smile curved his lips.

"However, as the very mention of the curse or magic, and I see now, fate tends to make the muscle on the side of your jaw"—she tilted her head, studied him then pointed to the left side of his face—"that one, right there, twitch—"

"I do not twitch." Damnation, she was going to make him laugh in spite of himself.

"Oh, you do when you're angry. You did a great deal of twitching last night. As I was saying, since I prefer to avoid any twitching on your part—"

He surrendered and laughed. "I do not twitch."

"And as you value things of a rational nature, I thought we could discuss our circumstances in a rational manner without mention of anything of an *unusual* nature."

"I'm not sure I understand," he said slowly.

"Nor should you." She smiled in a pleasant manner. What was the woman up to? She folded her hands on top of the papers in her lap. "Oliver, you are not averse to marriage. Indeed, you are apparently quite amenable to the idea."

He narrowed his eyes. "Did my mother tell you that?"

"She didn't need to, you've said it yourself. And goodness, everyone knows it." Amusement flashed in her green eyes. "Why, hardly anyone wagered on you to win."

"Wagered on me?" He stared in confusion. What on earth—abruptly the answer struck him. "You know about the tontine. How?"

"I shouldn't tell you," she said in a lofty manner. "It will only make you twitch."

"I shall endeavor to control myself," he said wryly.

"Excellent." She paused to collect her thoughts. "I consider myself every bit as sensible and rational as you consider yourself. So I certainly wouldn't have come to England to marry a man without knowing something about him nor would my family expect me to do so. My grandmother arranged for an investigation as to your background and I received a complete dossier upon my arrival in London."

"I see," he said slowly. "That's how you knew I was never much of a scholar."

"Oh well, Oliver, that was fairly—" She favored him with a bright smile. "Yes, of course."

He nodded at the papers in her hand. "Is that it?"

"No, this is something entirely different." Her brows drew together. "But you're not twitching. I thought surely you would be twitching by now."

"Admittedly, I find the idea of having my life reduced to a dossier annoying, even insulting. One likes to think one's life is too complicated to be summarized in a handful of papers." He thought for a moment. "Although I admit it is quite sensible."

"I thought so." She paused for a moment. "As I was saying, you are not opposed to marriage. Therefore I am . . . applying, as it were, for the position."

"What position?"

"The position of your wife."

"I was not aware I was seeking applicants," he said slowly.

"Perhaps not by placing an advertisement, but you are looking for a wife. You always have been."

"Perhaps but—"

"Goodness, Oliver, you weren't even pleased that you had won that silly wager." She paused. "Why you gave the coins you had won away at the first opportunity."

He stared at her. "Your investigator did an excellent job."

"That's neither here nor there at the moment. However, it seems to me that, as I know all the details of your life, it's only fair that you know all the details of mine." She tossed the papers in her hand onto his desk. "Last night, I compiled a dossier of my own about myself."

"You did?" He paged through the papers. "It appears quite extensive."

"As I said I couldn't sleep." She shrugged. "There before you are all the details of my life. You already know a fair amount. I am indeed well educated. You know I speak French but I also speak a smattering of Italian and Spanish. I have traveled but not extensively and I should dearly love to travel more. My lineage is noble and most respectable—"

"Given that your relations are all mad," he said under his breath.

"Now, now, Oliver we agreed not to discuss matters that are not of a sensible nature."

"I don't recall—"

"To continue, you are aware of my skill with bow and arrow as well as at croquet and I do enjoy games of golf whether that is indeed appropriate for a woman or not. I am, in addition, an excellent hostess. I have the skills to manage a household and have been trained since childhood to assume a proper position in life. That said," she smiled, "I am eminently suitable to be next Countess of Norcroft."

He stared. "Are you?"

"Oh, and I have a sizable fortune as well."

"Still," he chose his words with care. "There's more to selecting a wife than," he waved at the papers in front of him, "mere qualifications."

"Of course there is. Oliver." She met his gaze firmly. "When we didn't know who I was, I thought we got on rather well together didn't you?"

"When I wasn't being suspicious of you and you weren't slapping me—"

"I only slapped you once and you deserved it. I daresay it will never happen again. Probably." She grinned then sobered and drew a deep breath. "I didn't note this in my dossier, but you should also know the other night was, well, I would use the word *magic* but I don't want you to twitch. I thought it was . . . wonderful."

"As did I."

"And there too I thought we were perfectly suited."

"Yes, well . . ." He gestured at her dossier and forced a collected note to his voice. "I shall take this with me to London and give it due consideration."

"You're still going to go then?"

He nodded. "I think it's best."

"Oliver." She rose to her feet, braced her hands on his desk and leaned toward him. "I don't think I've ever met a man quite as stubborn as you."

He stood. "My mother says I take after my father in that respect."

"I find it most charming." Her voice was low and distinctly seductive. "Really quite endearing."

He swallowed hard. "I have his eyes too."

Her gaze locked with his. "A blue so deep one could lose one's soul in them."

"Did my mother say that?"

"No, Oliver." She smiled a slow inviting smile. "I did."

His breath caught. "Are you trying to seduce me again?"

She raised a brow. "Is it working?"

Yes. "No." It was all he could do not to grab her and pull her across the desk and into his arms. Into his life. "Perhaps I am my mother's idiot son after all," he murmured.

"Perhaps you are," she said softly, then sighed and straightened. "Do what you must, Oliver. As will I."

She turned and before he could say another word, left the room.

He sank back down in his chair.

He was exactly like his cousin. Staying here with temptation so close at hand was not conducive to making good decisions. And Kate was very nearly everything he'd ever wanted. Had he waited for love all these years only to lose it now? Still, if one accepted magic, curses, even fate, could one be sure one's feelings were real and not influenced by unseen forces? And for a man who indeed did want marriage, why on earth did the very thought now fill him with panic?

But was it marriage that made his throat tighten or was it love?

Chapter 19

"**H**ollinger." Oliver strode down the corridor toward the front door, Berkley trailing behind him. The length of his stride and the clipped note in his voice befit his foul mood. This was not the day to cross the Earl of Norcroft. "I shall be taking a carriage back to London today."

It was already nearly noon, the rain had at last stopped. It was a full day's drive back to London by carriage and Oliver was determined to get on the road. He had spent all day yesterday avoiding nearly everyone in the household, as well as reassuring himself that he was doing the sensible thing by leaving. Even if he wanted to marry Kate, and he still didn't know the answer to that, he wasn't about to be forced into it.

"Send word to the stables if you please."

Again last night he had scarcely slept a wink. He had, however, read Kate's dossier several times and had come to the reluctant but inescapable conclusion that she was indeed perfect for him. Although he had suspected it before she'd regained her memory, the details of her life confirmed it. She was everything he'd ever wanted.

It's fate, destiny, a match five hundred years in the making.

Utter nonsense.

"I am sorry, my lord," Hollinger said coolly. "But I'm afraid that's not possible."

Oliver stopped in his tracks. "What do you mean it's not possible? How can it not be possible?"

"There are no carriages available, sir."

Oliver drew his brows together in confusion. "No one has gone anywhere. Indeed, we've had no departures at all. By my count there should be at least three."

"There are, my lord, however," the butler paused, "they have no wheels."

"No wheels?" Oliver said slowly. "How can they have no wheels?"

"They were removed for repairs yesterday, sir. With the rain, it was thought to be an excellent time to take care of any problems."

"That makes a certain amount of sense I suppose."

He didn't especially want to ride a horse all the way back to London, but he had always thought well on horseback. And he had a great deal of thinking to do, even with Berkley beside him. "Very well then, Hollinger, if you would have horses saddled for us."

"I am sorry, sir." Hollinger shook his head. "That's not possible either."

Oliver narrowed his eyes. "And why not?"

"They're being reshod, sir."

"All of them? At the same time?"

"It seemed a good idea, sir. The rain and all."

Oliver narrowed his eyes. "And whose good idea was it?"

Hollinger hesitated. "Lady Norcroft suggested it, sir."

"Yes, of course. I should have known." Oliver willed himself to stay calm. After all, this was not Hollinger's doing. "She has gone to a great deal of trouble."

Hollinger wisely held his tongue.

"She needn't have had the wheels removed, you know. Simply incapacitating the horses would have done the trick."

"Trick, my lord?"

"Never mind." Oliver grit his teeth and wondered if his muscle twitched.

"Perhaps we should delay our departure then, sir," Mr. Berkley said hopefully.

"Both horses and carriages should be available tomorrow," Hollinger said. "Or possibly the day after."

"Mr. Berkley and I will walk into the village then and take the train."

"That will be difficult, sir."

"Why," Oliver snapped.

"The bridge at the foot of the drive over the river has been damaged, probably by the rain. Apparently several planks have fallen into the water and there are now gaping holes," Hollinger said. "It's not safe for horse or carriage or man today, sir. However, I have arranged for repairs. Unfortunately, they cannot begin until later today. Or possibly tomorrow—"

"Or the day after?"

Hollinger nodded.

"See to it that it is taken care of today." Oliver clenched his jaw, surely he was twitching at this point. "Is the boat that is usually kept tied to the bridge still in place?"

"I believe so, sir," Hollinger said slowly.

"Excellent. Then Berkley and I will row across the river, walk to the village, and take the train."

"You do realize there is only one train, my lord."

"I do indeed. Therefore we should be on our way."

"Do you wish me to have a footman accompany you to carry your bags, sir?"

"No, we have but one bag apiece. I daresay we are more than capable of carrying them."

"I would be happy to carry your bag, sir." Eagerness sounded in young Berkley's voice.

"I am not so old that I can't carry my own bag,

thank you," Oliver said in a sharper tone than he had intended.

"No sir, of course not, I didn't mean . . ."

"Lady Kathleen is in the parlor, my lord," Hollinger said. "If you wish to bid her farewell."

"That's not necessary. I shall be back in a few days at any rate."

"Of course, sir."

Oliver narrowed his eyes. "I'm not fleeing, Hollinger, if that's what you think."

"I would never think such a thing, my lord," Hollinger said coolly. "You are strategically retreating to a safe haven where you can determine if your familial duty requires marriage to break a curse you consider nonsense or whether you should follow your heart. Does that sum it up, sir?"

Oliver stared. "You're very good, Hollinger."

"Yes sir."

"Come along then, Mr. Berkley." Oliver picked up his bag and started for the door, opened immediately by a waiting footman. Oliver and Berkley took their leave and walked down the few broad steps to the drive.

Oliver started off and took but a bare step away from the house. Without warning, a slate from the roof shattered at his feet with a loud crack, missing him by mere inches.

He jumped back. "What on earth—"

Another two fell in quick succession sounding remarkably like shots from a gun.

"Are you all right, sir?" Mr. Berkley said quickly.

"Bloody hell, that was close. And decidedly odd." Oliver gazed upward at the roof. "We had extensive repairs done on the roof just a few months ago."

"Perhaps we should stay sir." Unease sounded in the young man's voice.

"Why?" Oliver shook his head. "Obviously the stone thackers simply left a few unsecured slates that were washed to the edge of the roof by the rain. I would think anything that was going to fall has now done so. I see no reason to stay."

"One might wonder, sir, if one believed in superstitious nonsense, which of course I don't," Mr. Berkley added quickly, "if perhaps this wasn't some sort of, well, of a sign that we should delay our departure."

"You have an excellent point, Mr. Berkley. If indeed one believed in superstitious nonsense, one might see a slate missing one's head by mere inches as a sign of sorts. But as we are agreed in that neither of us do hold such beliefs, we shall continue on. However, I have changed my mind." Oliver tossed his bag to the younger man. "You may carry this."

"I should be happy to, sir."

Oliver bit back a grin. There was something to be said for having a young man around who was eager to curry favor with the family of the young woman he was smitten with. Still, Oliver's mood darkened, he did wish Mr. Berkley hadn't brought up the idea of a sign. In and of themselves, the slates falling were not significant, but coupled with the rain, the disabling of the horses and carriages, and the damaged bridge, and one might indeed think a power greater than his mother had had a hand in it and preferred that he remain at the manor. If one wished to surrender to such superstition, which he had no intention of doing.

They reached the bridge and it was indeed impassable. Blast it all, the structure was old and probably well past its prime. Originally completely made of stone, it had collapsed when his father was a boy and rebuilt using the stone foundation and a wooden decking. And periodically it required attention. That it needed repair now was nothing but yet another coincidence.

For most of the year, the river itself was shallow and slow moving and, in truth, more of a wide stream than a river, but today it lived up to its name. The boat was indeed still tied to the bridge and crossing the mere fifteen feet or so to the far bank shouldn't be at all difficult.

"Go on, get in." Oliver grabbed the rope that secured the boat and began working at the knot. It was wet and far trickier than it appeared.

Berkley looked into the boat. "But there's water in the boat, sir."

"Of course there's water in the boat," he snapped. "It's been raining."

Berkley shook his head. "It doesn't look safe to me."

"Nonsense," Oliver muttered, the knot beginning to loosen. "It's perfectly safe. It's a short row to the other side. We'll be across in no time." The knot gave at last. Oliver untied it and tossed the rope into the boat. "There," he said with satisfaction. At least something was going as it should today. "Now, get in."

"Yes, sir." Reluctance sounded in the young man's voice but he tossed the bags into the boat and clambered in after them.

Oliver straddled the space between the bank and the boat then deftly hopped in, just as he had always done. His foot splashed in a good inch of water. Still, that was to be expected. The rain and all.

"I'll row." Oliver settled on the wet seat, winced with the unpleasant feel of water soaking through his trousers, and wished, belatedly, that he had thought to bring an oilcloth with him. Well, it couldn't be helped. His pants and shoes would dry on the walk to the village, if it didn't rain again.

He grabbed the oars and pushed away from the bridge.

"Sir," Mr. Berkley said uneasily. "The water is getting deeper."

"It might seem deeper but this waterway is very nearly the same depth all the way across and not very deep as rivers go. It's never been more than waist deep at best. Nothing at all to worry about." Oliver struggled to position the oars against a stronger than normal current. "Can you swim?"

"Yes sir, I can but I would prefer not to at the

moment. And I didn't mean the river." Mr. Berkley paused. "I meant the water in the boat. It's getting deeper."

"It's an illusion." Oliver's attention was focused on pushing away from the bridge and positioning the oars. He'd simply ignored how very wet his feet already were.

"I don't think so."

Oliver looked at the bottom of the boat and grimaced. The water that had come up only about an inch a moment ago had now washed over his ankles and was getting higher. Obviously, the boat was in no better condition than the bridge and the combined weight of the two men was sinking them. It was apparent the boat would be swamped in no more than a minute. At this rate they wouldn't make it as far as the middle of the river. And what had he expected anyway? "Perfect. Bloody well perfect."

Mr. Berkley stood, grabbed their bags and held them out of reach of the rising water. "I think we should abandon ship, sir."

"Careful, Berkley." Oliver cautiously got to his feet and took one of the bags. "I'd prefer not to fall in." Even as he said the words, the level in the boat was fast reaching the level of the river. In a minute or so, they'd be able to step directly out of the boat and onto the river bed. It struck him that if he were standing on the riverbank, watching two men sink slowly into the river, bags held high, it would be most amusing. Pity he wasn't on the bank.

"It seems we have no choice." He glanced at Berkley. "I suggest we jump."

"Very well, sir," Berkley said grimly. "After you."

"It's not that I wish to share this moment with you, but if we don't jump together, the boat will tip and we will both end up under water." He grabbed Berkley's arm. "Come on."

Berkley nodded and without another word they jumped into the river. The water was nearly chest high but both men managed to keep their footing.

"It's a good thing you can swim," Oliver muttered. He kept a grip on Berkley's arm and they struggled to make their way toward the bank.

"It's not the swimming," Berkley said under his breath. "It's the walking."

"I can't allow you to drown, you know. My cousin would never forgive me."

"Funny, sir, I was thinking the same thing about you."

They reached the bank and tossed the bags on the grass, then Oliver assisted Berkley to climb up. The younger man turned, gripped Oliver's hand, and helped pull him out of the water. The two collapsed, flat on their backs, soaked and exhausted, and stared at the dark clouds overhead.

So much for returning to London. "What am I to do now, Berkley?"

"I suggest we go back to the manor."

"That's not what I meant."

"Oh, you're talking about Lady Kathleen."

"Yes, I suppose I am." If one were a superstitious sort, which he was not, one might think everything that happened today was a conspiracy to keep him from returning to London and not mere coincidence. To keep him here to face . . . what? His fate? His future? All could certainly be explained away: the slates were an accident that could be blamed on careless craftsmen, the bridge was already in need of repair, the boat was ancient and should have been replaced years ago. Still, even a rational man might start to question the sheer number of coincidences. Oliver sat up. "Do you think it's magic, Berkley?"

The younger man sat up. "My father once told me love *is* magic, sir."

"No, that's not what I . . . never mind." Oliver scrambled to his feet then extended his hand to Berkley to help him up. "Do you wish to marry my cousin?"

Berkley chose his words with care. "I thought I was expected to ask you, sir."

"Life does not always happen as one expects." Oliver studied the other man. "You should know that. And be prepared for it." He rather wished he'd understood that sooner. What adventure could be had from the unexpected. With a start he realized that Kate had indeed been an adventure. "Well?"

"Yes, sir, I do." Berkley nodded with the eagerness of a young man in love. "Very much sir."

"Why?" A lovely, annoying, amusing adventure.

"Why?" Surprise crossed Berkley's face. "I love her, sir. I can't imagine a life worth living without her in it. I want to see our children, God willing, and their children. And I want her face to be the last thing I see in this world."

"Very good," Oliver murmured.

Berkley hesitated then grinned. "Will she like it do you think? Will it serve?"

"I know I worried that you might go down on one knee at any moment," Oliver said wryly and picked up his bag. "Don't you think she's too young for marriage? Or you are?"

"No, I don't. Besides—" Berkley picked up his bag—"it seems to me, when a man finds the one woman who is right, it scarcely matters what else is wrong." He nodded and started back toward the manor.

Oliver stared after him. The young man certainly had a better head on his shoulders than Oliver had at his age. Perhaps than Oliver did now. He hurried after Berkley.

"I can't simply give my permission, you know."

"I assumed as much."

"I need to know about your income, your prospects, that sort of thing."

"Of course you do." Berkley reached into his waistcoat pocket, pulled out a folded, wet piece of paper and handed it to Oliver. "I made a list of my good points, my faults, my prospects."

"You are well suited for Genevieve." Oliver examined the soggy paper. "It's wet and illegible."

"I should be happy to discuss it with you, sir."

"You don't happen to have made a list of her good points, have you?"

"No sir," Berkley said indignantly. "I have no need to."

"We can discuss it all later I think. For now." He smiled. "I don't see any real reason why I would withhold my permission."

Berkley grinned with relief. "Thank you, sir."

"The final decision is of course up to her but you're right." Oliver nodded. "When a man finds the one woman . . ." He stopped in mid-step.

When a man finds the one woman who is right, it scarcely matters what else is wrong.

"Sir?"

Was he blind? Or was he indeed his mother's idiot son? Kate or Lady Kathleen or whatever she called herself was the one woman who was right. Did it really matter how she had come into his life or why, only that she had? What difference did it make if everyone else believed in a curse or magic and he didn't?

Didn't he want to see their children and their grandchildren?

"Sir?"

Didn't he want her face to be the last thing he saw before he died?

Berkley cleared his throat. "Sir?"

Could he imagine a life worth living without Kate in it?

"Lord Norcroft?"

"No, Berkley," Oliver said firmly. "I most certainly cannot."

"I beg your pardon."

Oliver picked up his pace. "I have been, I don't know, afraid I suppose is the proper word, to see what was right in front of me."

Kate had been an adventure and always would be. His adventure.

"I must thank you, Berkley. You've been a great deal of assistance."

"I couldn't let you drown, sir."

Oliver laughed. "For that too."

They approached the manor. Once again, a scant foot or so from the front steps, a slate whizzed by Oliver's face and exploded at his feet, then half a dozen more.

Oliver froze.

"Sir, are you all right?"

"Yes, Berkley, thank you for asking." Oliver drew a deep breath, glanced upward and yelled. "That's quite enough. I believe."

"In the curse, sir?"

"No, Berkley." Oliver grinned. "In the heart."

Chapter 20

"Hollinger!" Oliver strode through the front door and handed his bag to a footman.

Hollinger appeared so quickly one might have thought one was expected to return. "Yes, my lord?"

"Is Lady Kathleen still in the parlor?"

"Yes, sir."

"And my mother?

"She and Lord Dumleavy are in the conservatory I believe."

"Excellent. Tell them I wish to speak to them in the parlor."

"At once, sir." Hollinger paused. "You do know you're dripping on the carpet."

"I am aware of that, yes. It is not my primary

concern at the moment." He started toward the parlor, then paused. "Oh, and find Miss Fairchild, Genevieve, for Mr. Berkley." He grinned at the young man. "Best of luck, Berkley."

Berkley nodded. "You too, sir."

Oliver started toward the parlor. He wasn't sure exactly what he would say but he wasn't going to worry about it now. The right words would come.

He pushed open the door to the parlor. Kate stood by the far window, gazing out over the back gardens. There was something in the set of her shoulders that looked almost defeated. His heart twisted. Had he done this to her? No, surely it was a trick of the light. He couldn't imagine anything that would defeat Kate. His Kate.

"Kate." He stepped toward her.

She whirled around and her eyes widened. "You've come back."

He nodded.

"Why?"

"I couldn't leave."

A slow smile spread across her face. "Oh, Oliver."

"No." He shook his head. "I mean it was impossible to leave. There are no horses, no carriages, the bridge is impassable, the boat sank and I was nearly killed by falling slate."

Her smile faded. "I see."

"No, you don't." He moved to her. "It wasn't until it was impossible for me to go that I realized." He pulled her into his arms. "I couldn't leave . . . you."

"Oh my." She gazed up into his eyes. "You're . . . you're very wet."

He laughed. "I know." He kissed her fast and hard and then released her. "My apologies."

"Accepted." She framed his face with her hands and kissed him, a kiss long and soft and right. And when she released him, he was hard pressed to catch his breath.

"I gather this means you're not leaving." His mother's voice sounded from the doorway.

"I should hope not," Lord Dumleavy growled.

Oliver stepped away from Kate. "You made it damn difficult for me to do so."

"One does what one can for one's children," his mother said in a lofty manner and seated herself on the sofa. Dumleavy moved to stand behind her. It struck Oliver that the two had formed an alliance of sorts. Whether it was for the purpose of seeing her son and his niece wed or something else entirely he wasn't certain he wanted to know. "You should thank me."

"Thank you?" Under other circumstances he would still be angry at her interference. But as her meddling had at last made him realize what he truly wanted he couldn't muster anything more than amusement. "For disabling the horses and the carriages?"

Mother grinned. "I thought it was brilliant."

He studied her closely. "I'm assuming you had nothing to do with the gaps in the bridge—"

"There are gaps in the bridge?" Surprise colored his mother's face. Oliver wasn't sure he believed it.

"It's impassable." He nodded. "And there are apparently holes in the boat. It sank. With Mr. Berkley and I in it."

"Really?" She traded glances with Lord Dumleavy. "Imagine that."

Oliver narrowed his gaze. "Mother."

"Goodness, Oliver, you needn't look at me like that. By the way, do you realize you're dripping on the carpet?"

"Do you realize I could have drowned?"

"Nonsense." She huffed. "The river has never been very deep and you've always been an excellent swimmer. But I assure you I had nothing to do with the bridge or the boat."

"He might as well blame her for the rain as well," Kate's uncle said under his breath.

"I would if I thought it possible," Oliver said.

"I will confess to making sure there were no horses or carriages available but the rain was in the hands of a far greater power than I." She paused. "Still, I am rather proud of the falling slates."

Oliver stared. "You were responsible for the slates? What? Did you crawl out on the roof?"

"That would be extremely foolish." She waved away his comment. "I simply took the time to go through some of those family papers in the attic as you should have done years ago." She glanced at Kate. "I discovered very old references to the curse as well as evidence that yours is not the only family to occasionally toy with"—she aimed a pointed look at her son—"magic."

"Perfect," Oliver muttered, all sense of amusement gone.

"Therefore, as there was a precedent and certainly a need, I thought I might try my hand at"—she raised her shoulder in a casual shrug—"a spell."

Oliver groaned. "Good Lord."

Mother directed her words to Kate. "Your uncle helped me, dear. He's very good at this."

"Uncle." Kate turned stricken eyes to Dumleavy. "You too?"

"When faced with an army one cannot defeat, one needs to ensure at the very least, equal force," Dumleavy said.

Kate's brow furrowed. "What?"

"It seemed to me that if all the women in my family were pursuing the magic arts, I'd best look into it." The Scotsman grinned. "If only for protection."

Kate stared at him. "But it never has worked for them."

"Nor has it ever worked for me. But perhaps." His eyes twinkled. "It was not the right time."

"You're mad. All of you." Oliver turned an angry glare on Kate. "He's corrupted her, you know."

"Nonsense." Kate bristled. "He taught her a . . . a parlor trick. It's nothing more than that."

"That parlor trick came bloody close to killing me. It missed me by inches. Twice!"

"Well, if it missed you, they didn't do it right, did they?" Kate said sharply.

"I do apologize if the slates came too close," his mother said. "It's not an exact science you know."

"It's not a science at all!"

His mother ignored him. "It was meant as nothing more than a warning shot across the bow as it were. To keep you from leaving and bring you to your senses."

"It took being sunk in the river to do that."

His mother raised her chin. "I am not to blame for that." She paused. "I didn't think of it."

"That's something at any rate. And mind you, I do not believe magic is responsible for the slates either. There is a rational explanation for everything that has happened today." Although the sheer number of coincidences was beginning to strike even Oliver as too convenient. Still, it scarcely mattered at the moment. He ran a hand through his wet hair. This was not at all how he thought this would go. Kate should be in his arms by now, not glaring at him as if he were . . . unreasonable. He drew a steadying breath. "Kate."

She raised a brow.

"Is there anything magical in the way I feel about you?"

She crossed her arms over her chest. "I should think it's quite magical. It's supposed to be."

"No, I mean have there been any spells cast?"

He met her gaze and held his breath. "Any charms concocted? Any parlor tricks?"

She straightened her shoulders. "No."

"Mother?"

"Another excellent idea but again, one I didn't think of so the answer is no. I certainly haven't done anything." She shook her head. "Dislodging a few slates from the roof is the only spell I've tried." Mother cast a puzzled glance at Dumleavy. "Twice?"

Dumleavy shrugged.

"What do you mean by twice, Oliver?" his mother asked slowly.

"Twice. I mean two times. The slates fell once when I was leaving and again when I returned," he said impatiently. "The second time was unnecessary by the way. I had already decided what to do."

Mother traded glances with Lord Dumleavy. "Twice was not intended."

"Perhaps you don't know your own power," the older man said in an off-hand manner that belied the uneasy look in his eyes.

Oliver ignored them both, moved to Kate, and took her hands. "I know the circumstances are not the least bit romantic and I should get down on one knee but I am wet and chilled and I have waited too long already. I don't believe in the curse but I am grateful that it brought you into my life. And I think any talk of magic is absurd save for the magic I see in your eyes. In spite of the fact that we may well disagree on all of that, Kate," he drew a deep breath, "will you marry me?"

"Oliver." She stared at him for a long moment then shook her head slowly. "I don't think I can."

Shock coursed though him. "What?"

She pulled her hands from his and turned to his mother. "You had nothing to do with the bridge or the boat or the slates falling a second time?"

His mother shook her head. "No."

"Uncle?"

"Not I."

Kate looked at Oliver and fear shone in her eyes. "You could have drowned. You could have fallen through the bridge. The slates could have killed you."

"But they didn't. I'm fine. A little wet perhaps—"

"You could still catch your death of cold." She wrapped her arms around herself. "I should have realized it before."

He stared in confusion. "What are you talking about?"

"I should have known better." She paced the room. "This has nothing to do with love."

"I haven't mentioned love," Oliver said quickly. "I intended to but I haven't had the chance."

Kate ignored him. "I should have realized what might happen as soon as I knew I loved you."

Oliver grinned. "You love me?"

"Kathleen," Lord Dumleavy said. "What are you thinking, lass?"

"It's the curse, Uncle." She stared at Dumleavy. "Don't you see? It won't be ended if I marry Oliver."

"But aren't those the terms of the curse? That the families have to join in marriage?" Mother said. "You're the last of your line just as he is the last of his. There is no one else to end it."

Kate chose her words with care. "The original match, the one that started all this, was for duty and responsibility. They never wanted to be together. Marriage for them was a sacrifice."

"I certainly don't consider marriage to you a sacrifice," Oliver said quickly.

"And therein lies the problem." Kate shook her head. "The curse, the real curse is that the marriage that was to join our families together five hundred years ago was for duty not love. Love would have made it perfect. It would have been what they wanted and not a sacrifice at all. Now, marriage with love won't end the curse. Only sacrifice will end it."

"But I don't believe in the curse!"

"It doesn't matter what you believe. Don't you see?" Kate shook her head. "The bridge, the boat, the slates falling a second time, perhaps even the fact that your mother's spell worked the first time, it wasn't to keep you here, it was a warning."

"I don't believe that," Oliver said staunchly. "I won't believe it."

"I'll not marry you if I cannot love you and it's

impossible for me not to love you. But I will not be the cause of your death."

"That's absurd, you're talking about a curse, something that doesn't exist."

"One man who loved me died for it. Three more who might have loved me died as well. I will not take that chance with your life."

"Very well then." He had to think of something. He couldn't let it end this way. "What if we admit there is a curse. If we don't marry, the curse won't be broken."

"And if we do you'll die in some horrible, ridiculous way."

"What happened to marry the Englishman, break the curse?"

"I'm not supposed to love the Englishman!" She shook her head. "It's an endless circle. Oliver. There is no answer. No way to resolve this. It is a most efficient curse."

He stared in disbelief. "There has to be a way out of this."

"I wish there was." She gazed at him for a long moment. Tears glistened in her green eyes. His heart cracked.

"But if we don't marry terrible, dreadful things will happen."

"My darling Oliver." She swallowed hard. "They already have." Kate drew a calming breath and turned to her uncle. "We should leave as soon as possible."

"It might be a few days," Mother warned.

"That cannot be helped, I suppose." Kate started for the door. "I shall remain in my rooms until then."

"Kate." Oliver stepped toward her.

She paused in the doorway but did not turn around.

He moved closer. "I don't believe my life is at risk but even if it is, I don't care." He rested his hands on her shoulders and resisted the need to pull her close and tell her all would be well. "I would rather live a short time with you than an entire lifetime without you."

"And I could not bear to lose you and live the rest of my days knowing your death was because of me." She shrugged out of his grasp and left the room.

He stared at the door. For a long moment no one said a word.

"When we leave," Dumleavy said at last, "I would very much like for your mother to come with us."

Oliver turned. "Why?"

His mother stared at Dumleavy. "To Scotland? I've never been to Scotland. What a lovely adventure a visit would be."

"Not as a visitor," Dumleavy said slowly, "as my wife."

"No," Oliver said without hesitation.

"Does no one in this house know how to propose properly?" Mother huffed.

Dumleavy chuckled then knelt on one knee and took her hands. "Edwina, you have touched something in my heart I did not know could be touched again. I should dearly like to spend the rest of my days having adventures with you."

"No." Oliver glared. "You scarcely know one another."

"Oliver." His mother shot him a firm look. "This is my proposal if you don't mind."

"I promised Father I would look after you."

"And I promised your father I would take care of you. I think we have both done an outstanding job but the time has come"—she paused as if choosing the right words—"for me to decide what's best for my life. My apologies if that is selfish."

He stared at her and wondered why he hadn't noticed before. Since Dumleavy's arrival his mother had seemed, well, happy, not that she'd ever seemed especially unhappy. Still, at this moment, she was radiant. He'd obviously been far too involved in his own affairs to pay any attention. He shook his head and smiled. "Not at all. Mother." He nodded at the older man. "You have my approval, Dumleavy."

"I don't recall asking for it, lad," Dumleavy said. "Edwina, you've not answered my question."

"Didn't I? And I thought I had." She favored Dumleavy with a brilliant smile. "I should dearly love to be your wife." She leaned forward and kissed him. "To share your adventures and your magic."

"It might never work again, you know."

"That's not the magic I meant."

He chuckled. "Can I get up now?"

She laughed. "Yes, dearest Malcolm, you can."

"Good." Dumleavy rose to his feet with a wince. "Now that that's settled." He met Oliver's gaze. "What are you going to do about Kathleen?"

"I don't know." A knot clenched in his stomach. "But I do not intend to give her up without a fight." He sank into a chair and tried to think. "It's pointless to try to convince her the curse doesn't exist."

Dumleavy settled into another chair. "A dead husband and three dead suitors tend to make even a sensible woman believe in something she might otherwise find absurd. Kathleen's always been a sensible lass."

"Do you believe in the curse?"

"I don't know that it's real," Dumleavy said thoughtfully. "But I don't know that it's not."

"It seems to me, at this point, it only really matters whether or not Kathleen believes." His mother stood, crossed the room to the whisky decanter and poured two glasses. She handed one to her soon-to-be husband and another to her son. "Although I must say, I would prefer you not marry her if it means your death."

"It doesn't," Oliver said firmly. "Although the only way to prove it is to marry her and not die."

"There's a risk there," Dumleavy said.

"But well worth it."

Dumleavy swirled the whisky in his glass. "If you survive."

"There is that." Oliver thought for a moment. "Tell me this, Dumleavy—"

"You can start calling me Father if you'd like." Dumleavy grinned.

"I think not." Oliver took a long swallow of the whisky.

"Or Malcolm if you prefer."

"I think I shall check on Kathleen. Oliver, you need to get out of those wet clothes before you catch your death of cold and poor Kathleen thinks it's her fault." Mother looked from one man to the next. "I am counting on the both of you to come up with a solution to this mess." She favored Malcolm with an affectionate glance. "I should feel quite bad if I was blissfully happy when those I love are miserable."

"Then I shall endeavor to make certain you remain happy." Malcolm grabbed her hand as she passed by and drew it to his lips. Mother cast him a private sort of smile, entirely too private and distinctly intimate, and took her leave.

Oliver cleared his throat. "About you and my mother—"

"None of your business, lad."

"I'm not a lad."

"Then you should know better." Dumleavy sipped his drink.

Oliver started to reply and instead took a long drink. "Tell me more about the curse."

Malcolm shrugged. "Not much more to tell. Five hundred years ago, two warring families tried to end the bloodshed by marriage. When it didn't happen, both sides were cursed."

"So, anyone from my family and anyone from your family could have married at any time during the past five centuries and ended this?"

Malcolm nodded. "Probably."

"How would we know?"

Malcolm's eyes narrowed. "How would we know what?"

"When the curse is ended?"

"Oh." Malcolm sipped his whisky. "There's a sign."

"What is it?"

"You won't like it," Malcolm warned.

"There's very little about this that I do like. Go on."

"Very well." The Scotsman tossed back the rest of his drink. "It's lost in the mists of time." He grimaced. "I can see where that's a problem."

"Not at all." Oliver got to his feet, collected the whisky decanter and returned. Malcolm held out his glass and Oliver obligingly refilled it. "My mother said you and she found references to the curse in the papers in the attic. Did you look through all the papers?"

"No, there are trunks full of them, some extremely old. We only managed to look through a handful, we were . . . distracted." Malcolm grinned. "Your mother can be a most distracting woman."

Oliver winced. "I didn't need to know that." He downed the rest of his whisky. "Then there could be reference to this sign somewhere in those papers."

"It's possible I suppose."

"If we can find that, unless the sign is something of a celestial nature." Oliver thought for a moment. "We can make certain the sign appears."

Malcolm studied him. "Go on."

"Then we can convince Kate the curse is broken. Convince her that she was wrong, that love doesn't enter into it. That her willingness alone to marry me was enough to break the curse. Or better yet, that her willingness to give up love to save my life was the required sacrifice."

"It might just work." Malcolm sipped his drink, his brow furrowed in thought. "And if we don't find this sign?"

"If we don't," Oliver leaned closer to the other man, "then we're free to come up with any sign we wish. I'll tell Hollinger not to hurry those repairs. That should give us a good three days."

Malcolm's eyes narrowed. "You're talking about tricking my niece."

"Indeed I am."

"I think it's a grand idea." Malcolm chuckled. "I couldn't have come up with a better plan myself."

"Thank you." Oliver stood. "To the attic then?"

Malcolm nodded and got to his feet. "Let me ask you one question, lad." He hesitated then blew a long breath. "What if you're wrong and she's right? By my guess, that would give you no more than a year before the curse killed you."

"Malcolm, I meant what I said." Oliver met the other man's gaze directly. "I would rather live a year with her than a hundred without her."

For a long moment the men's gazes locked, then finally Malcolm nodded. "You're a good man. I confess I didn't expect that. Not that you've asked for my permission to marry my niece but you have it. You've earned it."

"Thank you."

"To the attic then." Malcolm grabbed the whisky decanter and headed toward the door.

"To the attic," Oliver said and followed after him.

It was indeed a good plan, maybe even a great plan. And hopefully it was a plan that would work.

Chapter 21

$\mathcal{K}$athleen couldn't recall the last time, if ever, she had been this weepy or felt this fragile. She was not a fragile sort of female. Indeed, she had always prided herself on her strength and her sensibility. That she had come to this—this frail, puffy-eyed, creature hiding in her rooms, a virtual shadow of her true character—was almost as upsetting as everything else.

She sat curled up on the chaise in her sitting room, absently shifting the four shillings Oliver had given her in her hand, their weight oddly comforting, and gazed out the window. It was another dreary day, as befit her mood, and once again rain threatened. In the distance, she could see men working on the bridge. They didn't seem to be making much progress but from here it was difficult to determine. Kathleen did wish they'd hurry. The sooner she and Malcolm could leave the better. She hadn't taken a step outside her rooms since she'd left Oliver in the parlor yesterday, she didn't dare, but she wasn't sure how long she could remain in her self-imposed prison before she went stark raving mad.

But what choice did she have? She couldn't see him, not ever again. Leaving him was already hard enough. If she saw Oliver again, listened to his laughter, felt the press of his lips against hers she might well weaken and that would not do. If she believed in the curse—and God help her she did—then she had no choice. She loved Oliver with a passion she had never expected, never dreamed she'd know again. Damn Hannah anyway. If Kathleen hadn't lost her memory she would have guarded against losing her heart.

Or perhaps, if this was a match five hundred years in the making, she would have lost it anyway. It was so blasted unfair. She'd been willing to marry a man she didn't know, a man she didn't love, and an Englishman at that to end the curse and save both their families. Now, she had to sacrifice her family's future as well as her own happiness to ensure the safety of the man she had foolishly fallen in love with.

In many ways, refusing to marry Oliver was selfish of her. She had been devastated when Kenneth had died, but she'd been young and strong with, at that time, no knowledge of the curse. No idea that his death was due to something ancient and unforgiving and irrevocable. Even in the midst of her sorrow then, she'd known there was an entire lifetime ahead of her. But to lose Oliver as she had lost her first husband would be a heartbreak she would never recover from. Better to lose him now and know he was safe and well and living his life.

As for her life, she heaved a heavy sigh, she would go on as she always had. She would live in Dumleavy Castle with her grandmother and Malcolm and Hannah until one by one, they passed on. And then she would be truly alone. There would not be another man in her life nor would there ever be children. She would grow old, finding her only solace in the study of ancient Rome as she herself became ancient and forgotten.

And what of Oliver? Regardless of whether or not he truly believed in the curse, there would always be a doubt in the back of his mind and he was not the type of man to risk a woman's life. He too would end his days alone.

Last night had been especially difficult as tonight no doubt would be and every night she remained under Oliver's roof. Every time the floor boards in the corridor had creaked she had feared or hoped it would be Oliver. Come to try to change her mind or say goodbye or make love to her one last time.

A knock sounded at her door and she got to her feet. It was probably luncheon although she hadn't touched her breakfast. She slipped the coins into her pocket, crossed the room, and pulled open the door.

"Good day, Kathleen," Lady Norcroft said with a pleasant smile and entered, followed by a maid with a tray. "Ellen, put that on the table and take the breakfast dishes." She cast Kathleen a chastising look. "You must eat, my dear. It won't do anyone any good if you waste away to nothing."

"I'm really not hungry but thank you."

"No." Lady Norcroft sighed. "I suppose you're not." She waited until the maid had cleared the dishes and left the room, closing the door behind her. "Now then, my dear, we need to talk."

"Again?" Kathleen mustered a weak smile. Oliver's mother had come to her room shortly after she'd left everyone in the parlor yesterday. The older woman had held her and let her cry, much as her own mother might have done, until Kathleen had thought she had no more tears left. "I wish to apologize for yesterday. I am not the type of person to weep uncontrollably."

"My dear child, yesterday seemed to call for nothing less than uncontrollable weeping. Today, however, is a new day. Do you feel at all better?" Lady Norcroft eyed her critically. "Although I must say you look dreadful."

Kathleen laughed in spite of herself. "Thank you, I feel dreadful."

"Heartbreak will do that to you. Now." She waved at the table. "I do not intend to leave until you eat something."

Kathleen glanced at the offering. There was a platter of cold meats and cheeses, a small bowl of fruit, a basket of breads and a plate of sweets. "That's rather a lot."

"I didn't know what might tempt your appetite." Lady Norcroft shrugged in a helpless manner.

"It looks wonderful." Kathleen seated herself at the table and Lady Norcroft joined her. Kathleen selected a fruit tart and took a bite. It was as wonderful as it looked. Perhaps she was hungry after all. She ate in silence for a few minutes then sat back and studied Lady Norcroft. "If you have come to change my mind, you should know I have no intention of doing so."

"Of course you don't," Lady Norcroft said firmly. "You're not the type of woman to frivolously change her mind because you're not the type of woman to make it up frivolously in the first place."

"No," Kathleen said absently, surveying the scones. Were they are good as the tarts? "I'm not."

"However, I believe I owe you an apology of sorts as well."

"Do you?" Kathleen slathered clotted cream and strawberry jam on a scone. Good Lord, she was famished. She hadn't really eaten since yesterday. "Whatever for?" She took a large bite and savored the sweet, rich flavor. "These are very good."

"Cook does an excellent job. As I was saying—"

"You should try one." She took another bite.

"I have, dear, they are indeed very good. Now then—"

"Oh no," Kathleen said between bites. "Good does not do them justice. They are so much better than—"

"Kathleen," Lady Norcroft snapped. "I am trying to offer my apologies."

"Yes of course." Kathleen took another scone and gestured with it. "Go on."

"I fear I expected too much of you."

"Wha—" Kathleen mumbled then swallowed. "What?"

"You are not behaving at all like the type of person I thought you were. I had thought that you were a woman of strength and intelligence." Lady Norcroft shrugged. "I see now that I was simply hoping you were."

Kathleen stared. "Leaving Oliver takes every once of strength I have. It is the hardest thing I have ever had to do and probably the most intelligent."

"Of course it is, my dear."

"It's not something I want to do."

"No, that's obvious."

"I see no other choice."

"Nor does anyone." Lady Norcroft paused. "Still, one would think a strong, intelligent woman would not give up so easily. Without a fight."

"I did not give up easily." Indignation sounded in her voice. But had she?

"Without exhausting all the possibilities."

"There are no possibilities."

"Without trying to find some sort of solution short of running away."

Kathleen's voice rose. "I am not running away. I am saving Oliver's life."

"And I can't fault you for that, he is my son and I would certainly hate to see him felled by a curse he doesn't believe in." Lady Norcroft paused. "Or any curse for that matter."

"There is no answer." Kathleen shook her head. "No solution."

"Are you absolutely sure?" Lady Norcroft met Kathleen's gaze directly. "Without a doubt?"

"Yes." Was she?

"It seems to me if the details of something like this are lost in the mists of time then the mists of time are where one needs to look for an answer." Lady Norcroft rose, walked to the door, and opened it.

Kathleen stared. "I have no idea what that means."

Lady Norcroft waved a footman carrying a large trunk into the room. "Set it there if you please." The footman set the trunk down then took his leave. "What it means, Kathleen, is that the fight is far from over. If that's what you wish."

Kathleen nodded at the trunk. "What is that?"

"That is a trunk filled with the mists of time. Or some of them anyway."

"You have me at a disadvantage, Lady Norcroft.

Once again, I don't know what you're talking about." Kathleen was almost afraid to hear the older woman's explanation.

"This trunk is one of several in the attic." Lady Norcroft unlatched the trunk and flipped open the lid. "And there you have it, the mists of time."

Kathleen peered into the trunk. It was filled with papers bundled and bound with twine, letters tied with ribbons, ledgers and what appeared to be journals and diaries. "Is this where you and Malcolm found references to the curse?"

"No, we found that in another trunk. There are a good half dozen or more in the attic. Unfortunately, my husband's family, while very good at record keeping, was quite bad at keeping those records in order. Malcolm and I found papers from as recently as forty years ago together with documents from hundreds of years past. We only managed to get through a portion of one trunk before we were . . . distracted." She glanced at Kathleen. "Your uncle can be a most distracting man."

"So I've heard," Kathleen murmured. "You think there might be information about the curse in here?"

"I have no idea." Lady Norcroft shrugged. "But it's certainly worth a look. Oliver and Malcolm seem to think so. Something about a sign they said. They've been in the attic searching through the trunks since yesterday."

"Have they?"

"Oliver has no intention of giving up. He loves you, my dear."

Kathleen stared at the trunk. "What if there's nothing there?"

"Then there are more trunks in the attic."

"What if—"

"Goodness, Kathleen." Lady Norcroft huffed impatiently. "It's better than doing nothing at all isn't it?"

"I can't—"

"Sometimes, Kathleen, all we have is hope." Lady Norcroft's voice softened. "What do you truly want, dear?"

What did she want? Children, a future, living a long and happy life with the man she loved. She met Lady Norcroft's gaze. "Oliver."

"Is he worth fighting for?"

Kathleen stared at the older woman. She was right, of course. Kathleen wasn't behaving at all like herself. She had indeed always been willing to fight for what she wanted. And she had never, ever given up on something she had truly wanted to accomplish, be it scholarly pursuits or archery. She squared her shoulders. "Most definitely."

"Then I suggest you begin." Lady Norcroft turned toward the door. "I have a wedding to prepare for."

Kathleen grimaced. "Lady Norcroft, don't you think that's a bit premature?"

"Oh, I'm not talking about your wedding, dear."

Lady Norcroft smiled. "And you may call me Aunt Edwina if you wish."

Kathleen drew her brows together in confusion. "Aunt—" She gasped with realization. "You and Malcolm?"

Aunt Edwina beamed. "I'll be returning with him to Scotland. I never thought I would be a bride again, you know. I thought perhaps I might still have the occasional adventure with a gentleman, but—"

Kathleen bit back a grin. "Aunt Edwina!"

"Your uncle and I are extremely well suited." She smiled in a decidedly wicked manner, opened the door then looked back. "And do remember, child, there is only one reason to stop fighting." She met Kathleen's gaze directly. "Victory." With that she left the room, snapping the door closed behind her.

Kathleen eyed the trunk for a long moment. She wasn't used to feeling sorry for herself nor was she used to giving up. It was probably pointless. There was, no doubt, nothing of significance there at all. Still, for the first time since she'd realized Oliver remained at risk, something that might indeed have been hope flickered within her.

Very well then. She'd always considered herself something of a scholar and this might well be the most important scholarly pursuit of her life. She selected a packet of letters from the trunk, grabbed the plate of scones as she passed by the table and moved to a ladies' desk that was going to be entirely too small for her purposes. Still, it would have to do. She might need more scones as well.

Kathleen sat down, untied the ribbon, and started to read. It wasn't long before she was immersed in the long and varied history of the Leighton family and the earls of Norcroft. It was most annoying that nothing was in a chronological order but that, Kathleen decided in a no-nonsense manner, only made it more of a challenge.

For the rest of the day and all of the next and a good part of the day after that, Kathleen pored over yellowed documents and fragile letters and journals falling apart with age. As a strictly scholarly pursuit, it was fascinating to catch glimpses of one family through generations and centuries. She went through three more trunks without finding a single reference to the curse.

On the third day, she noticed the sun was at last shining. It scarcely mattered. Her attention, her very future, was confined to this room and these papers. She refused to give up, still it was disheartening. If the bridge was repaired and she was able to leave before she found something of worth, she didn't have much choice but to go.

Kathleen paged through a diary, brittle with age and a passage caught her eye. Dated 1632, it wasn't exactly what she'd been looking for. She had to read it three times before she realized what it meant.

Victory.

Chapter 22

"*H*ollinger?" Kathleen tried to maintain a sedate pace even though she could scarce contain her excitement. "Do you know where Lord Norcroft is?"

"I have apparently misplaced him, my lady," Hollinger said. "However, Lady Norcroft was in the parlor but—"

"Excellent." Kate cast the butler her most radiant smile, turned toward the parlor and fairly burst into the room. "Aunt Edwina!" She stopped short and sucked in a hard breath. "Grandmother?"

"Good afternoon, my dear." Her grandmother, tall and stately and every inch the Countess of

Dumleavy, chuckled. "I gather you did not expect to see me."

"No." Kathleen stared. "You're the last person I expected to see. What are you doing here?"

"Malcolm sent word when he discovered you weren't in London. I thought you might need our help."

"Our help?"

"Good day, Kathleen," a familiar voice said absently.

Kathleen's attention jerked to the woman standing by the window. She narrowed her gaze. "Hannah."

Hannah stared out the window. "That gardener is carrying a potted tree. And he's the second I've seen. How very odd."

"I don't care about the gardeners." Kathleen approached her aunt. "Do you have any idea what you did to me?"

"I daresay I do." Hannah turned from the window and smiled in a satisfied manner. "I took your overly practical and far too sensible nature and replaced it with—"

"You replaced it with nothing! You took my memories, my history! You stole my life!"

"Nonsense," Hannah shrugged. "I simply made it possible for you to follow your heart."

"Follow my heart?" Kathleen stared with disbelief. "It was a dreadful thing to do to me. You're not even sorry are you?"

"First of all, Kathleen, I had no idea if it would

work at all let alone work so well. As for being sorry," Hannah thought for a moment. "No. I'm actually rather proud."

"Proud?" Kathleen turned to her grandmother. "Do you have any idea what she did to me?"

"We've been here for a good half an hour," Grandmother said, "and Lady Norcroft has told us everything. She's gone to find Malcolm." Grandmother chuckled. "That is something I didn't expect but a lovely turn of events nonetheless. I understand you've had an interesting time of it."

"Interesting?" Kathleen nearly choked on the word.

"If you're going to repeat everything we say we shall never get anywhere," Hannah said in a lofty manner.

"Aren't you going to chastise her?" Kathleen stared at her grandmother. "Or shall you leave it to me to strangle her?"

"It's extremely difficult to chastise a woman in her fifty-second year as if she were a child. But if it makes you feel better." Grandmother fixed Hannah with a firm look. "It was not at all right of you, in a moral sense, to do what you did to Kathleen." Grandmother paused. "Although I should like to know exactly how you did it."

Hannah smirked.

"Grandmother!" Kathleen snapped. "It scarcely matters how she did it only that she did."

"Yes, of course. I lost my head for a moment in the excitement of realizing that a spell might actually have worked. It's a first you know. Although I suppose that's neither here nor there at the moment." Grandmother shrugged. "However, all's well that end's well as Shakespeare said."

"It hasn't ended well. Surely Lady Norcroft has told you—" Kathleen stopped. "Did Lady Norcroft tell you everything?"

Grandmother nodded. "It seems to me she left nothing out."

"We heard every *interesting* detail I would say," Hannah added.

"I see." Kathleen considered her grandmother thoughtfully. As far as Lady Norcroft knew, Kathleen intended to save Oliver from the curse by refusing to marry him. If her grandmother was aware of that, and certainly Lady Norcroft would not have left out such an important point, why wasn't her grandmother concerned? Unless of course, she already knew what Kathleen had just discovered. "Grandmother."

"I believe you and I should have a long talk, child," Grandmother said coolly.

"Yes, I believe we should."

"In the garden perhaps?" Grandmother smiled. "It's a lovely day and I understand the gardens here are quite extensive. It is nearly autumn after all, and who knows how many more pleasant days there will be."

"Excellent idea." Kathleen's cool tone matched the older woman's.

A few minutes later they strolled side by side

along the main garden pathway flanked by tall hedges.

"Well?" Grandmother began. "What do you wish to ask?"

"How do you know I want to ask anything?"

Grandmother chuckled. "I raised you, girl. I know when there is something on your mind."

"It's about the curse."

"Ah, yes it would be wouldn't it?"

"You believe in it don't you?"

"You know the answer to that."

"Nonetheless—"

"It would be foolish not to believe in it." Grandmother paused. "Life is full of all sorts of tragedy, Kathleen. Accidents happen, clumsy men tumble off roofs or drown when one wouldn't think it possible. People one loves die too young, others one hopes to love are never born. It's a comfort to believe in a reason, even as unpleasant a reason as a curse, rather than accept the random nature of life." She sighed. "I've never been good at acceptance."

Kathleen chose her words with care. "Then you're saying—"

"Nothing of any particular significance," Grandmother said in a brisk manner and shifted her parasol. "Now then, what do you wish to know?"

"I have been looking through some old papers, documents, diaries, that sort of thing, that have been in Oliver's family for generations." She studied her grandmother closely. "I found an interesting passage in a very old diary."

"About the curse?"

"Not exactly. It appears that in 1632, the illegitimate son of a Leighton married the widowed daughter of an Armstrong. Wouldn't that satisfy the curse?"

"Why yes, I suppose it would."

"Did you know about this?"

"I imagine if he wasn't acknowledged by his family his name would not have been Leighton and, as she was a widow, her name wouldn't have been Armstrong." Grandmother shrugged. "They could have been easily overlooked. In terms of the curse that is."

Kathleen widened her eyes. "You did know about this didn't you?"

"I really can't say. I'm getting very old and my mind . . ." The older woman heaved an overly dramatic sigh. "Wanders."

"Hah! Your mind is as sharp as a tack."

"Don't forget wise," Grandmother murmured.

"If indeed you did know—"

"And I can't remember one way or the other."

Kathleen ignored her. "Then tell me why you encouraged me to believe in it? If it was simply a plot to find me a good match—"

"A match five hundred years in the making," Grandmother said pointedly.

"Don't say that!"

Grandmother smiled in a satisfied manner. "I understand you let him call you Kate."

"That's not the least bit significant." Kathleen waved away the comment.

"When you were nine years old you announced Kate no longer suited and your name was Kathleen. You've permitted no one to call you Kate since except your husband." Grandmother chuckled. "As I said, this is a match five hundred years in the making."

"The only thing that is years in the making is this plot of yours!"

Grandmother shrugged. "One does what one must for those one loves."

Kathleen shook her head. "I still don't understand."

"Nor do you need to." The countess stopped and stared her granddaughter straight in the eye. "Shall we simply say there was a curse and perhaps now there isn't."

"What do you mean perhaps?"

"It seems to me, marriage between our families some two hundred or so years ago would certainly have ended the curse unless of course you are right."

"Right?"

"In that it didn't take marriage itself to end the curse but a sacrifice. As you are willing to sacrifice both your family's future and love to save Oliver, I would think any curse worth the name would be satisfied by that."

"Do you?"

"I do indeed." She nodded firmly. "At this point, if we take the curse as we know it—that simply marriage between families would satisfy it—then it no doubt ended with the bastard son marrying the widowed daughter and you can safely marry Oliver. If you're right—and true sacrifice is required—then again your sacrifice is enough to end it and again you can marry."

"But we don't know."

"Kathleen." Grandmother sighed in exasperation. "In spite of my best efforts, you have grown up to be a practical, sensible, intelligent woman with a good head on your shoulders. You are exactly like your mother and I am very, very proud of you." Grandmother cupped Kathleen's chin, exactly as she had done when Kathleen was a small girl, and stared into her eyes. "There are no assurances in life, my dear child. Hope and love are the only things that can sustain us." She released Kathleen, readjusted her parasol, and continued. "Of course a sign is always nice."

"A sign? What kind of sign?"

"I don't know, it could be anything. That's the awkward thing about signs but we shall surely know it when we see it." They reached the intersection of two pathways and Grandmother stopped and glanced around. "That's what the curse says. There shall be a sign." Grandmother folded her parasol and pointed down the path to the right. "And that, my girl, is a sign."

Kathleen's gaze followed the parasol and she caught her breath.

At the end of the hedge, where only a few days ago, the last blossoms of the season were fading, now flowers bloomed in profusion. There was no rhyme or reason to their arrangement, it was simply a glorious explosion of color, blues and yellows and pinks, all the hues of spring. And all most familiar.

"Imagine that. Spring flowers blooming when it's nearly autumn." Grandmother nodded approvingly. "A sign if ever I saw one."

"Grandmother." Kathleen leaned closer to the older woman and lowered her voice. "Those flowers are all from the greenhouse."

"Yes, well there are signs that a curse has been broken and signs of a man willing to do whatever is necessary for the woman he loves. If I were you, I would accept this as both." She smiled with satisfaction. "And I suspect he's waiting for you."

Kathleen took a step down the path then hesitated. "Do you really think he'll be safe?"

"I do." Grandmother nodded. "Now go."

Kathleen started toward the flowers, the pace of her step increasing with the beat of her heart. There were tulips and hyacinths, daffodils and jonquils and anemones. It looked and smelled like spring, like a beginning, and was nothing short of enchanting. This, indeed, was magic. She spotted a few small flowering trees, a cherry and a dwarf apple. There was probably nothing left in the greenhouse at all. Kathleen noted even a rhodo-dendron in bloom and caught her breath at the wonder of it.

In the midst of it all, Oliver stood studying the display as if trying to decide if it was sufficient. He didn't hear her approach.

She paused. She could certainly tell him she was well aware that he was behind this outbreak of spring. Or not.

"Oliver?"

"Kate!" His face lit at the sight of her and that too was magic. "Look at all this." He waved in a grand gesture. "Why it's amazing."

She bit back a smile. "It is indeed."

"Spring flowers blooming at this time of year?" Astonishment rang in his voice. He was very good. "Why it's—"

"A miracle?"

"Well, yes, that." He paused. "But what I think it really is is . . . a sign."

"A sign?" She adopted an innocent tone. "That we will skip over autumn and winter altogether and go directly to spring?"

"No, no that would be absurd." He chose his words with care. "I think it's a sign that the curse is ended."

"Why would you think that?"

"We found references to the curse in papers in the attic that said there would be a sign when the curse was at end." He shook his head in a somber manner. "I think this is definitely a sign."

"Do you?"

"I do indeed." He nodded firmly. "What do you think?"

"Oh, well." She glanced around. "It is most unusual."

"Yes?"

"And I would say there is no other rational explanation."

"No," he said quickly. "None that I can think of."

"Therefore, it simply stands to reason that this must mean"—her gaze met his—"the curse has indeed ended."

He stared at her for a long moment. "Then there's no longer any reason why you won't marry me?"

Her heart thudded. "None that I can think of."

Relief washed across his face and then joy and he swept her into his arms. "Are you sure?"

She swallowed hard and gazed into his blue eyes. "There isn't a doubt in my mind. Or in my heart."

He grinned. "I love you, Kate."

"And I love you, Oliver."

"And I shall love you every day for the rest of our very long and happy lives." His words were reflected in his eyes and she thought her heart might burst with the joy of it. "I think I loved you from the moment I first saw you lying unconscious in the manor."

She laughed. "And I might well have loved you the moment you gave four shillings to a woman you thought needed them with a wish that they would bring her better luck than they did you."

He narrowed his eyes. "How did you know—"

She grinned. "I really must get a new cloak."

He raised a brow. "You?"

She nodded.

"And did they bring you luck?"

"Indeed they did." She brushed her lips across his. "They brought me you."

With that his lips met hers and she knew without question or doubt that the curse was indeed at an end. And was grateful that it had, in one way or another, whether it had anything to do with her grandmother or whether it was truly fate, brought her to him. And she knew she would live the rest of her days and never tell him that she was certain this sign, this spring, this magic that surrounded them was his doing.

And knew as well, she need never tell this sensible, practical man who didn't believe in silly things like magic or curses, who would surely find a rational explanation, that there had never been rhododendrons in the greenhouse.

Epilogue

Spring 1884

"This is excellent cognac." Warton studied the liquor in his glass in an appreciative manner. "I can't believe you've waited all these years to drink it."

"What I can't believe is that it's taken us this long to be in the same place at the same time," Cavendish said wryly.

Sinclair chuckled. "It does seem whenever I have been in England one or more of you have been out of the country."

"It didn't seem right to open it without you here.

Apparently, gentlemen," Oliver raised his glass, "there is indeed a time and place for everything."

At long last, the four old friends sat together again in their favorite chairs in their favorite club. The facility was little changed, although past due for refurbishing. One might even be able to believe, if only for a moment, that it had been no time at all since they had formed the tontine and had wagered a handful of shillings and this fine bottle of cognac. That it was scarcely longer than yesterday since Oliver had been the last one of them to marry, the last man standing. If, of course, one squinted one's eyes and ignored that there was among them a few more pounds and a bit less hair.

"There never seemed to be an occasion important enough to warrant opening the bottle until now," Oliver said.

"I would say the joining of two of our children in marriage is certainly an occasion." Sinclair nodded. "That too is something I never imagined."

"Life, my friends," Cavendish said in a sage manner that had only come with age, "is full of the unexpected."

"Not to mention adventure." Warton saluted with his glass.

Between them, they had certainly had their share of both adventures and the unexpected. All four were successful as the world judged such things. Indeed, they had all known triumph in business or politics or both. The three Englishmen had all made their mark in Parliament and Sinclair had truly become a captain of American industry. And in the process of building his own fortune, had endowed the rest of them, his investment part-ners, with considerable wealth. In their private lives, each and every one of them had known great happiness and great sorrow, great loss and great love. Such was the way of life.

As for their wives, in spite of the demands of their positions and children, they too had left their mark on the world. Lady Warton had continued her study of orchids and was now a recognized expert in the field at home and abroad. Lady Cav-endish was credited with the co-discovery of a minor comet. She seemed content enough with that, al-though Cavendish never failed to mention that she shouldn't have been made to share the honor and only had to do so because of the stature of the man who claimed the discovery as well. Mrs. Sinclair's travel books had become a necessity for female and male travelers alike and she had kept her hus-band busy discovering the world with her.

Kate had turned her scholarly pursuits toward their families. It had taken her years to decipher and catalogue the papers in the attic as well as similar documents regarding her own heritage. She had compiled it all into histories of both families and was currently working on her third massive vol-ume, which Oliver fully intended to read someday.

She had never asked him if he was responsible for the planting of the spring flowers in the garden, the sign that the curse had ended but he had long suspected she knew the truth. And, even as absurd as he had always thought the curse to be, he had to admit, if only to himself, he had breathed a sigh of relief with every year that passed that he remained on this earth.

There had been no more dabbling in magic, at least as far as he knew, by any of the ladies in his family. The only magic in his life had been, and continued to be, that to be found between a man and the wife he adored who had made his life whole and well worth living.

"Do you see those gentlemen over there?" Warton nodded toward a table in the far corner of the room. There sat four young men, obviously friends, sharing a bottle, deep in jovial conversation. "Do they remind you of anyone?"

"Not at all," Cavendish said staunchly. "There's not an American among them."

Sinclair laughed. "And yet, even from here, one can sense an attitude that seems remarkably familiar."

"In that case, gentlemen." Oliver got to his feet. "As once was our custom, let us propose a toast."

"Excellent idea." Warton nodded and stood, the others followed suit. He held up his glass. "To our young friends in the corner then. May their friendship sustain them through the years to come and last as long as ours."

Sinclair thought for a moment then raised his glass. "May they find the ladies who will make their lives complete and with them the happiness I doubt they suspect exists in this world."

Cavendish paused. "May they have the grace to accept the sorrow in life as well." He lifted his glass. "And may they have the strength to carry on."

"And, gentlemen," Oliver began. "May they know love and adventure and, most of all." He raised his glass. "May they know magic."

In the following pages
you are cordially invited to a tea party
in which the author has invited some of her
favorite characters to discuss all sorts of things.
Join the discussion already in progress . . .

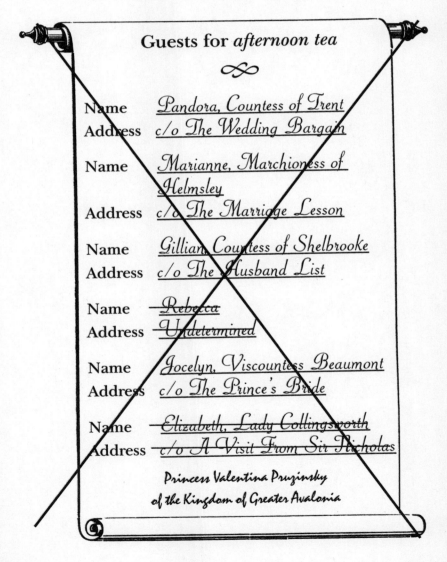

Guests for *afternoon tea*

Name *Pandora, Countess of Trent*
Address *c/o The Wedding Bargain*

Name *Marianne, Marchioness of
Helmsley*
Address *c/o The Marriage Lesson*

Name *Gillian, Countess of Shelbrooke*
Address *c/o The Husband List*

Name ~~*Rebecca*~~
Address ~~*Undetermined*~~

Name *Jocelyn, Viscountess Beaumont*
Address *c/o The Prince's Bride*

Name ~~*Elizabeth, Lady Collingsworth*~~
Address ~~*c/o A Visit From Sir Nicholas*~~

*Princess Valentina Pruzinsky
of the Kingdom of Greater Avalonia*

Continued from Secrets of a Proper Lady . . .

" $\mathcal{I}$ don't know what I expected." I looked from one fictional face to the next. "Each and every one of you is exactly as I wrote you." From Marianne Shelton Effington (Marchioness of Helmsley) to her sister-in-law Gillian Effington Marley Shelton (Countess of Shelbrooke), to Gillian's cousin, Pandora Effington Wells (Countess of Trent), to last, but never least, Princess Valentina Pruzinsky, of the Kingdom of Greater Avalonia, they gazed at me with a shared look of expectation. A look known only to fictional characters hoping for something from their author. I ignored it. "I shouldn't be the least bit surprised that this whole afternoon has gotten completely out of my control."

It had started innocently enough when I had invited some of my favorite heroines to join me for tea in my living room. Which isn't nearly as weird as it sounds. Sure, they're fictional and I'm real but, aside from that, we have a great deal in common. Maybe at first glance it might not seem like wealthy, nineteenth-century British aristocrats have anything in common with a former television reporter who lives smack dab in the middle of a country only one of them had ever seen. Admittedly, they thought my lack of servants was shocking, the size of my house pitifully small, my inability to properly pour tea pathetic, and they would never, ever say *smack dab*. Okay, so maybe we didn't have much in common but I had made them up, they were my fictional creations, and I thought it would be fun if they visited my world for once. After all, I lived in theirs fairly often. But it really hadn't worked out.

One of my guests, Rebecca, had faded away because I had never written a book for her and the others were kind of awful about what they saw as a failure on my part. Another, Elizabeth, had left because she didn't want to hear her mother and her aunts talk about men. I had invited these characters at the point I knew them best—at the end of their stories. That made the Elizabeth visiting my house older than her mother and more than a little uncomfortable. I can see where that might be a problem. Then there was the princess who had popped in because the other ladies wanted to talk to someone who had more experience with men than they had. Her arrival had prompted a third guest, Jocelyn, to leave in an indignant huff because Valentina had once kind of, casually, nearly had her killed.

It all went downhill from there. Valentina, who I have pretty much reformed by the way, started insisting on her own book. She has always been a secondary character and she's not happy about it. And since Jocelyn had called her a witch, Valentina jumped on the idea of having magical powers. She wanted a wand too. Well, before I knew it, my other guests, all sane and charming and intelligent women, were insisting on a new book in which they'd all have magical powers and wands and, oh yeah, a book of spells.

Clearly, this had not turned out as I had expected. Now I have to say, I usually give really good parties. People have a great time at my parties. Sometimes, I have themes. You know, Evening in Italy, Watch the SuperBowl commercials, Dress like a pirate (not my best idea—too many eye patches and not nearly enough peg legs but that's a different story), that sort of thing. But I have to admit, having ladies who don't exist for tea might not have been as brilliant as I had originally thought. And, at this point, the party was over.

I drew a deep breath. "As much as this has been fun, in an awkward and uncomfortable sort of way, I think I've had enough. More than enough."

"As have I." A distinctly male chuckle sounded behind me and, just like in my books, an actual shiver of excitement raced up my spine. Even though I had never heard his voice in anything other than my head before, I knew exactly who it was. I didn't even have to look.

Crown Prince Alexei of the Kingdom of Greater Avalonia had a voice deep and rich and sexy, with just the right hint of accent to add a touch of mystery. That voice was enough to make any normal woman melt. I had written it really well.

"I cannot believe this." Valentina huffed and addressed her cousin. "What are you doing here?" Then her glare shifted to me and I realized, while I had reformed her, there was a lot of the old Valentina left. "What is he doing here?"

"Hey, I didn't invite him," I said quickly although I was delighted. Maybe this party could be saved after all. "I don't know why he's here."

"I, or rather I should say we, are here to rescue Victoria."

We?

"Cool," I said under my breath, not quite believing my luck. I can't remember the last time I was rescued by a prince. No, wait, that would be never.

"Ladies, if you please," Alexei said in that charmingly imperious manner of his.

"Oh, I don't think—" Pandora vanished.

"Surely you can't—" Gillian disappeared.

"If I had magical powers, you wouldn't dare—" Valentina blinked out of sight with a strange sort of sizzling noise. I wasn't sorry to see her go. She could be a little scary.

Alexei stepped in front of my chair. Tall with broad shoulders, dark hair, and an arrogant look in his brown eyes, he was all I'd written him to be. Without a word, he took my hand and raised it to his lips, his gaze locked with mine. Now, I had written this particular seduction technique any number of times but I'd never been on the receiving end before. If I hadn't been sitting down, my knees would have buckled. It was that good.

From out of sight behind him, Marianne cleared her throat. "Well, then, if you don't mind, Victoria."

"No, no, not at all." I wouldn't have minded anything at the moment. Had I written that there were gold flecks in his eyes? I should have.

"I shall take my leave as well if you're certain you don't need my assistance," Marianne said and it struck me how very nice I had made her. As well I should. She was destined to be a duchess and the kind, wise matriarch of her family in some future book.

"I daresay she doesn't need any assistance," Alexei said smoothly. I don't think I've ever seen eyes with gold flecks in real life. Only in fiction.

Of course, he was fictional.

"Very well then." A shrug sounded in Marianne's

voice. "I suppose I—you're here too? I must say I am not at all sure—" Her voice cut off in mid sentence and I knew without looking she had followed the other ladies.

Which left just me and the prince. Worked for me.

Alexei released my hand and seated himself in the chair Marianne had vacated. I noticed we had been joined by three of my other heroes. There was no need for introductions, I would have known them anywhere. They were exactly as I had written them.

Richard Shelton (Earl of Shelbrooke) was on the sofa between Maximillian Wells (Earl of Trent) and Thomas Effington (Marquess of Helmsley). Here in my living room, in the flesh—more or less—were my first Effington heroes. And let me tell you, you always remember your first.

I stared, I couldn't help it. They were all, well, *fit* is the right word. Their shoulders were broad and I knew they were sitting on really nice butts. Their hair ranged in shade from a sandy brown to a deep, almost black color. Their eyes varied in hue but from man to man held an amused, slightly wicked look and promised, well, all sorts of things. They were, each and every one the composite of all the British influences of my formative years. The Highlander and the Beatles (mostly Paul), Mr. Darcy and, of course, James Bond. They were, to put it simply, hot. Exactly as I had written them.

"Oh," I said with a sort of breathless disbelief. "My Lord."

"Yes?" they all said in unison.

"No, that's not . . ." I laughed. "You are all exactly as I pictured you. Absolutely perfect."

"Oh, we may look perfect." Alexei glanced around the circle. "Yes, I would say we are a good-looking lot but we have any number of quite annoying flaws. Your fault, I might add."

"We are, one and all, stubborn," Richard said. "And proud."

"Arrogant," Max added. "Prone to making decisions, devising plans that are often less than brilliant."

"And not one of us easily admits when he is wrong." Thomas paused. "As rare as that occasion might be."

"And last but certainly not least," I said reluctantly. "Not one of you is—oh, what's the word—I know, real."

"You wouldn't be at all pleased if we were." Max cast me a pointed look.

"Oh, maybe for a minute . . ." I smiled weakly.

"You wouldn't put up with any of us for the equivalent of ten pages." Richard heaved a frustrated sigh. "You're exactly like the rest of your kind."

"My kind?" I stared at him. "Do you mean women?"

"Not merely women." Thomas's manner was grim. "Nonfictional women."

"You have a point there." What was great fun to read about would be really, really irritating to actually live. "Although you don't know anything about my kind."

"You're absolutely right." Amusement gleamed in Max's eye. "We know nothing whatsoever about women not of a fictional nature living in"—he glanced out my front window at the cars passing by—"a time that is obviously not our own."

I nodded at the window. "That doesn't shock you?"

Max shrugged. "Apparently not."

"My dear Victoria," Alexei began. "We are well aware of who and what we are."

"We are exactly what you wish us to be," Thomas said. "Part and parcel as it were of your imagination.

Richard leaned forward. "I don't think you wrote us to be easily shocked."

"Of course not. I don't mind you having a few endearing flaws but I'd hate for you to actually be stupid."

"And that is most appreciated. Now then," Max said, "tell us about your kind."

Thomas nudged Richard. "Although I daresay women probably haven't changed all that much."

"No, in many ways we haven't. Most of us want love, romance, commitment," I began.

"Marriage." Thomas nodded in a sage manner. "Some things will never change. Women will always need a man to take care of them."

"Not exactly." I chose my words with care. "Women today are free to make choices. There are many who choose to stay home and take care of their children and their households—"

"With the appropriate nannies and maids and cooks and so forth, of course," Max said.

"Most of us don't have nannies and cooks and maids and so forth," I said. "Very few of us have servants. We do it all ourselves."

"No servants?" A look that might have been horror washed across Alexei's face.

"All of it yourselves?" Richard's eyes widened in disbelief. "How very daunting."

"No kidding. It's hard. And brace yourselves now, boys." I leaned forward as if I was about to impart some great confidential information. "There are just as many women today who take care of themselves. Who have jobs and careers and make their own living."

Max stared. "Earn their own money you mean?"

I nodded.

"There's nothing worse than a woman with her own finances." Richard shuddered. "Unless it's an intelligent woman of independent means."

"Oh that's never good." Alexei shook his head. "A clever woman who earns her own way can lead to all sorts of dreadful consequences."

"Making their own decisions and that sort of thing." Max drew his brows together. "It can be bad, very bad."

"The next thing you know they'll want to vote!" Thomas stared at me. I grinned and his expression fell. "You vote don't you?"

"You betcha. We vote and we run companies and countries and serve in the military and do everything men do. There has even been"—I paused for dramatic effect and to savor the moment—"a female prime minister of England."

Thomas winced. Max paled slightly. Richard looked as if he had eaten something bad. Actually, I was kind of proud of them for their relatively restrained responses. After all, their stories were set in the Regency, from a time before Victoria took the throne. They were not used to the idea of females at the helm of a ship of state or anything else.

"Come now, gentlemen," Alexei said. "There have been great female rulers throughout history." He looked at me hopefully. "No servants at all? Surely your husband has a valet?"

"He prefers to dress himself."

"But you must have gardeners?"

If he'd seen my yard, he wouldn't have to ask.

"Oh no, we're not doing this again." I shook my head. "I already went through this with the ladies. I have no servants. No gardeners, no footmen, no maids, no stable boys, no carriage drivers, no cooks. It's a different world, boys, than the one you inhabit. Now, let's talk about something else."

"Very well then." Alexei paused. "Let us talk about how the blue of your eyes is like the sky on a fine summer's day."

I stared at him. "Huh?"

"And your hair is the color of spun gold," Richard said.

"It's my natural color," I murmured. Okay, maybe it isn't natural now but it is my *original* color.

"And your hands." Max took my hand. "Are as soft and delicate as a breeze in spring."

"I thought they were a little chapped . . ."

"As for your voice," Thomas added. "It is music to my ears."

I would have raised a brow but that's a trick I've never been able to master. "Music to your ears? Is that the best you can come up with?"

"No," Thomas said with an indignant raise of his own brow. How did he do that? "It's the best you can come up with. You wrote it."

"No one seems to be saying much of anything I wrote at this little gathering. In fact . . ." I narrowed my eyes and looked from one man to the next then pulled my hand, as reluctantly as any heroine's, from Max's. "What do you all want?"

"What any hero of fiction wants." Max shrugged. "A good story."

"You've all had good stories," I said firmly. "And you are all living happily ever after, exactly as I left you."

"And we do appreciate it but . . ." Richard paused. "Happily ever after is not terribly exciting. We'd all rather like another story."

"A new book," Alexei added. "For each of us."

I shook my head. "Oh, I don't think so."

Thomas leaned forward and stared into my eyes. "You finish with our books, Victoria, and unless we pop up again in a later book—"

"Much older and only rarely wiser," Richard said.

"We're done. Finished. Relegated to the back of the bookshelf." Alexei sighed.

"And we are all agreed"—Max glanced around the group and the other men nodded—"given everything that you put us through, that you owe us a second chance."

"After all, Victoria." Thomas met my gaze directly. "You had me pretend to be a poetry-spouting highwayman. And not especially good poetry either."

I bit back a grin.

"And I seduced my wife while thinking she thought I was another man." Richard huffed.

I smothered a laugh.

"You made me come up with ways to emulate the labors of Hercules." Max's eyes narrowed. "And if I recall, in the writing of it, you made me do one task two different ways."

I shrugged. "Rewrites. It happens."

"You took away my title, my country, my heritage." Alexei shook his head. "It wasn't at all nice of you."

"Sacrifices must be made for a good story," I said in the lofty manner usually reserved for my characters. "And I did let you keep your money."

"And much appreciated. Still . . ." A tempting note sounded in Alexei's voice. "Another book—"

"No."

"A novella perhaps?" Thomas said hopefully.

"No."

"What about a nice short story?" Richard said. "A bit of adventure to keep life interesting?"

"Absolutely not." I laughed. "You're a pushy little group, aren't you?"

"You wrote us this way." Max sighed. "Well, if you're not going to give us all new stories, the least you can do is offer us proper refreshment."

Richard cast a disgusted look at the tea pot. "Is tea all you have in this world run by women?"

"No brandy? No whisky? No ale?" Thomas said. "No interesting beverages of an alcoholic nature?"

"Interesting beverages of an alcoholic nature? Well, I have wine . . ." I stared at them for a moment then realized. As there was a bit of James Bond in all of them, what would he drink? "I think I have just the thing, boys."

I got to my feet and sauntered—I don't remember ever having sauntered before but the occasion did seem to call for it—to an antique reproduction liquor cabinet that would have indeed fit into their world. "Let me introduce you to a little something we call . . . the martini."